The

INHERITANCE

By RHONDA BLACKHURST

The Inheritance

Carpe diem

To Clint, who has been my strongest
source of support. Thank you for your
endless patience.

Acknowledgments

Family, whether "normal" or not, is a gift. These are the people we get to share life with—we see the good and bad in one another, love each other anyway, and in the end are still family. I would like to thank my family, my support system, the people who have enriched my life beyond measure.

To Clint, my husband and best friend, the soul mate I've waited my entire life for. Thank you for believing in me even when I'd stopped believing in myself. You've pushed me onward and upward, helping me to achieve my dream of becoming an author. You've made my dream a reality.

To Ben and Alex, my precious boys who have grown into amazing men. You, my sons, have given life a whole new dimension, showing me how to truly love completely and unconditionally. My journey through life as your mother has been my most cherished role by far. I love you more than you could ever imagine.

To Jennifer and Becky, my stepdaughters. Jen, I am blessed to have you in my family circle. You are an amazing mother and wife. Becky, my angel, there isn't a single day I don't think of you and miss you, and at times I can feel your presence with me. I find comfort in knowing I will get to be with you again someday.

To my grandchildren—Spencer, Morgan, Jayden, Cassie, Cody, and Zoey—each of you has placed a memorable handprint on my heart. I love each of you to the moon and back.

An inheritance gained hastily at the beginning will not be blessed in the end.

Proverbs 20:21 (NKJV)

Prologue

The stars shone brilliantly above, sparkling through the moonroof of the Mercedes. The countryside sped by on this crisp October night as the car hugged the road's twists and curves neatly and tightly. The evening's benefit event that Victor and Vivian had hosted had been a huge success, and they were both reflecting upon the amount of money they had raised to feed the poor. It was a cause they both cherished and held near to their hearts. The outpouring of kindness from the hearts of so many strangers wanting to give to something other than their own bank accounts had astonished them.

Victor's mind traveled to his beloved wife of thirty-six years. He loved the way she gracefully made her way through the crowd of those who were eager to get their chance to meet her. She had spoken so eloquently at the podium, creating powerful images of her trips to third-world countries to work with children living in devastating poverty, that she seemed to have moved the hearts of everyone in the room.

He had never seen her look more beautiful than tonight. Her simple black dress had fit her curves perfectly, and her chin-length black hair had reflected radiantly in a halo of soft hues beneath the overhead lights that had been dimmed to create the perfect ambiance.

Vivian had been the love of his life since high school. He remembered how nervous he'd been when she'd finally agreed to go to a movie with him in their junior year—and look how far they'd come from that day.

What a journey their love had taken. He now had a private practice that had netted him more money than was even fair for one person to earn. Vivian's love for art and her own pieces she was able to sell for handsome amounts further enabled their travels to other countries. Together, they found that visiting those much less fortunate than they placed into perspective what life was really about. These experiences had changed the entire way they lived their own lives. They had managed to put away a considerable amount of money for each of their three children.... He sighed as his thoughts became more clouded. Stormy clouds after the brilliant sunshine.

Vivian turned and studied the lines of her husband's handsome face as he stared ahead into the endless stretch of road that led into the night before them. She noticed his furrowed brow, the seriousness—almost sadness—that had settled there. She suspected he was thinking of their children, and her heart ached for him. She knew Victor considered it his personal failure that their children had become so estranged from them, from each other, and from God. Each was so lost in life, on roads that would surely carry them through much heartache.

She placed a warm hand on his leg, a simple yet solid assurance that they were in this thing called life together. Though it looked more like a deep valley than a mountaintop at times, especially lately, they were still in it together. In good times and in bad. Sickness and in health. They had weathered a lot of storms throughout the years, and this was one they would survive as well. As long as they had each other.

Vivian and Victor looked at each other, her warm smile reaching deep into his soul. Then she turned to look forward as the headlights from an oncoming car illuminated her face. He didn't see the car itself—it careened around the corner entirely too fast. What he did see, though, was the look of surprise on Vivian's face as she reached for the dashboard in front of her. As if in slow motion, he turned his head to see the oncoming car right before it crashed into his.

The sound was deafening—metal on metal, screeching, sliding, and Vivian's screams. He felt her hand grab his arm in panic, and then a pain beyond anything he had ever known shattered his thoughts into a million pieces. And just like that, there was nothing. Nothing but silence in the dead of night. The inky black that covered the night sky enveloped his mind and body as he drifted away toward the most penetrating, whitest light he had ever imagined. Something so beautiful it couldn't possibly be real. And so strong and magnetic...he couldn't possibly resist it. Especially when he saw his beloved Vivian standing there, holding out her hand, beckoning gently for him to join her.

Chapter One

Madison, Max, and Molly were all scheduled to arrive on Sunday at their parents' home. It had been a long time since they'd all been together at the beautiful old farmhouse they'd grown up in. With the tensions between them, it had been easier to spend more and more time apart than together. Until now they rarely saw each other at all. Madison accomplished a brief weekly phone call to her parents, but she was sure Max hadn't been home or phoned for quite some time—his firm and his ladies kept him too busy to be bothered with family. Molly rarely went home, for reasons of which Madison had no idea. Molly had always seemed like the one on the outside looking in, like she just didn't quite belong.

Madison couldn't help but wonder where and when they had all taken such opposite turns on life's highway, each speeding at an alarming pace away from one another. And what had her parents thought? The distance between them all must have been painful.

Madison pulled her car into the driveway, tears springing to her eyes as the harsh realization of why she was here hit her full on. The news of her parents' death, until that moment, had seemed almost surreal. She'd heard the words the estate attorney had told her over the phone, but her mind still fought against fully absorbing them. In fact, as she'd listened to Stephen's voice telling her what had happened, she'd begun to feel as though she was levitating above her own being, looking down on someone else having a conversation on the phone, someone else turning shock-white at the grave news being transferred across phone lines. It had taken a good long while before she'd felt present in her own body again, before she realized it was she who had replaced the phone receiver in the charger, she who was standing before the window watching the drops of rain trail down the pane of glass, and no one else but she who had been stricken with the unpleasant news from the caller at the other end.

Madison blinked through her tears, looking up at the farmhouse once again. A house that once had held so much life now stood empty, dark, and lifeless; the looming, gray, October sky painted in the background made the house look even more cold and empty.

Cautiously, she let herself in with the house key she had been given by her mother so long ago and nearly forgot she had. She noticed the familiar creak when the door opened, the same creak that had destroyed Max's hope of sneaking in the house unnoticed when he was in high school. She wondered if her dad had ever considered fixing it or if it was in some odd way a cherished memory.

She pushed the door open a bit wider, afraid of what she would find and hoping somehow to find who she knew she wouldn't. She stood just inside the door and looked around. The kitchen looked as if her mother should be coming through the entryway from the family room at any moment, greeting her with the warm, welcoming hug she always had for Madison. Usually, she'd just be stopping by long enough to drop off Zoey and Oliver for one of the overnight slumber parties they enjoyed having with their grandpa and grandma.

For a moment, she thought she could smell the faint scent of cherry tobacco from the pipe her father smoked at Christmastime, but he must have smoked it more recently than that for the smell to still linger in the air.

She realized things were likely just as they had been when her parents had left for the fundraiser that night. The wilting yellow Asiatic lily her mother tried to nurture in the warmth of the house each bitterly cold winter caught her eye, and tears began to run freely.

Her mother had taken such joy in this big, sunny yellow kitchen. The farm-style butcher-block table with its heavy wooden benches waited patiently for the children and grandchildren who seldom came by. The same table had hosted the family meeting they had all coined "The Talk"—the one that had changed it all. The one in which her father had sat them all down to let them know that as of that very moment, things would be changing. There would be no more free rides, no more getting anything and everything for nothing. There would be chores, expectations, and privileges taken away for noncompliance. It had been such a drastic turn from what life was up to that point that they all did a one-eighty in trying to figure out what had happened.

Madison wished she could turn the clock back several years. She knew she couldn't control what her brother and sister did, but she could have made an effort to come by more often. She could have carved time out of her chaotic schedule somewhere, allowing her children to get to know their grandparents better. Of course, truth be told, her parents probably knew Zoey and Oliver better than they did her these days. At least Zoey and Oliver had spent occasional weekends with her parents—which was more than the brief phone calls that Madison made.

The carousel of copper pots hanging from the ceiling caught her attention. They sparkled in the sunlight, and she realized the gray skies had given way to clear. She looked around at the warmth of the cream-colored cabinets, the candle that sat atop the cream-colored stovetop…. All of it was in sharp contrast to the coldness that engulfed her.

She made her way to the table and sat down gingerly on the end of one of the benches, afraid the weight of her soul would topple it end over end. She ran her finger lightly over the grooves that had been there since Max had carved them so many years ago. She remembered her mother scolding her little brother behind a hint of a smile she tried to conceal. And she remembered listening from the family room as her mother told her father that those grooves only added to the character of the table, that she wasn't going to cover them up because they would always remind her of Max's mischievous spirit.

Madison half-laughed at the memory, remembering thinking way back then that it wasn't a mischievous spirit, but a devilish one. But her mother had always exuded such grace. Would she have been as understanding if that had been Oliver carving into their table at home? She could only hope so.

She sat quietly, reminiscing, until she heard a car drive in. The sound of a car door closing drew her to her feet, and she walked to the big bay window to look out in time to watch Molly stand next to her car, staring up toward the windows of what used to be her bedroom. Madison watched her, wishing she knew what was circling in her sister's locked mind. She continued watching for a moment longer, and then Molly turned her head toward the end of the driveway. Madison's gaze followed to see Max turn the corner in a sleek little sports car. It rolled to a stop next to Molly.

Madison didn't move but continued to watch as Max emerged from his car, phone to ear, hanging up once he closed his car door. He said something to Molly. The two of them looked at each other for a long moment. A sadness tugged at Madison's heartstrings, and she made her way to the front door to go join them. She wiped the last tear dry as she went, determined to be strong.

She crossed the front yard, and both Max and Molly turned in her direction. She caught Max in an awkward, unfamiliar sort of hug and then folded Molly into a snug embrace that lasted just a moment longer than she sensed Molly was comfortable with.

"Come on," she said. "Let's go in the kitchen, and I can make us some coffee."

Chapter Two

"What time are we meeting the attorney?" Max asked, all business as he sat at the kitchen table. Madison bristled at his detachment.

"Not until three o'clock." She turned to see him frowning at something he'd pulled up on his cell phone. "We have time to talk awhile first and try to reconnect for a bit." She glanced at Molly who was leaning against the counter, close to the door, as if she wanted to be close enough to bolt should the need arise.

"What time did you get here?" Molly asked Madison.

"Not long ago. About long enough to open the door and sit at the kitchen table and consider making a pot of coffee, but not long enough to actually make it." The smile she aimed at her little sister was met with a stoic gaze.

Madison began searching through cabinets for the coffee, finally finding it in the pantry. She felt Max's gaze hot on her back, and she turned to see him looking amused. She felt her cheeks flush as she anticipated Max's silent judgment. It was obvious that she didn't stop by very often, but neither did he. He was likely jealous that she was more at ease here than he was, she thought, enjoying his insecurity.

Madison watched as his gaze traveled to Molly, detached from all of them as she stared out the window. And she continued to notice as his eyes quickly reverted back to his cell phone, his eyebrows knit back together as he frowned.

"Some things never change," she said quietly, just loud enough for him to take notice.

"What's that supposed to mean?"

"Nothing."

"Oh, it meant something," he countered. "So have the guts to tell me instead of this passive-aggressive shit."

"You have always used your cell phone as a means of escape, Max. You—"

"—have no right to judge me," he interrupted. "This may be where I grew up, Madison, but I outgrew it a long time ago."

"That's right," she retorted, turning to meet his eyes straight on. "You're the big-city lawyer who's too good for the rest of the world."

"I never said that."

"You didn't have to. Your actions speak much louder than anything you say."

"Who appointed you God, judge, and jury?" He accused her. "My place is in the city. In Denver. Where there's lights, action, civilization."

"Yeah, because you're so civilized," she said, her sarcasm filling the room. "When was the last time you took the time to even call Dad to see how he was? To let him know you were okay and not dead somewhere?"

"I called him last summer and invited him to a baseball game. He would have loved Coors Field."

"Oh wow, that recent, huh? Almost a year ago. I'm impressed."

Molly left the room, and Madison instantly felt guilty. At a time when they should be at least trying to get along, she and her brother were at each other's throats. And she couldn't even fully blame it on him. He just had a way of getting under her skin, and her nerves were already raw.

She knew Max's love of sports and the fact that he enjoyed being so close to both Coors Field and

Sports Authority Field at Mile High; both were a short five-minute drive from his loft. She was never sure why he chose to move so far away, but he seemed to feel at home in Denver.

She knew she could maybe understand, if even a little, if she spent time to ponder at all. She had accompanied Phil on a business trip to Denver once before the kids were born, but she hadn't let her brother know they were in town. Instead, while Phil was in his meetings, she'd toured the city with its lights, listened as the fans erupted in cheers at an ongoing baseball game, and enjoyed the smells of hotdogs and onions wafting toward her. She'd seen the rides in motion at the Elitch Gardens Theme Park, lights and laughter filling the air. Denver was a city ablaze with life and diversity, but she had been ecstatic to be away from it all and back home at the end of the trip.

"How long are you expecting this to take?" he asked Madison, bringing her back to the moment. His detachment from the reality of what was going on saddened her . "Have you already spoken with the folks' attorney?"

"Only for a moment when he called to set up the appointment."

"Why did he call you?" he asked, his voice tight.

"I don't know, Max," she sighed. "I don't think that really matters, do you?" She turned to glance at him as she poured the water in the coffeemaker.

"Just odd, is all. I'm the attorney. It would have made more sense for him to call me."

Madison took a slow breath before turning to face him. "Max, what does that have to do with anything? This is about Mom and Dad, not you and what you do for a living. In fact—news flash, little brother—this isn't about you at all. Funny, isn't it? That not everything is about you and how wonderful and successful you are?"

"Just sayin'…" He looked up as Molly wandered back into the room, beer in hand.

"Molly, how have you been, sweetie?" Madison interrupted, changing the direction the conversation was inevitably going.

"Fine."

"Yeah?" Madison questioned. "Are you doing okay?"

"Yup."

Madison noticed she was answering only the questions, offering nothing further. She reached out to touch Molly's hand as Molly deftly moved just before contact. "How has your writing been coming along?"

"Fine."

"Wow, quite the conversationalist, aren't you?" Max added his two cents as he met and held her eyes in what Madison thought looked to be a challenge. Molly glared at him, her cold eyes shooting daggers at him. "Ouch," he murmured under his breath. "This is going well."

The three fell into an awkward silence until Madison spoke again, sadly. "What happened to us?"

"Oh, please." Molly looked up and rolled her eyes. She tossed her hair over her shoulder. She was hard to read as she looked around the room at all that had been a part of her mother.

"Molly,' Madison continued, "help me to understand. What on earth could you possibly have to be so bitter and angry about? You could have the world by the tail."

"Ya think? I'm nothing but the red-headed stepchild of this family."

"Says who?"

"Says the people who stared at me when we used to get together with Mom's side of the family for Christmas. Says the people—like Mom, for instance—who used to ask me why I couldn't be more outgoing like you. I guess being me wasn't acceptable." Her words dripped with bitterness.

"Molly, maybe Mom was just worried about you."

"Whatever."

"Hey, Moll," Max suddenly said, "have you gotten a job yet?"

"I've always had a job, you jerk. Don't even go there," she warned.

"Go where?" Max asked, feigning innocence.

"You know where," Molly stated, her voice hard. She left the room abruptly, ending the conversation the way she had always done best. Madison and Max remained silent until Molly emerged from the cellar with a bottle of vintage merlot.

"Wouldn't you rather have a cup of coffee, Moll?" Madison asked. "It's not even quite noon."

"It's noon somewhere," Molly murmured, proceeding to open the bottle, then pausing to look at Max who was watching her with a smirk. "What? What are you looking at?"

"Nothing at all, Moll. Nothing at all."

Madison moved to the window, looking out to where a huge cottonwood tree used to stand. Max joined her a moment later.

"I see Dad had that big old tree taken down," he stated.

"Yeah, I guess he did." Her mind traveled years back.

"Hey, remember the tire swing that used to hang from that tree? That was fun."

"Yeah, it was fun. And I remember you pushing me right off that swing." She smiled wistfully at the memory.

"Only once," he countered.

"Yeah, but that once landed me a broken arm." She looked at him, her eyes wide in disbelief that he'd choose to ignore that part.

"Man, I got in trouble for that," he chuckled.

"As well you should have. If Oliver did that to Zoey, he would get in trouble too."

"Speaking of which, where are the kiddos? How am I supposed to get to know them if you don't bring them around?"

"They're at home with Phil. When he comes up for the funeral, they'll stay with the nanny. I didn't think it would be good for them to associate all this sadness to their grandparents." Madison cast a sideways glance at her brother. "You could make an effort to come visit once in a while, you know."

"Ditto."

"You don't have a family to schedule around. And at the rate you're going"—Madison added without thinking—"you never will."

"What's the rush?"

"There isn't one. I just want you to find happiness, Max," she sighed.

"Who says I'm not happy? I have everything I could ever hope for."

"Do you? Really?" She studied him, trying to get a read on what he wasn't saying.

"Yeah, I do. Really," he answered with enough sarcasm to make Madison decide not to respond but to simply let it go. "What about Molly over there?"

"What about me?" Molly asked.

"When are you going to finally get it together and settle down?"

"When cows fly."

Max laughed at her sarcasm. "Isn't that supposed to be 'when pigs fly'?"

"Don't you, of all people, dare to correct what I say," she said, her voice tight.

Madison felt a twinge of fear for what was happening. Put all three of them in a room for the first time in years, and they didn't know how to relate. She placed the palm of her hand against the warming flesh of her forehead. "You guys, why are we doing this?"

"Doing what?"

Madison looked at Max, eyes wide with disbelief. "Doing what?" she mirrored. "Did you seriously just ask that? You can't even look at me. You just sit there at the table looking at that darn newspaper and spout off stupidity." Max looked up at her, and she was sure she saw a spark of...something...in his eyes. Joy that he was getting her riled up? Anger? She couldn't tell. "Why can't we just reconnect like the adults we supposedly are? Why can't we try be friends?"

Molly snorted, "Friends?"

"Yes, friends." Madison sighed. "You and Max can't even stand being in the same room together. And I for sure wouldn't want to leave the two of you alone, for goodness sake. I fear there would be a homicide."

It saddened Madison that this is what it had come to. Her heart twinged with pain at what her parents would think if they could see their children—their blood and the product of their fierce love for one another—acting the way they were beneath the very roof under which they were raised. Beneath the same roof that once, a very long time ago, had held laughter, giggles, and a real family. It would break their hearts, she thought sadly.

Max broke the lingering silence. "So if you want us to 'reconnect,' as you say, what do you propose we do? All hold hands and sing Kum ba yah? 'Cause I don't much like to sing."

"Max, you're such an ass," Madison hissed. Unbelievably, she saw a tiny smile tug at the corner of his mouth, and she felt an angry heat rise to her cheeks. "I hadn't planned anything specific, Maxwell." Her voice was tight as she tried hard to stay calm and in control. "I just thought it would be nice to catch up with one another, maybe try to revive some of the fun times we had growing up. To honor our memories of Mom and Dad."

"Hmmm," he pretended to ponder the idea. "Yeah, see, I don't so much remember any fun times."

"For once we agree," Molly mumbled.

"How can you say that?!" Hot tears stung Madison's eyes.

Molly looked up and met Madison's gaze. "I don't know, Maddie. All I do know is that it feels like I shouldn't even be here."

Her openness surprised Madison. As little as she had spoken with Molly over the past several years, every time she had, Molly had been anything but open. In fact, she was careful not to reveal anything. "Why, honey?"

"Dunno. Just because," she murmured, looking out the window again before turning back to Madison, ignoring the fact that Max was even in the room. "I've never felt like I've fit in this family. All I've ever gotten is grief for not being you and for doing what I love. What makes me happy. I've never been able to be enough just being Molly." She turned to glare at Max. "And *you*," she paused. "You are just plain *evil*. I hate you."

"Maybe Mom and Dad just wanted the best for you," Madison suggested, trying to rein the conversation back in. "Did you ever take the time to explain to them what it is you do?"

"For what? I shouldn't have to do that. Mom was an artist, for Pete's sake. She should have understood."

"But did you try? Did you give them a chance rather than just writing them off as being the enemy?"

"You never gave any of us a chance," Max interrupted. "You hibernated in your room whenever you were home, like a hermit. If you weren't in school or hanging with the cast of characters you called friends, you were locked in your room. Hell, even having a conversation with you was impossible."

"You just couldn't stand to keep quiet any longer, could you, Max?" Madison asked.

Molly took a gulp of her wine, draining the glass. "Well, at least I didn't monopolize every conversation like you've always felt the need to do."

"And you would know that how? Jeez, kid, have you and I ever even *had* a conversation?" He paused for only a moment before pressing further. "Besides, you couldn't, because you were never in a conversation long enough to monopolize it."

"Whatever."

"That's your answer for everything, isn't it, kiddo?" He scoffed.

"Back off, Max," she warned.

Madison had been silently watching their exchange and finally spoke up. "Guys, enough! Neither of you have ever tried to get along with the other. Beside, we're not getting anywhere by disputing things that no longer matter. I was hoping we could mend fences, pave new roads, build bridges. Not further destroy whatever we have left." Madison's eyes brimmed with unshed tears.

"We won't be here that long," Max retorted.

Madison got up to pour them each a cup of coffee. She made sure to place Molly's directly in front of her. She was well into her third glass of wine.

"We can at least start, Maxwell. A start is better than nothing at all." She was silent for a moment before adding, "Maybe we could take a few moments to take a breath, unpack, and settle into our rooms. We can reconvene at one o'clock. Would that be okay with you guys?" The tension in the room felt like an over-tightened guitar string, and Madison wondered which of them would end up with the biggest wound when that string finally snapped.

"Madison—always the planner and scheduler," Max said dryly.

Molly got up and left the room, suitcase in hand, leaving the cup of coffee untouched. She paused at the foot of the stairs when Max called after her.

"Hey! Where's my hug?" His voice dripped with sarcasm.

"Never gonna happen in this lifetime," Molly retorted.

A hint of a smile tugged at Max's grim look, and it offered Madison the glimmer she needed to breathe new life into her dying hope. This might work after all, she thought. It would take a lot of biting her tongue and self-restraint to keep from reaching out and strangling her little brother and shaking her little sister, but there was hope. She smiled and exhaled slowly, not realizing she had been holding her breath.

Madison unpacked, then headed to Molly's room. The door was ajar, and she peeked in. She was going to assume the open door was a sign of acceptance and ask for forgiveness if she was wrong. She'd heard long ago that it's better to ask for forgiveness than permission, and she was going to use that wisdom now. She just hoped Zoey and Oliver would never hear that saying before the age of thirty.

She nudged the door open just enough to squeeze through, catching her breath when it creaked, afraid it would wake up Molly who lay sleeping on the old familiar gray and purple patchwork comforter. Her head was nearly buried among the throw pillows and stuffed animals that she'd clung to as far back as Madison could remember. She smiled as she remembered the pet net her father had hung in the corner of Molly's room as a place to hold all of her stuffed animals. They never stayed there long before they made their way back onto Molly's bed again. Madison wondered if that was her sister's way of finding comfort in a world that made her feel so insecure.

She slowly eased herself onto the bed beside Molly, feeling the mattress depress beneath her weight. Molly's eyes flickered, and then she startled, eyes flying wide open. Madison chuckled as she stretched out on her stomach beside her sister, propping herself up on her elbows, chin in her hands.

"What the…Dang you! You're creeping me out, Maddie. How long have you been there?" Molly tried to catch her breath.

"Just got here," Madison grinned. "Did you just call me creepy?"

"Waking up to find someone watching me *is* creepy," she clarified, smiling despite herself.

"I've missed you, Molly. I miss my little sister," Madison twirled a strand of Molly's brown hair around her finger wistfully.

Molly lay there looking up at the ceiling, chip back in place. "You don't even know me, Madison."

"I know you could stand to put on some weight," she said in an attempt to lighten Molly's dreariness. Seeing she was unsuccessful, she said, "You need to get over that and stop feeling sorry for yourself for something you've brought on yourself." The minute the words were out, she regretted them. She remembered telling Zoey not too long ago, "Words are like toothpaste, honey. Once it's out of the tube, you can't get it back in no matter how hard you try." And now she'd proven it.

She braced herself, waiting for a fight to come from her sister who hadn't even flinched, she was lying so still. She waited a moment before saying softly, "Let me in, Molly. Let me into your life instead of dead-bolting the door of your soul."

"Dead-bolting the door of my soul?" Molly asked, looking at her sister like she had lost her mind. "What's that? Shrink jargon?"

Madison chuckled. "No, it's just me, begging." She rolled onto her side, her elbow burrowing into the mattress and her head resting in the palm of her hand. "And I'm still begging…and waiting…and begging…"

"Shut up." Molly smiled the first real smile Madison could remember in a long time. "Maddie, wanna know somethin'? I don't even know what I'm feeling. If anything at all. I mean—when I think about what was way back when we were little…and what was after Max turned evil…and what could have been if he hadn't—"

Madison waited patiently for her to continue, watching her struggle to capture events from the past, even as her gaze remained vacant.

"It's just—well, why does Max always have to be such an ass?" Molly's soft brown eyes stared at the ceiling. "Sometimes—no, most of the time—I…I really hate him."

"Hate's a pretty strong word, don't you think?" Madison asked gently.

"Sometimes it doesn't feel strong enough."

"Maybe he's that way because that's his role as an attorney. I mean, come on. It's not like he's even a prosecutor—he's a defense attorney!" They both laughed. Madison was enjoying Molly's presence and the rare opportunity to really talk with her. Madison rolled over on her back to lay side by side next to her little sister.

"You know, I've tried to trace the trail of where things got so messed up, and every time I try, I get lost before I'm even out of the gate. And most of the time? Well, most of the time I don't even care."

"What do you remember most about Mom and Dad?" Madison asked, looking at the navy-painted ceiling, at the stars that glowed in the dark covering the entire space. She remembered when Molly had insisted on placing them there by herself, not accepting anyone's help. She was so stubborn even back then. Madison's gaze traveled the make-believe sky until she noticed the slightest crack in the corner. Or maybe it's a finely spun spider web, she thought as she studied it.

"I remember that Dad didn't stand up for me when Max was being...Max. It was like I wasn't even in the room. Or in the entire house, for that matter." Molly's voice brought Madison back to their conversation.

"How sad that that's the one thing you remember. How about something positive. Anything?"

"Maybe the Sunday dinners Mom always used to make. The pot roast, potatoes and gravy, and dessert. She always made dessert. And the smell in the house when Mom canned tomatoes. Do you remember that? I loved that smell. So sweet. And if something can smell warm, that was it."

"Hmmm. Yeah, I do remember that," Madison whispered, a small smile playing on her lips. "Why didn't you let me help you put these stars on your ceiling? You were such a stubborn little snot."

"I thought we were talking about memories."

"We are. So why didn't you let me help?"

"Cause you already thought of me as helpless. Always have. Letting you help me would have only proven that."

"I never thought of you as..."

"Don't even say it, because, yes, you did."

"Hmmm. Maybe..."

"There's no *maybe* about it. You did," she insisted.

Madison decided not to pursue what was sure to be a power struggle and chose to stare at the stars. "See that little star?" Molly asked, pointing to the furthest corner of the ceiling.

"Yeah. What about it?"

"Bet you didn't even notice that one, did you? That one has always been my favorite."

Molly's face was sober, her eyes took on a distant look, and Madison wondered if their conversation was over. If she was losing her again. "Why was that your favorite?"

"Because that star is so small it gets lost among the larger ones. That's exactly how I felt. Lost among all of you."

"Why did you..."

"What about you?" Molly interrupted. "What's your favorite memory of mom and dad?"

"The same thing. It was always so special to come in after playing outside with friends to the smell of Mom's Sunday dinner. And the canned tomatoes. And, yes," she turned and smiled at her sister, "I think warm can be a smell. It was especially yummy smelling on cool fall evenings,"

"So yummy can be a smell, too, then?" Molly chuckled.

"Of course. And do you want to know why?"

"Not really. But I'm sure you're gonna tell me anyway."

Madison elbowed her playfully. "Because I said so, that's why." Madison peeked at Molly out of the corner of her eye, relieved to see a small smile. "Know what's so ironic? My favorite memory is mom's roast beef Sunday dinners and now I don't even eat meat."

"At all?" Molly asked in disbelief.

"Not red meat. If it has fins or wings, I will."

"Me either. Except I don't eat *any* meat. It grosses me out."

Madison laughed as she looked at sister's scrunched face. "Why doesn't that surprise me?"

They lay side by side for a moment. Madison looked at Molly, lying there looking relaxed for the first time in years, and she smiled. "I really did miss you, Moll." Molly was silent. "I know you and Max couldn't stand to be in the same room and you wrote him out of your life, but did you have to edit me out as well?"

Molly stayed quiet, and it seemed to Madison that she was a million miles away. But Molly had spent a lot of years locked within herself, and it would likely take time to break free of those chains. Madison was intent on helping that happen and committed herself to the challenge.

"I guess we should probably go back to the kitchen and see if Max is there yet."

"Do we have to?" Molly groaned.

Madison playfully tugged Molly's hair that splayed around her in a halo, and pretended to scold her, smiling. "Yes, young lady. We do. We're going to see if we can get through this day without the two of you killing each other."

"I'm making no promises."

"There will be no casualties today," Madison held her hand out to help Molly off the bed.

"Well, tomorrow's a new day, and all bets are off."

"By golly, sis. I think you're lightening up a little. If I'm not mistaken, I think you just made a joke."

"No. You're mistaken."

Molly accepted Madison's hand and stood up. Madison smoothed her hair, Molly pulled hers into a ponytail and slipped on her flip-flops, and they made their way downstairs. Just before they crossed into the kitchen, Madison felt Molly's cool, slim hand on her arm.

"Maddie?"

She turned to see Molly looking at her, reminding her of a frightened deer. "Yeah?"

"I'm sorry, ya know."

Madison feigned shock and dramatically jerked away from Molly. "Oh my gosh! Is that what I think it is? Like a real apology?"

"Don't make it a big deal," she said, making a face at Madison. "Just sayin'…I didn't mean for you to get caught in the crossfire. It was never about you."

Madison looked at her sister, joking aside. "Thanks, sweetie."

They were surprised to see Max already in the kitchen, beer in hand, reading one of the newspapers that Madison had picked up off the front porch when she arrived.

"You two look like you're up to no good," he said, glancing at them from the corner of his eye, then immediately refocusing on the paper.

"Let me guess. Sports pages?" Madison asked.

"Nope, comics."

"Yeah, right," she chuckled. "Although it would probably do you good."

"And you would know this how?" He countered.

"Older and wiser."

"I'll give you one of the two. You are older."

Madison shot him a look and noticed Molly smile despite the rigidity and tension that seemed to happen simultaneously with Max's presence. And it was a smile that warmed Madison's heart. Her little sister was such a beautiful, gentle soul. But that soul had so many injuries and scars. Although as much as Molly would deny it, many of those wounds were self-inflicted.

Chapter Three

Madison and Molly made small chit-chat on the ride to Stephen's office. Madison swung the car in next to Max's little black Jaguar already parked in the lot. She saw him hang up his cell phone when he saw them pull in.

They opened the door to the small reception area, and Madison watched as Max openly checked out the receptionist. Madison thought she somewhat resembled Julia Robert's character in the movie *Erin Brockovich*, raw, sexy beauty that renders surprise at the sign of immense intelligence.

When the receptionist let them know that Stephen was finishing up a phone call and would be with them momentarily, Madison was taken aback at how much she even sounded like the character. By the look on her brother's face, she assumed he saw and heard the resemblance as well. She groaned inwardly, certain her brother's attention would be on the receptionist rather than what they were there for. He was such a player, she thought as she watched him trying to catch the poor woman's eye. If the girl wasn't careful, she would be caught like a fly in a spider's web.

The three took a seat, ironically each with their backs against opposite walls. Max sat so he was facing the Erin Brockovich look-a-like, who was now filing her nails. For no other reason than to be somewhat entertained while she waited, Madison continued to watch Max as he picked up a copy of *Sports Illustrated,* then glanced at the pages while watching the receptionist blow big pink bubbles through her perfectly pink lips.

The woman looked up and smiled at her brother, who was doing nothing other than making himself look like a teenaged idiot. Madison shook her head and looked away in disgust. She turned her attention to Molly who sat staring out the window. How predictable they both were. It was as if they had been playing the same role for years. But then again, they had been, so why would she expect anything different.

Madison studied each of them, trying to decide who they looked like most, their mother or their father. Max, she decided, with his coal black hair and sharp blue eyes, was a picture of their mother when she was younger. He could pass as a twin of her mother's brother, Uncle Alex, back in the day. His build was tall and lean, but not shy in the muscle department. He was the wrong one to be blessed with such masculine attractiveness. It only heighted his arrogance.

Molly, on the other hand, had some of her father's features, though not as much as Madison herself had. Molly had frequently said she was the milkman's kid, because she didn't look like either of her parents. And unless one really looked and knew what to look for, she was right. Her brown hair and brown eyes could blend into a crowd unnoticed. She felt pity for her sister, but only for a moment. What Molly lacked in stand-out beauty, she made up for in her figure, though Madison thought she looked a little on the thin side now. She hoped someday Molly would stop feeling sorry for herself long enough to see that she truly did belong and was loved. Though, in truth, none of them were acting very loveable at the moment.

Elevator music piped through the speakers in the ceiling, and Madison was surprised to find it irritating instead of soothing, as it was likely intended to be. She couldn't put her finger on why, though. Rather than overanalyzing as she was often guilty of (a by-product of her job as a psychiatrist, she figured) she let it pass as just being what it was—elevator music that she had never been fond of. Either it didn't affect Molly and Max or, more likely, they weren't even aware of it. In fact, Max wasn't aware of anything except the bubble-blowing, nail-filing woman who was now openly flirting with him with her eyes. Madison was pretty sure an earthquake could happen, and neither Max nor Molly would notice.

Madison looked around the room, taking in the synthetic greenery, the lamp in the corner, and the harsh overhead lights that made the lamplight nearly invisible. There were two corner tables with magazines and a tiny nook that held an array of toys and children's books. Things Madison would never allow Zoey and Oliver to play with if they were here. She wouldn't want to risk her own children getting sick from the germs she could almost see growing. She visibly shuddered.

"Cold?" Molly's voice surprised her. She hadn't even realized Molly had been watching her.

"Just got a sudden chill," she lied, smiling gently at her sister, noticing again how thin she looked.

As Madison surveyed the rest of the room, she realized the décor, like the music, was likely an attempt to soothe whoever came in. For Madison it had the opposite effect. She just wanted to get this over with and get back to her parents' house. The place where she felt closest to them.

Phil would be coming up tomorrow, but the kids would be staying with Natalia, their nanny. Madison didn't think it would be good for them to be at the funeral. They were too young to be exposed to the finality of death. But she battled with herself if that was what she truly thought or if she was simply trying to protect them from the unpleasant realities of life. Suddenly she wished Phil would bring the kids with him. It would be such a beautiful distraction for her. She needed a distraction from the unpleasant emptiness within her.

She felt a sudden urge to wrap her arms around her children and hold them tight. And perhaps they'd drive the short distance into the city to buy them a special treat. Something that would help them all feel better. She pictured Oliver's chubby little hands and cheeks from not so long ago, slimming as he grew older. And Zoey. Sweet yet feisty Zoey. Dressed in the smart little dresses she has always been so fond of, her blond curls up in a ponytail tied with a little ribbon, and a whole lot of attitude as she walked in a way that made her ponytail swing wide from side to side. Madison was deep in thought, thinking of something special she could buy them to make up for coming here without them, when she heard her name.

"Hey, earth to Madison," Max's voice came through loudly. She startled and looked up to see Max, Molly, and Stephen all looking at her. For a moment she wondered if she'd dozed off and was dreaming. The visions of her children seemed so vivid.

She stood, shook Stephen's hand, and followed the rest of them into an office decorated much like the waiting area, minus the toys, and much smaller, forcing them to sit near one another. Madison took Molly's cool, slim hand in her own, felt Molly's muscles tighten at her touch, and waited for Stephen to begin.

Stephen took a seat behind his desk and shuffled some papers around. When he was satisfied that everything was in its proper place, he removed his glasses, laid them on the desk in front of him, and folded his hands, leaning slightly forward.

He looked up and made eye contact with each of the three people in his office. It had been years since he'd seen them, that they had now become relative strangers. Victor had mentioned them frequently, both the good and the bad, the bad slanted to be as good as Victor could make it, of course. He knew Victor and Vivian loved their children more than life itself, but had realized after it was much too late that they had been too generous in giving them things, making sure they never wanted for anything. All in the name of love. Victor eventually realized it was a selfish drive that led him to never say no, and accepted the bitter pill that it was much easier for him to give them what they wanted rather than deal with their disappointment. He'd been feeding his own ego as others looked at his family with envy, and that's when Victor decided to make some serious changes and called the fateful family meeting that had transformed Max into the selfish man he was today, and caused Molly to retreat even further.

He had been Victor's best friend and confidant, and he'd listened and watched from and saw how Victor had become so wrapped up in Max's behavior that he'd noticed little else, including the two girls. Stephen had attempted to bring it to Victor's attention a time or two, but Victor just waved his hand in dismissal.

Maxwell had developed the intense drive for success no matter who he had to step on to get it. His insatiable appetite for women had confused Victor, however. Victor had hoped that he and Vivian had modeled a relationship that each of their children would someday desire for themselves. That hope for Max vanished as soon as he began dating.

And Molly…Victor had told Stephen once that Molly had shut all of them out, refusing to allow anyone in except her friends. And even those were few. She wanted nothing to do with family, but spent any time at home alone in her room writing, and that troubled them. Especially Vivian. She had tried talking to Molly; she had tried backing away and giving her space. But no matter what she tried, it only seemed to push Molly further away.

After studying these grown children of his friends for a moment longer, Stephen pushed his glasses up with his forefinger and finally turned his attention to the matter at hand. The reason they were here.

He cleared his throat. "Before we begin, do any of you have anything you wish to say or ask?"

"Just get on with it," Max barked.

"Max!" Madison scolded.

"Let's begin, shall we?" Stephen said, stopping an impending sibling squabble. His hands that were a mere moment ago folded, now pushed his glasses up yet once more upon the bridge of his nose. He opened a file that lay in front of him and took another moment to silently prepare himself for reactions he was sure would transpire. He studied the top paper for a moment until Max's voice broke the uneasy silence.

"Why are you stalling? Let's get on with it already."

Stephen simply looked at him over the rim of his glasses, cleared his throat again, and began to read.

"Our dearest children: We had two separate wills drawn, one in the event we die at different times and another in the event we die together in one of our travels. If you are reading this one, it is as we would have wanted to go into our next life. Together. This will, however, is not what any of you are going to expect. Once you hear what we have to say, you will understand why it was necessary for you to make time for the reading of the will before our burial.

"Our funeral has been fully planned so as not to cause any potential disagreements between the three of you. It has also been paid in advance, down to the smallest detail. Nothing has been left out; no stone left unturned. You may think this extensive planning is morbid. We, however, know you will have other, more important things to attend to and didn't want you to have to worry about our burial. Be patient for a moment as"—Stephen cleared his throat—"Uhh...as Stephen reads this, and you will understand.

"To Madison. Our beloved oldest and firstborn. You have always been such a joy and bright light in our lives. You've always had such a generous heart and spirit, giving so much of yourself. In an odd way, and one which you may not understand to begin with, we are trying to save you from yourself. We realized much too late the damage that can be done in giving children everything they could want in the name of happiness."

"Huh," Max said dryly. "I believe they just called us damaged."

"Max!" Madison hissed. "They most certainly did not. Can we please just listen to what Mom and Dad want us to hear without your commentary?" Her voice was quiet but firm, preventing Max from saying anything more.

Stephen took a moment to stop and look over the top of his glasses at Max then Madison, making sure they were done, before he continued reading.

"You will receive a third of our estate upon completion of two tasks—tasks which have been given careful consideration. We have discussed them with Stephen in great detail just in case our instructions, which we've tried to be very clear in writing, are not clear to you. It is our hope that you will understand the intent behind these requests.

"First, you are to choose a child from an underprivileged third-world country to sponsor financially and to nurture an ongoing relationship with. You are to do this with both Zoey and Oliver, so they can understand and see how privileged they are and see how others less fortunate are forced to live. There are several organizations that are reputable and trustworthy from which to choose. Stephen has agreed to help you research them and choose one, if you so desire. And you are to allow Phil in on the process as well.

"Why this request, you're asking? It's because—" Stephen saw Madison shiver and paused.

"Are you okay, Madison?"

"Yes," she whispered. "It's just strange how they seem to be right in this room with us, knowing what I'm thinking."

A sad smile tugged at his lips and he continued reading.

"It's because you've worked so hard to make sure your children have everything they could ever possibly want, just as we did before we realized the harm in that. You're doing them no favors by spoiling them. On the contrary, our sweet girl."

Madison interrupted, her brows furrowed. "I'm not sure I'm understanding all of this." Madison knew she was on the defensive but couldn't stop herself. "What's wrong with making sure my children are well cared for?"

"Cared for? Try spoiled," Max interjected with sarcasm.

"And you would know that how? Because you spend so much time with them?" she asked with sarcasm of her own.

"Maybe it has something to do with the pony you bought Zoey for her seventh birthday."

"Ninth," she corrected him.

"Ninth what?" he asked, confused.

"Ninth birthday, genius. And what's wrong with buying her a pony? You should have seen the smile on her face when she saw him. It was priceless."

"Sis, who takes care of that pony?"

"Why? What are you getting at?"

"Does Zoey take care of it?"

"Heavens, no. She's too young."

"No need to get defensive," Max chided her. "But if she's too young to take care of it, she's too young to have it," Max stated in the most matter-of-fact tone.

"Seriously, Max? You're the last one to be giving parenting advice."

Molly sat watching her brother and sister bicker, not getting involved. Stephen had seen enough to know that Madison was a little stung by the conditions of the will. And they hadn't even gotten past the first condition. He also knew Max was taking advantage of his sister being down to gain the upper hand, trying to be what to him represented the man of the group—the one with power. However, from all Stephen had heard from Victor and Vivian, it sounded as though it was a little too late for that. They had made excuses for Max even up to the last time he had met with them, blaming themselves, but Stephen had his own opinion of the young man. An opinion much less esteemed than Victor and Vivian's, though he would never have admitted that to them.

"Shall we continue?" Stephen asked the trio who were now avoiding each other and looking directly at him to end what they had only just begun. "Right."

Clearing his throat again and placing his glasses back on the bridge of his nose, he continued.

He read, "Madison, we understand you love Zoey and Oliver with your whole heart, and that is a good thing. You are such a good mother, and we are very proud of you. But we want you to learn the difference between selfless love and selfish love. The difference between needs and wants. The children should never need for anything, but allowing them to want things is a good and healthy boundary to set. One we didn't set until it was too late, and we couldn't go back."

Stephen looked up from the paper to Madison. She sat with one leg crossed over the other at the knee, her foot swinging back and forth. Her arms were crossed tightly in front of her. A combination of pain and confusion covered her face. But it wasn't Madison's expression that bothered him. It was Maxwell's. He was looking a bit too smug, enjoying his sister's predicament. That is until the next sentence.

"Maxwell," Stephen continued reading, "before you think Madison is being picked on and you choose to gloat over her situation, yours is yet to come. You, too, dear boy, will have your turn." Stephen paused and looked up to see a look of surprise pass over Molly's usually blank expression. He looked at Max and watched as a slight flush in his cheeks spread to the tips of his ears. Stephen smiled without it reaching his lips, enjoying the moment. To see Max humbled, if even just a little. He knew it could be construed as unethical on his part, but after what Max had put Victor through, it seemed deserving.

Stephen continued on. "And the next thing, Maddie, the second and last for you, is that you are to mentor an at-risk youth. Where will you find the time, you're asking us in that mind that's always thinking and planning?"

"What is this?" Madison whispered, her voice laced with disbelief. "How can they know what I'm thinking?"

"They knew a lot more than any of you thought they did," Stephen replied and continued reading.

"Take one or two fewer clients a week. If you're honest with yourself, you'll admit you don't *need* the money; you simply *want* more. In fact, cutting back one or two clients per week will give you an opportunity to spend some priceless, quality time with your children, doing things together that will imprint permanent lessons and memories in their minds. Don't just give them things with the money you're making, Maddie. Give them the gift of your time and life lessons that will help make them even better people as they grow and venture out into the world. Before they are forced to make life-changing, even life-saving, decisions for themselves. What could possibly be more important than that? You have so much to give, but you're giving everything to those who already have everything. Step out of your sterile, organized life long enough to spread your heart and love to those who need what you have to offer."

Stephen put the packet of papers down for a moment so Madison would know that his next words were coming from him and not her parents' will. He took his glasses off and began turning them over, back and forth, with one hand as he asked, "Madison? Do you have any questions?"

"No," she answered, a combination of politeness and tightness. "It's crystal clear."

Stephen had a strong hunch that had Maxwell not been sitting in the room, Madison would have been more forthcoming with her questions and concerns. As it was, he suspected she wasn't about to give Max the satisfaction of her discomfort. She would likely contact him to discuss it at a later time, after she had time to process and try to make sense of what was happening. He also suspected the inheritance didn't matter as much to her as the fact that her parents were telling her she had to jump for it and, in a way, how high. He could see the irritation and perhaps a bit of anger in the lines on her face. Stephen knew that anger was an emotion Madison typically did not display, but at this precise moment, he could sense it was bubbling below the surface. She was probably fighting with everything she had not to let it erupt, to flow like hot lava from an active volcano.

Madison straightened in her seat, visibly regaining composure and putting her anger in check. She turned to glance out the window and inhaled deeply, then exhaled slowly.

"Very well," Stephen continued. "We'll move on then. Maxwell, you're next."

He picked up a different stack of papers, flipped to the second and third pages then back to the first. He placed his glasses once more upon the bridge of his nose and began reading.

"Maxwell, our beloved son and middle child, I think you were born with a cell phone in one hand and a little black book with the ladies' names in the other. Son, there's more to life than your job and latest conquest, proving your worth by winning, not learning the lesson when you lose, and always finding somewhere else to place the blame. You have a good heart, boy, but it's gotten a tad hard over the last several years. It is our wish and deepest desire that you work on that to find the peace and contentment that has eluded you for far too long. We are hoping to help you achieve those things, even though we're no longer physically with you."

Stephen paused a beat and looked over the top of his glasses at Max who was impatiently waiting for the conditions that were to be laid before him in order to get his inheritance. He guessed Max would already have a plan in place as to how he would invest his money.

"Time's a wasting," Max stated abruptly.

"Max, could you be any more rude and insensitive?" Madison scolded.

"The sooner I find out what hoops need to be jumped, the sooner I can get it done and invest the money."   "That's cold even for you," Molly added.

Stephen spoke up, interrupting once again the escalating emotions. "In case you're thinking you can hurry and get this done in order to *win* your inheritance, as you strive to win at life, it won't be that easy."

Stephen saw Molly smile—the first since she'd arrived—as she and Madison watched the expression change on Max's face to one of disbelief.

"What the hell?" Max muttered under this breath.

"They know you better than you think," Madison answered the unspoken part of his question, mirroring what Stephen had told them just a moment ago.

"Well, it's creepy as hell," Max said quietly, looking about the room as though he expected to see his parents in there with them.

Stephen smiled and continued. "Maxwell, unlike your sister, you and Molly will each have three tasks to perform." Max began to protest, but Stephen cut him off by continuing to read. "Before either of you has a chance to wonder why, let us explain.

"Madison has a husband and two children to care for. Someday each of you will find how much time it takes to invest in a family. And one of the purposes of our requests is to help you understand the importance of family, not to take Madison away from hers."

Stephen looked up to see Max staring at the ceiling as he exhaled sharply, shaking his head slowly with a smile that reeked of sarcasm. Stephen would have been lying to himself if he didn't admit he felt a great deal of satisfaction in Max's discomfort.

He continued. "Max, you are to volunteer forty hours at a homeless shelter. Not doing pro bono legal work for them, but physical work that involves interacting with people."

Madison and Molly each stifled a giggle. Max shot them both arrows with his eyes.

"Why forty hours you're asking?" Stephen continued. "Because we want you to put in a full week's worth of work on something you won't get paid for. Something that fosters relationships with others who are less fortunate than you. One week's worth of work that will build and grow your character and empathy for others."

"Tell me that's all I have to do," Max asked Stephen, more hopeful than he'd been about anything in a long time.

"Sorry, Max," Stephen answered, but actually not sorry at all. "As previously stated, there are three conditions each for you and Molly," he smiled, truly enjoying this arrangement. Victor and Vivian had planned this to the last possible detail.

"The second requirement for you," he went on to read, "is to help build one complete home for Habitat for Humanity. Get your hands dirty; work up a sweat. And for God's sake, son, don't wear your suit. Go buy yourself a pair of jeans and a T-shirt that you're not afraid to get dirty. And don't worry, the dirt will come clean from beneath your fingernails after enough time."

At that Madison and Molly both burst out laughing. Even after they were gone, their parents had a sense of humor. Max, however, found it not the least bit entertaining. His face was a bright crimson.

"And third," Stephen continued, "you are to use your business sense to organize and spearhead a fundraiser for AIDS research. You remember your uncle Chris whom you wrote off because he had AIDS? In fact, you said it was a gay disease and something he'd brought on himself. You wrote him out of the pages of your life and never allowed yourself to know him. The real Chris—his love for people and the welfare of others, the tireless work he did for those less fortunate than him—was amazing. Yes, son, even though he was sick, he saw himself as fortunate. Fortunate that he knew love for and from others. Fortunate that he had such a blessed and happy life. Fortunate that he was close to his sister—your mother—and would have given his own life for her. He died a year and a half ago. Your mother never told you because she needed to grieve the loss of this good man and celebrate the life they shared without disapproval from you. Science has come a long way in AIDS research, but has yet a long way to go. Had there been funding to enable further research, your uncle's life might have been spared, if even for a little bit longer. The world would have been a much better place for it. Maybe by raising money to assist in further research, you can make that happen for others. If even for one more person, it will have been worth it."

"You girls didn't see fit to tell me about Chris?" Max asked them with a mix of accusation and hurt.

"Yeah, not really," Madison answered blandly.

"I didn't know about it either," Molly added.

"Mom didn't need you talking negatively about Uncle Chris when she was trying to deal with her own pain, Max."

"Oh, I get it," Max sneered. "So it was your job to protect Mom from me? Such a martyr you are."

Seeing they were getting nowhere but further irritated with one another, Stephen continued in an attempt to distract them from their bickering.

"As you can see," he read, "these things will not cost you anything unless you choose to invest monetarily. It will only be necessary to invest your time to refocus and redirect your thinking, and to challenge your comfort zone. I've already spoken with your boss at the writing of this will, should this event transpire."

Stephen allowed a moment for Max to experience the sting of humiliation and anger at Victor's taking the liberty to talk to his boss. Stephen knew that Max's pride had likely just taken a huge hit, and had he not known Max as he did, he might have felt sorry for him.

He finally continued reading.

"And, son, I know speaking to your boss was a risky thing to do. I understand this will probably make you resentful of my intrusion into your affairs—professional affairs, that is—but I had my reasons for doing this. Reasons you will discover as you travel along the journey. If you even choose to travel that road. That, of course, is up to you."

Max straightened in his chair and ran his finger around the collar of his shirt. "What the hell?"

The room gave way to silence as each of them absorbed what had been laid out before them so far. Molly squirmed in her chair, as if knowing all eyes would be on her and her life in a moment's time. Stephen looked at her over the rim of his glasses. "Molly?"

"Yeah?" Molly crossed one slim leg over the other, her flip flop dangling from her foot. She tossed her long ponytail she'd been playing with over shoulders that were back, displaying what Stephen assumed was a defiant sense of bravado. He was sure that she wasn't going to give way to weakness any more than she had to. She would stand up tall with everything she had in her right now. "I'm ready," she encouraged him to carry on.

Stephen picked up the papers and studied the top page for just a moment before reading.

"Molly, our strong-willed baby, you have tried so hard to be independent. You've been so busy making sure you didn't need anyone else in the world that you've made a victim of yourself. Honey, life could be so much easier for you if you'd get out of your own way and allow it to be." Stephen glanced up briefly and saw Molly's pride force her sit a little taller in her chair, a little bit straighter, even as the chip on her shoulder became almost visibly heavier. Stephen continued.

"You, as well, will receive one third of the estate, provided you follow through with three conditions. And this may be the hardest of all for you. More so than for Madison and Max. You will understand why in just a moment.

"First, you are to mentor someone in the adult literacy program. Reading and writing are things you are passionate about, so helping an illiterate adult to enjoy a book or be able to write feelings to paper will allow you to do what you love while working on letting a little of yourself go. We want you to place your focus on another person rather than hide behind the walls you've erected so high around you. You'll get a taste of a freedom you never knew existed.

"Second, you are to take our dog, Lily, and care for her. What on earth for, you ask?"

"Dog?" All three asked in unison, clearly surprised.

"Oh, that's right," Madison said. "The kids did say something about Grandpa and Grandma's dog."

"Since when have the folks ever wanted a dog?" Max asked, clearly confused.

"Seriously? A dog?" Molly scoffed. "Been there, done that. And not doing it again," she stated adamantly. Stephen watched her as he tried to read what she was thinking—why she would deny such a simple request. Unable to do so, he continued reading.

"You'll understand after we tell you the third. The two intertwine somewhat."

Max couldn't resist commenting at this. "You're getting off easy, as usual, little sis. What's the big deal about taking a dog? Still being pampered even after Mom and Dad are gone." He scowled. Molly raised her eyebrows slightly, and a small trace of a smile pulled at the corner of her mouth as she looked at Max.

"Max, you've been jealous of Molly since Mom and Dad brought her home from the hospital," Madison snickered. "I would have thought you'd have outgrown it by now."

"No, I haven't," he countered. "I just wish they would have left her there."

"Maxwell," Stephen looked at him sternly. "Allow me to finish. You may change your mind after I'm done."

He looked at Molly and saw her posture stiffen. He knew she wasn't going to want to hear the next item on the agenda. Especially when she wasn't happy about the dog, something that seemed like it would be rather easy and pleasant. Stephen sensed her fear and smiled gently at her as he continued.

"Third, our sweet girl, you are to attend a twelve-step program for your drinking." Molly's face paled. Stephen suspected she wanted nothing so badly at that moment than to crawl under her chair to escape the scrutiny of Madison and Max's stares, four eyes asking her a thousand questions. Stephen continued quickly to alleviate some of Molly's discomfort.

"Madison and Max, don't be so surprised. Had you taken the time to call her once in a while, you would have figured it out as well." And again, an eeriness came over the room. Even he could feel it this time—that his friends could have predicted what was going on within the confines of each head within that room. "Molly, whenever we've called and you decided to answer the phone, your speech was a dead giveaway. We feared that if we said something, you would stop answering the phone altogether. And we wanted to prevent that from happening. Oh how we loved talking with you." Stephen looked up to see Molly blink away tears.

"Molly," Stephen read her parents' words, "we didn't feel it would help to interfere. But since you're hearing this letter, it means our time has run out. We don't want to be responsible for giving you yet one more reason to drink your pain away. You have always suffered in silence. Suffered about what and hidden from whom, we're not sure—you've never allowed us to get close enough to know. And we're not even sure that you know. But it is our hope that a twelve-step program will help you figure it out. Help you stop drinking and get to know yourself. If you choose not to actively participate, that is up to you. All we ask is that you attend at least six meetings and see where it leads you."

"They seriously think I have a drinking problem?" she asked incredulously, the first obvious sign of emotion Stephen had seen since they'd started. "And they want me sit in a room with a bunch of cigarette-smoking drunks? I thought you said they knew us," she directed angrily at Stephen. "This is what I've always said—they didn't know the first thing about me."

"Who's the one who got drunk first thing when we got to the farmhouse?" Max accused.

"I wasn't drunk," she shot back at him. "Everyone uses to medicate when needed and to cope with difficult circumstances. And seeing you is beyond difficult, believe me. But that hardly makes me an alcoholic."

"Damn, Moll, you just put a complete sentence together instead of mumbling incoherent words. I'm proud of you."

Stephen could see the pleasure Max was taking in humiliating Molly and decided to put an end to it. The rate this was going, Molly would go back to the house and ingest the entire contents of the wine cellar, and that would be the exact opposite of what Victor and Vivian intended the result of this to be.

"And this is where adopting Lily comes in," Stephen continued. "All you have to do is love her, and commit to taking care of her. Animals are such therapeutic little creatures. They see us at our ugliest and still have nothing but love to offer. Having her will keep you from always focusing on your problems and isolating yourself."

"Molly." Stephen looked up at her. "Do you have any questions?"

"No. I believe it's all been said."

Stephen paused, then placed the paper from which he had read to Molly behind the others in his hands. He looked at the three siblings who sat quietly while their body language screamed their frustration. He rested his forearms on his desk and folded his hands. Each couldn't possibly be more different from the others. And the sad part was, none of them knew what made the other tick. None of them truly knew what the other liked or disliked, what made each happy or sad. Max and Molly were too preoccupied by anger and resentments. Max's arrogance, Stephen suspected, was simply a cover for a lack of self-esteem. And Molly with a brick wall firmly encasing her heart, being a victim of something she didn't even know. Sheer fear and nothing else. And Madison...she was the most level-headed and stable one of the three. She at least had returned the love of her parents, but only with what she had left over. Leftover time, leftover energy, leftover love. She was so busy making sure her children had the best of everything, that she had completely lost touch with reality. How the common people live. Putting herself and her children above the rest of the world.

Stephen stopped his analytical thinking and said, "There's just a bit more to read before you go. As they indicated in the beginning," he explained, "they were very thorough and left no stone unturned."

Max rolled his eyes and Molly sat on the edge of her chair looking like she was ready to bolt out the door. Madison had a blank, tired look as she waited for him to continue.

"In order for these requested items of action to have maximum effect, we ask that you continue them for a full year."

Max gasped and the girls remained silent.

"After a year's time," Stephen continued, "provided you've attended to each of your items, Stephen will issue a check for your portion of the inheritance. Each of you will be receiving half a million dollars. We've been blessed to earn more than we ever deserved, being sure to live frugally where we had to, so that we could save this inheritance for our children.

If, however, any of you don't complete your requested items or simply choose not to participate, your third will go to a charity of our choice. Stephen has that information in the event that it should come to that.

"In addition, Stephen will be monitoring progress on an informal basis. He will be available for any questions or concerns that should arise over the upcoming year. Think of it as a challenge. A treasure hunt of sorts. Make it fun for yourselves."

Max retorted, "Fun. Yeah, I'll get right on that. Not!"

"Stephen will also be taking care of the house for the next year, making sure it is available in the event any of you want to use it or if the three of you would like to gather occasionally. Or often, if you so choose. Nothing would make us happier. If after the first year you will all commit to using the farmhouse as a gathering place at a minimum of once a year, the title will be transferred into all of your names in equal shares. But if even *one* of you chooses to disengage from gathering, Stephen will sell the house and the money from the sale will go to charity. This time, however, the charity will be up to the three of you to agree upon, with Stephen as the mediator."

"At least something is up to us," Max commented under his breath.

Madison looked at him and rolled her eyes. "Max, *shut up*."

"One final thought," Stephen read. "We're not telling you money is bad. But when it becomes your focus in life and you center your life on it, it affects your character. It is our hope that your character will reflect God, not money."

"And with that"—Stephen put down the paper, got up from behind his desk, and walked around to where the three remained seated—"here is a business card for each of you. Please, feel free to call me for anything at all."

"I just have one question," Max asked tightly, barely civil, revealing the extent of his hostility. "How much have my parents given you to take care of this and babysit us for the next year?"

"Given me?" Stephen felt heat rise up his neck, into his cheeks, and to the tips of his ears. He visualized one of those cartoon characters with steam coming from his ears, and had he not been so angry, he might laugh. But Max had hit a raw nerve. His eyes narrowed and through thin lips, he answered, "They gave me their friendship. Nothing financially. I'm doing this pro bono." His eyes met Max's in a hard stare. "Being an attorney yourself, Max, I assume you know what pro bono work is?"

Max's cheeks turned crimson, and both Madison and Molly cracked a smile, looking at one another.

"Touché," Max said quietly as he walked out of the office, leaving Stephen's business card on the end table that was beside the chair where he'd been sitting.

Madison shook his hand, though she still appeared somewhat in shock and exhausted.

"Thank you, Stephen. I'm assuming you will be at the funeral?"

"I wouldn't miss it," he replied as he shook Molly's cool hand and watched the two women until they drove away.

Chapter Four

Madison and Molly let the radio dominate the ride back to the farm. Neither felt like speaking. They were surprised that Max wasn't back when they pulled in the drive -- he'd been long gone by the time they left Stephen's office. In fact he'd left so quickly it was obvious he'd forgotten about the object of his flirtation just two short hours earlier. Madison supposed he was driving around the city, getting rid of some attitude. At least she hoped he was getting rid of it somewhere. She wasn't in the mood for his sarcasm and bitterness. It would do no good at this point. There was a strong possibility he would decide not to follow through with the requirements to collect his share of the inheritance. Then again, she knew how much he hated to lose. He just might decide to do it to win the challenge if nothing else.

"Should I make us some dinner?" Molly asked her.

"You cook?" she asked, eyebrows raised.

"How do you think I eat if I don't cook?"

"Since it's just you, I thought maybe you did take-out, fast food...I don't know." She shrugged. "I guess I didn't think of you cooking."

"Uh...no. Take out and fast food got old a long time ago. I cook." Molly looked at Madison. "Sit. I'll show you."

Madison smiled through her exhaustion. She watched as Molly poured herself a large glass of merlot and began opening cupboards, drawers, the pantry, orienting herself with the kitchen. She realized how little she really knew her sister anymore. Somehow, somewhere she'd grown up into a beautiful woman, yet Madison still pictured her as the rebellious teenager who'd driven her parents crazy with worry. Before she knew it, Zoey would be cooking too. If Natalia hadn't already begun teaching her how to do that. She would have to remember to ask.

Max walked in shortly after, rubbing his hands together for warmth. The sun had long since gone down, and it was getting cold outside.

"Molly's making dinner. Want some?"

"Not hungry," he answered.

"Good. 'Cause hell will freeze over before I make anything for you," Molly interjected.

"Hunger strike?" Madison asked, an attempt at humor. Humor none of them felt at the moment. It had been an odd day, fraught with emotions that ran across the entire spectrum. Madison felt as though she were suffering from an emotional hangover. Molly must be feeling that way too—she was working hard at medicating and drowning, now well into her second large glass of wine. She'd have more than just an emotional hangover come morning.

"Molly, when did you start drinking?" Madison asked more from curiosity than anything else.

"Too bad you can't ask Mom and Dad. They seem to know more about my drinking than I do," she retorted.

"Do you think you have a problem with it?"

"Not a problem with drinking, no. If I had to live without it...? That might present a problem." She smiled a small, sad smile, then sighed. "I don't know, Madison. I do know I don't want to think about it right now." She finished what she was doing over the stove and began tossing a salad.

"So are you going to quit?"

"Quit what?"

"Duh!" Madison laughed. "Drinking, you dork."

"It doesn't look like it to me," Max interjected, nodding toward her glass.

"I'm pretty sure she wasn't talking to you, big brother." Molly glared at him, then looked at Madison briefly and answered, "Not a second before I have to. And then I still don't know. I'll see."

"Hey, Molly." Max's unwelcome voice invaded the room again. "Why is it you'll talk to Madison and have an actual, real adult conversation with her, and you only throw me hostile darts?"

"Like the dart you threw at me when I was twelve? I still have the scar from the stitches to prove that one. And when you stop *playing* an adult and start *acting* like one, I will talk to you too. But since that'll never happen, guess I won't have to worry about it."

Madison fought back the surprising threat of tears as she continued to watch Molly move effortlessly, noticing how comfortable she appeared in the kitchen. Natalia did most of the cooking at their house, and Madison wondered if she should do more herself. Maybe even with Zoey. Make it a team thing. And truth be told, Oliver would probably like it more than Zoey. She could picture Oliver having fun creating his own recipes. But it looked like she may be busy doing other things now, thanks to her parents' requests. She felt the sting of bitterness and quickly brushed it away. After all, she had gotten a lighter load than the other two. It was more the fact that she felt like she was being punished. Not approved of. That was what irked her the most. Is this what Molly felt for so many years?

Max grabbed a beer from the fridge and planted himself at the table opposite of Madison. "So tell me, sis, are you going to jump right in on your tailor-made bucket list?"

"I'm going to think about it and plan it before I jump in with both feet."

"Of course," he chuckled. "How very like you."

"What's that supposed to mean?" she asked wearily, too tired to really care.

"It means even when we were kids, your life always had to be organized, planned, and orchestrated. You never could just do something without a full-blown plan."

"That obviously bothered you." She watched him, waiting for a typical smart-aleck Maxwell remark.

"Nah. It's just the way it was." He took a swig of his beer. "Just one of the things I remember. See girls? I paid attention no matter what you may have thought."

"You have to admit that comment Mom and Dad made in their will about you being born with a phone in one hand and a little black book in the other was pretty funny," Madison grinned.

"Yeah, hysterical," he retorted.

"Come on! Admit it." She pressed him.

"I will not." He stated firmly, standing his ground.

Molly turned to them and asked, "What time did you say we're meeting the funeral director tomorrow?"

"Three." Madison could see Molly visually lighten as she continued to swallow her wine, reaching to pour another glass.

"What's the purpose?" Molly questioned. "According to Stephen, everything has been done, planned, and paid for. And since Mom and Dad were cremated, it's not like we can see them."

"That's just sick," Max interrupted. "I don't want to be cremated."

"That's your vanity talking," Madison told him.

"So what is the purpose of meeting with the funeral director?" Molly asked again.

"To choose the urns, go through the planned arrangements, tie up any loose ends..." she trailed off, looking out the window at the darkness beyond.

"And, no, Moll, you can't sneak in a flask," Max retorted. "Unless you share it with me."

"That'll be a cold day in hell," she shot back. "You better start being a little more human. It wouldn't look good if you showed up with a black eye."

"Well, well..." he chuckled. "I think my little sister is getting some balls."

"Maybe you will someday, too." She threw the retort over her shoulder, and Madison let out a hoot.

"Gotta admit you opened yourself up for that one, bro," Madison laughed.

"Yeah, I just didn't expect it from *her*. That timid, meek persona she portrays is a ruse," he grinned, enjoying the banter.

Molly brought dinner to the table, putting a plate and silverware in front of Madison and for herself. Max looked dumbfounded as she sat down, leaving him out.

"What about me?"

"What about you?" she asked disinterested. "You thought I was kidding when I said I wasn't making anything for you? Surprise."

Madison remained silent, wondering if there was any hope for the two of them at all, believing it to be more unlikely than likely.

Max watched for just a moment before he got up and made himself a plate. "I dare you to try stop me."

"Take all you want. But I'm not serving you."

The three consumed the vegetarian pasta, salad, and bread sticks with garlic butter. They ate silently, each lost in their own memories. "Molly, you're a darn good cook," Max commented.

"Don't act so surprised," she said wryly. "Maybe you can get word to Mom and Dad that drinking isn't the only thing I'm good at." She smiled despite herself.

"You know, little sister, how come you don't smile more? You're a cute little brat when you do, you know."

"Maybe it's the company I'm in when you see me."

"Ouch!" he feigned hurt feelings.

Madison was relieved to see some of the day's tension melt away. "Max, would you mind starting a fire in the fireplace? I'm cold and tired. Not to mention emotionally and mentally on empty."

"I'm going up to my room," Molly said, getting up from the table, wine glass refilled and in hand. "Max, I remember you saying once that doing the dishes is women's work.... So I'm assuming you'll clean up?"

Madison flinched at the retort she was sure would come from her brother, but she had to admit to herself she was proud of her little sister. She really was getting brave to finally stand up to Max. When the response didn't come, she exhaled the breath she hadn't realized she was keeping in.

"I'll start the fire," was all he said. He began walking away before stopping to holler up the stairs. "Hey Molly, just for the record. You're a whole lot more fun after you've had a few. Maybe you should think twice about stopping."

"Maxwell!" Madison said loudly right behind him, making him jump.

"What?" he asked, pretending innocence. "Just making an observation."

"An observation no one asked for."

He put both hands up in defense. "Don't get so upset. I was just noticing how much more relaxed and fun she is after she's had a few. Maybe Mom and Dad are wrong about it being a problem. In fact, I actually see it as the solution to the problem."

"Like I said, no one asked for your observation. Or your opinion, for that matter. Start the fire," she ordered.

She stood for a moment, debating whether to let it drop or try to fix Max's insensitivity. Then she climbed the stairs and carefully poked her head into Molly's room. "You okay?"

"Yeah. He's just an ass."

"Can I come in?"

"As long as *he's* not with you."

She held up two fingers. "Scout's honor." She sat on the edge of Molly's bed and picked up a stuffed turtle, fluffing the fur on the dull mustard-colored head that used to be vivid yellow. "You know, I never did understand why you and Max hated each other so much. I mean, Max isn't easy to love—or even like, for that matter—but the two of you...I don't know. It's much more than a simple familial dislike."

"Do you even know the stuff he used to do to me when we were kids?"

"I know he felt tremendous jealousy because he wasn't the baby anymore. Or at least I figured that's what it was."

Molly scoffed and threw herself on the bed. "That's an understatement. You have no idea."

"Then fill me in. Sometimes I feel like I grew up in a different house than you did."

"Madison—"

Madison watched, holding her breath, as Molly seemed to contemplate whether to continue. She truly wanted to understand, but unless she knew what was going on, that was impossible.

"He used to torture my dolls—"

"He did that to mine, too. Don't you think that's just a brother thing?"

"Seriously?" Molly asked incredulously. "You sound like Dad. Not only did he torture my dolls, he used to punch me so hard it would bruise my arms and legs. He would pinch the back of my arms and pull the hair at the nape of my neck. And after Dad delivered his spiel? Yeah, well, that just made it ten times worse."

"Geez! And I thought it was bad when he made one of his dinosaurs take life and pull one of my dolls apart, leaving broken limbs and patches of hair scattered around the floor in the family room."

"See?" Molly's eyes were wide. "See what I mean? He's sick!"

"Why didn't you tell Dad?"

"I tried. Ya know what he said?" She laughed bitterly. "He said, 'Boys will be boys, Molly.' "

Madison couldn't help but chuckle at the sound of Molly imitating her father's voice, until she saw Molly's scowl. "I'm not laughing at you. Well—not really. You just make a great imitation of Dad."

"After hearing it enough times, knowing Dad wouldn't do anything about it, I gave up. What was the use?"

"Didn't you tell Mom?"

"Why? So she could take Dad's side?"

"To give her a chance," Madison explained, sadness in her heart. "Molly, I had no idea this was all going on. For crying out loud, girl, why didn't you tell me then?"

"You were too busy with all of your yuppie friends, being prom queen, class valedictorian, boyfriends…"

"Wow," Madison smiled, "you make it sound like I lived such a glamorous childhood."

"You did."

"And that's my fault?" she asked Molly, not understanding what Molly was getting at.

Molly exhaled slowly. "Noooo. I just wished I could fit in like you did. Everybody from our family liked you; you had tons of friends; you were always the teachers' pet—"

"Max didn't like me so much," Madison countered.

"But he didn't pick on you like he did me. Like he still does."

"Then stop hiding behind the bottle and stand up for yourself. Like you did today. Don't let him do it anymore," she ordered, her voice more firm than she intended. "I'm going to go down and sit by the fire. I'm exhausted. Feel free to come down and join me if you want."

"Nah, I'm good."

Madison smiled at her, put the stuffed turtle on the bed beside her, and headed to the door.

She stopped when Molly's quiet voice behind her, slurring slightly asked, "Do you believe in heaven?"

Madison turned to look at her sister, who was now hugging a pillow to her chest. "Yeah, definitely. Without heaven, what hope do we have to ever see Mom and Dad again?" She stood still for just a moment, then turned and closed the door softly behind her.

Madison descended the stairs to the family room where Max sat with his nose in the sports section of the newspaper. She sat on the sofa, watching the flames dance to their own music in the fireplace.

"Molly asked me if I believe in heaven," she said softly, keeping her eyes on the flames licking hungrily at the logs. "Do you?"

"Me?"

"I don't see anyone else in the room."

"No."

Madison glanced at him and back at the fire, waiting to see if he would continue, not sure if she even wanted him to. Silence was so beautiful and peaceful right now. But after a beat, he elaborated further.

"If there's a heaven, that means there's a God. And I don't believe in God."

Madison looked at him, not sure what to feel about his statement. Or even how to respond. Finally she simply asked, "Why?"

"Why what?"

"Why don't you believe in God? How do you explain our presence on earth? Or the miracle of life in general?"

"Science. Evolution," he explained matter-of-factly. "Tell me how you *can* believe there is a God. Can you honestly believe that a book written thousands of years ago is what actually happened? It's fiction, Maddie."

"I beg to differ. Everything good is God."

"So how do you explain all the suffering and pain in this world? Or the murdered or abused children that I see all too frequently in the course of a day with my job?"

"Your job is your worst enemy, Max. In every way. But to answer your questions, God is not the author of evil. Man is. God gave man free will, and it's that will of man that's evil." She paused before daring to press further. "Aren't you the one who defends the people who hurt and murder children? You're a defense attorney, right?"

"I am in a position to choose my clients. I would never choose someone like that unless I knew they were innocent. There are a lot of people who are falsely accused, and they deserve the best representation."

"No ego speaking there, huh? Or is that what you tell yourself so you can sleep at night?" She caught her breath, fearing she'd pressed too far. And maybe she wasn't being fair at all. "Sorry, Max." She didn't want to pursue a conversation that would surely turn into a bitter and heated argument. She was finally beginning to relax by the fire with a hot cup of chamomile tea.

Madison pondered the heaven and hell theory, wondering what Molly believed. As for herself, she couldn't imagine the thought of leaving this earth and never seeing her children again. That was a pain that she couldn't even begin to fathom.

"Do you go to church?" Max's voice startled her.

"Yes."

"Let me guess—Catholic, right?"

"Yes. Is there something wrong with that?"

"No, it's just predictable. You like rules and organization too much to be anything other than that."

Catholicism was all she'd ever known. And Max was right. It was organized and structured. Just like the rest of her life. "Life *is* about rules," Madison stated, confident she was right.

"Your life is," Max answered. "Not mine. I don't believe in rules made by men who say I have to confess my sins to a priest and attend church every single Sunday and any other day the church deems a holy day of obligation, or else I'll go to hell."

"Well, I think that's a little exaggerated, don't you?"

"Not even a little. Unless you can tell me otherwise. And prove it," he added. "Not to rain on your parade, but I'm done being entertained. Can we talk about something else?"

Madison grinned. "You want to have a nonintellectual conversation? Wonders never cease. You were born starting a controversial discussion."

"On my cell phone," he smiled. "And don't forget my little black book. I'm goin' to bed." He got up and headed for the stairs, but Madison stopped him.

"Uh uh. Oh no, you don't. You have a table and dishes to clean. It's women's work remember?"

Max snorted. "I still can't believe she had the guts to say that." He shook his head and walked up the stairs.

Chapter Five

Molly returned home from her parents' place and threw her suitcase on the bed. A moment later, she landed beside it. If it weren't so dark, she would go for a long walk. But she quickly realized that the dark was simply an excuse. As nice as it would feel to go for a walk, the safety and comfort of her own home, her own surroundings, felt even better.

She thought about the odd four days she had just spent with her brother and sister. They were the two people she was most closely connected to by blood, yet the two people she couldn't be more different from. In fact, they were all so different from one another it was hard to believe they were born from the same parents.

She thought about opening a bottle of wine, but the thought of her parents' will and the fact they had assumed she had a drinking problem stopped her. Where in the world did they ever dream that one up? Max had probably planted it in their heads.

"Will I ever be able to have a single drink again without feeling like I'm being watched or disapproved of?" She asked the empty room, feeling irritation and more than a touch of bitterness. She resented the fact that her mom and dad had assumed to know something about her and take it even further as to chalk it up to fact—and they had *no* facts to substantiate their accusation. This was exactly why she kept her private life private. And quiet. She hated the feeling of being judged and always coming up short.

By the time she left the farmhouse, she'd wanted nothing more than to just get out of there. Home. To *her* home. Where she could get away from it all and recover in silence, with absolutely no one to contend with. Not even Jo or John. At that moment, she didn't think she could stand the company of one single person. Just her own company, the safety of her apartment, and a good bottle of wine. Hell, it didn't even have to be good. In fact, she would take a bottle of Jack Daniels if she had to.

She remembered the first time she'd drank. It was in high school. The magic of the liquid made her insecurities vanish immediately. When she had a drink or two, it felt okay to just be Molly. And that felt good. To not want to hide behind false identities, to try be someone she wasn't, just so people would accept her.

She stopped to figure out what day of the week it was. This past week had been everything imaginable. Confusing. Educational. Sad. Lonely. The last made her yet more confused. How could she feel lonely when there were people constantly around her? The funeral, the gathering they had in the church basement afterward...always people. And yet she felt lonely. Except now. Now that she was home, the loneliness faded away and security enveloped her.

"Hell with it," she said aloud, getting off the bed. "I'm gonna open a bottle of wine and enjoy it." She popped some popcorn, poured her wine and thought about the conditions of the will. She toasted her parents, glass in the air before taking the first drink. She missed them so much and felt guilty at the same time. She couldn't even put her finger on why, she just knew it was overwhelming guilt. And yet, strangely enough, she felt numb, too.

She had refused to bring the dog home with her; she'd left her with Stephen until she decided whether she was going to accept the conditions of the will or write the whole thing off. Her life was so unsettled. Besides, unless she was at her computer writing, she was gone a lot. She wasn't sure that would be fair to an animal. Too bad it wasn't a fish. That would be easy enough. She chuckled and took a drink from her freshly poured glass, savoring the taste of the dry, dark liquid.

Her parents really had thought of everything. She loved animals, especially dogs and cats. She remembered begging them incessantly for a horse. When that was met with a resounding no, she'd moved on to requesting a monkey. And when that was met with an even more definite no, she decided she would settle for a dog or a cat. Until they got her a dog and the dog was hit by a car two years later. She remembered sitting with him on the side of the road as he breathed his last, remembered digging a grave and planting a large wooden cross her father had constructed for her.

She wasn't sure she could go through that pain again. As morbid as it sounded to be focused on that, it was reality. Animals didn't live forever. And she didn't want to have to feel that pain ever again.

Molly wandered back into her bedroom and opened her suitcase to unpack. There was a sealed envelope lying on top of her clothes. Her name was written across it in Madison's near perfect handwriting, loops and curves just so. She picked it up, touched the envelope to her lips, and sat down on the bed. She looked at it again, turning it over from front to back. She hesitated to open it, preferring for the moment to just let it be. To allow whatever was unsaid to remain unsaid for just a few moments longer. She leaned it against the lamp on her nightstand, her written name on the envelope looking back at her, reminding her that her sister wanted to say something to her. Molly just wasn't ready to hear it yet.

She continued unpacking, putting some things away, tossing some things aside that she didn't feel like putting away right at that moment. Finally she finished, closed the suitcase, and picked up the envelope from Madison again. She looked at it for a long moment, then placed it back against her lamp, picking up the phone to call John instead.

The phone rang the standard five times before going to voicemail. As she was preparing to leave a message, her doorbell rang. Molly opened the door to find John standing there, grinning and holding a bottle of Zinfandel.

"Wow!" She gave him a hug. "I was just calling you."

"I know," he grinned holding up his phone once he'd disengaged from her hug.

"Why didn't you answer?"

"Because I was standing right outside your door, genius. If you'd been listening, you would have heard it." They both laughed and she gave him another hug, this time melting into his strength and comfort. She was happy to have company after all. Sometimes being by herself was her own worst enemy.

"Man, is it good to see you! These past few days have been beyond weird. I don't even know how to explain it."

"First off, how are you doing?"

"Fine, why?"

"You're lying. You just buried your parents. There is no way you can be fine," he stated a bit cautiously. "What gives?"

"John, I am so strung out on trying to be strong, keeping it together despite the most difficult events I've ever had to go through—well, since the last time I had to be in the same room as my brother, anyway. If I let go now, you'd witness a complete meltdown. You would walk out that door and never come back. In fact, you'd have me taken to the psych ward." She looked at him through tears rimming her eyes, threatening to erupt. "I'm on overload right now and just really need to relax with a drink and my best friend. Can you just give me that?" John stared at her, silent. "What?"

"I'm just trying to decide what's best. Make you get it out or give you space." He paused, continuing to look at her. "Fine, you win. Those beautiful brown eyes get me every time."

"Thank you," she purred, batting her eyelashes.

"Yeah, yeah. But after you've had time to de-escalate, you have to tell me what's going on."

"And I will. I promise." She pretended to salute him. "I just don't have it right now."

She couldn't reveal the conditions of her inheritance yet. Saying it out loud would make it too real. All of it. Her parents' death, their will, her pain and humiliation from so many things and from so many years—all that had bubbled to the surface in the past several days. It felt like she had so many balls in the air, combinations of thoughts and feelings and emotions, that she was afraid they would all come crashing down around her, smashing to the tiniest shards, and she would never be able to put them all together again. She needed to process all of it on her own.

Besides, if she told John about the will, it would force her to be held accountable to something she wasn't even sure she wanted to follow through with yet. Was money really worth it? And yet there was an overriding voice in her head telling her to do it, just to prove them all wrong. If she didn't, that was like admitting defeat.

She shuddered when she realized how much that thought sounded like Max.

"Earth to Molly." John's voice called her from her reverie. She realized he was watching her again from the chair across from the couch where she was perched. "If you want to be by yourself there, kiddo, just say the word."

"What?" she asked, confused. She had just told him she wanted him here. Needed him here.

"You're having a party of one with yourself, Moll. Do you mind if I turn on the television and see if there's a game on?"

"No, I don't mind."

She knew her irritability showed just beneath the surface of her answer. But for the next half hour, Molly drank the majority of the bottle of wine John had brought, and met his questions with short answers.

He abruptly stood, threw the remote on the couch and turned to face her. "You know what, Moll? I'm feeling like an intruder here and it's not comfortable." He ran his fingers through his prematurely thinning hair, his hand coming to rest on the back of his neck, color rising in his cheeks as he now faced her. "I feel like we're playing a game, and it's a game I don't want to play. It's too risky, and the stakes are too high. I think I'm just going to head on home. I have an early day ahead of me tomorrow." He got up and began putting on his coat.

"What's wrong?" She knew she'd been shutting him out, but she didn't think he would leave.

"Nothing is wrong with me, Moll. But you're acting weird, and you won't let me know why. Let me know when you're ready to talk."

"So 'nless we do what you wanna do and talk about what you wanna talk about, you're leavin'?" She emptied the last drops from the bottle into her glass and took a big swallow. "I wasn't aware a friendship worked that way. I thought it was a two-way."

"That's not fair," he said quietly.

"No? You're sayin' 'nless I tell you what's on my mind at this moment, when ya know I'm not up for

it, you're leavin'. I'd say that's a pretty one-sided deal."
She was angry now. And she was going to make sure he
knew it. But she was right, dammit. She took another
gulp. "Jus' leave then."

"I didn't say we had to talk about anything
specific. Just something. Anything. I feel like I'm
walking on eggshells right now, and that's not a good
feeling."

"I told you to jus' leave then." She knew she
was being ugly, but she didn't care. He was just
bringing more ugliness bubbling to the surface.

John walked over to her and gently kissed her
forehead. She turned her head away from him and
walked into the tiny kitchen so the bar was between
them. She watched as he looked at her one more time.
She knew she was hurting him, and still she didn't care.
And then he turned and opened the door, quietly closing
it behind him as he left.

Molly stood leaning against the counter for a
moment for balance. She drained the rest of her glass
then poured another from an already open bottle in the
cupboard. She made her way to her room and threw
herself on the bed, sobs taking over her entire being.
The phone began to ring, but she ignored it until it
finally stopped and then began ringing again. She
finally picked it up.

Her nose was stuffy from crying, but she
managed to slur, "Jus' leave me alone, John. Go home.
I'm too tired to fight." She tossed the phone, aiming
for the nightstand but making the floor. It was the last
thing she remembered doing.

Molly awoke and lazily stretched after pressing
the snooze button on her alarm clock for the third time,
squinting at the too-bright blue numbers telling her it
was past the time she had planned to rise. She needed to

stay busy today until the scheduled photo shoot this afternoon, so she could shut out the discomfort of the last few days. The effects of last night's wine weighed her down in a blanket of fog. Why in the hell had she drank so much when she knew she had so much on her plate today? When will I learn to only have one glass of wine on nights before a big day, she wondered. The thought fled as quickly as it came, though. She had too much to do to waste time thinking about something so insignificant.

The phone rang, forcing her to untangle herself from the warm blankets of her bed to reach the receiver where it had landed from the night before.

"Ello?" She folded herself back into the still warm mattress.

"Molly, it's me. Joanna. Did I wake you up?"

"Hi, Jo. No, I was awake. Just getting ready," she lied, flinging her arm across her eyes.

"Ready for what, to take a nap? You sound groggy."

"Busted," she chuckled. "What's up?"

"What time did you get in yesterday? I kind of expected you to call me."

"By the time I finished unpacking, I was exhausted," she lied, feeling instantly guilty.

"What time will the column be ready? I hate to push, but it needs to be in my inbox before noon."

"And you'll have it before then, Jo. Trust me. Have I ever missed a deadline?" She hesitated a beat before adding, "Wait, don't answer that."

"Molly, I wish you would have just agreed to let someone else do it instead of insisting on doing it yourself. You had a darn good reason to ask someone to cover. But it's a little late now." Jo paused and took a breath. "Listen, I don't mean to sound insensitive, but I still have a business to run. And you insisted—"

"Jo, stop. I told you I would have it to you. I won't miss the deadline. Again."

"I realize it was only once, and I'm not trying to beat a dead dog, but that one time put us in a bind. It made everyone else scramble trying to cover your butt. Or I should say the paper's butt."

"I know. And I've said I'm sorry about a hundred times. I don't know what else I can say."

"I know. I'm sorry. I know I need to let it go and not keep throwing that ball back into play, but sometimes you remind me of one of my own kids, and it's my job to be sure you fully learn the lesson. Just keep producing quality work. Your health and fitness advice column is one of our best-rated pieces. And it just keeps getting better with the holidays approaching. And speaking of holidays," Jo rambled on, "what are you doing for Christmas this year since your plans of making a rare visit to your parents—Oh my hell, Molly. I'm so sorry."

"Don't worry about it, Jo," she said, trying to comfort her boss but rolling her eyes. "Besides, I haven't decided yet," she replied absentmindedly, taking her favorite pair of jeans from the shelf in her closet, rifling through the tops hanging beneath the shelf, and finally choosing a loose-flowing white gauzy number. "It's too far away to even think about."

"Let me know when you decide. We'll need your column in advance if you'll be gone."

"No prob. You'll be the first to know. But I do have a laptop that travels." She threw her clothes on the bed and headed for the shower. "You want my column by noon, right?"

"Yes, that's what I said."

"Then I need to go and finish getting it done." Joanna laughed, a sound that right now pierced Molly's ears. "By all means, do that. Talk to you later. And Molly?"

"Yeah?"

"Maybe spending the holidays with your sister and brother would be a good idea, given what you've all gone through."

"I said I'm not even thinking about it yet." That would be the last thing she would do—spend Christmas with Max. "You'll be the first to know, okay?"

"Don't get smart with me, Moll. You remind me of myself when I was your age. Wandering aimlessly, trying to find a purpose and be accepted for being different. I never was one to follow the rules or color within the lines. I always thought outside the box. We're just artists at heart."

"Thanks for your concern, Jo. I'm impressed you can remember back that far." She smiled through her sarcasm, her warmth for Jo crossing the phone lines.

"And you're a brat."

Molly hung up and headed for the shower, stubbing her toe in the process. "Damn!" she yelled, falling on her bed to assess the damage. Broken or not, she had a column to get done. And fast.

After her shower, Molly pulled the white blouse over her wet hair, then slipped into the soft cotton of her jeans, the knees shredded just as she liked them. And just as her parents hadn't. She was so different from the rest of them that sometimes she swore she was adopted. Maybe Max hadn't been teasing when he told her she was the milkman's kid. Except milk delivery went out of style way before she came along. The mere thought of her mother having an affair made her laugh. Her parents had been hopelessly devoted to each other, backing each other anytime she or her sister or brother tried to get what they wanted by playing one against the other. It didn't take long to know never to try that again. Except Max learned that if he went to their father, he would get whatever he wanted.

She continued thinking about her family as she padded barefoot across the tile floor to the kitchen for coffee and toast smothered in cinnamon butter. Her toe still throbbed, reminding her to avoid putting any pressure on it.

She wondered why she never felt comfortable at home. It was like she could never quite fit in. A square peg trying to squeeze into a round hole. Tight, uncomfortable, and restricted. Not only was she not a perfect fit, she didn't fit at all. She knew her parents loved her, but did they really love *her*? They didn't even know her. Who she was, really, was never acceptable. How she dressed, her hair, her choice in friends, her career. Sure, her parents said they were proud of her, but were they really? Especially her father. He treated her like she would someday find her mind and do what he would like her to do. It was one of the reasons she rarely went home. The pain of not being accepted by her own parents—people who were supposed to love her unconditionally—was just too great. It was easier to stay busy with her own interests and surround herself with people who knew her and loved her anyway. People like Jo. And John.

Her mind segued to John and the previous evening as the phone rang again, a harsh reminder that her headache from her wine the night before was in stiff competition with the ache in her likely broken toe. She looked at the number on caller ID.

"Speak of the devil," she answered timidly. "I was just thinking of you."

"Uh-oh. What'd I do now?"

"Not a thing. It's what I did."

"Yeah, that. Well--you know I can't stay mad at you."

"Whew!" she exhaled loudly, instantly wincing as pain sliced through her head. "Man, I have a headache. How much wine did I drink last night?"

"Obviously too much. When I left I thought you would go straight to bed. I take it that's not what happened?"

"Nah. Did a little writing. A little drinking. A little writing. A little drinking..."

"I think I'm getting the picture," he interrupted.

John was her best friend. They'd met in college, attempted dating a couple of times, but found it awkward. They used to tease each other that their friendship got in the way of their dating, and they'd mutually agreed to keep it platonic. Their friendship grew and survived the jealous girlfriends he had gone through and crazy boyfriends she'd had. They were to each other that one person the other could count on, come hell or high water. If the world were to crash down around them, she would throw all one hundred and ten pounds of herself over him to protect him and knew he would do the same for her.

"Whatcha doin' today?"

"Same as you. Working. Provided you ever get your butt moving," he answered warmly.

"I'm at my computer right now as we speak. Wanna stop by later, or do you have a hot date?"

"Hot date." Molly's disappointment began to take hold. She didn't want to be alone. But then he added, "with my co-worker's dog."

She hadn't realized she was holding her breath until she exhaled. "Dog sitting?"

"No, that's all I've been able to get to date me lately," he laughed.

"Maybe I'll stop by. If you're lucky."

"Knock before you enter. Just to be safe."

"You are a sick man. Just in case I haven't told you that lately," she said, the fondness she felt for him laced throughout her words.

"That's why you love me."

"Yeah, you just keep believing that," she laughed. "Gotta run. See ya later."

"If you're lucky."

Molly worked furiously in her home office, getting up only to cross the hall to the kitchen to refill her coffee mug. She had thought more than once about moving the coffeemaker into her office since she spent most of her time there anyway, but realized she depended on that distraction to get her away from her desk at consistent intervals. Once she sat down, she lost track of all time and could sit for hours at a time without even realizing there was a world beyond her computer screen.

Today was a treat. As soon as she sent her column to Jo's computer, she'd be headed across town for that photo shoot. Her freelance photography work kept her busy enough and nicely supplemented her income from the newspaper and her freelance writing. She thrived on the thrill of being in the make-believe world of her books, creating characters whose lives she loved and hated, traveling to market her work, her speaking engagements and book signings, as well as producing her weekly column at the newspaper. Her occasional photography gig was an added bonus. It allowed her creativity to expose itself through yet another medium, and it helped her feel balanced.

She finished the final touches of her column, hit the button, sending the column off to Jo and stood up, stretched, and gathered her camera and supplies. She slung the camera bag over her shoulder, grabbed a

Honeycrisp apple and headed out the door to her little black Honda for her journey to the family's home, a good forty-five minute drive away. Norah Jones kept her company on the radio.

Today's shoot was a family photograph session in preparation for holiday gifts. The family was a friend of a friend and by all appearances, was the perfect family. Given her background, Molly couldn't decide whether she was looking forward to it just to somehow prove it was actually all a lie, or out of envy for how a family not as dysfunctional as hers actually functioned. Were there actually normal families out there? That was the million dollar question. And whose definition of normal was even normal? In all the writing she had done, it had never once crossed her mind to put the words "normal" and "family" in the same sentence.

She was doubtful at this point. Jo's relationship with her daughter seemed foreign to her, and she had to admit, she'd felt pangs of envy more than once. She had wished a few times that Jo were her mother. And now she felt guilty for that. "You're such a Debbie Downer," Molly scolded herself aloud.

Pulling into the long driveway, Molly admired the huge, perfectly maintained home and manicured lawn in front of her, placing the chip on her shoulders securely in place once more. She told herself this was not a perfect family, but just one more that wanted the world to think they were. "It's all a big charade," she muttered as she got out of her car. She stretched and realized her headache was now completely gone, but her toe continued to ache horribly.

She reached for her camera and saw the most serene landscape off to her right. It seemed to cover miles—horses lazily wandering, gracefully dipping their heads occasionally at the lush green carpet beneath, a Palomino catching a glimpse of her and looking back for just a moment before returning to its task of doing nothing but looking beautiful.

She heard a voice behind her, and she jumped. A quick glance at her watch told her ten minutes had somehow gone by as she stared at the open land in front of her.

"You're Molly?" asked the woman as she extended her well-manicured hand.

"I am," she answered, offering her own plain hand to the woman.

"I'm Sharon, wife and mother to the brood you'll be photographing today," she said warmly.

Sharon spoke with ease and peaceful joy, pure contentment with being mother and wife. But Molly had gotten so good at being who she needed to be in order to not rock the boat, who's to say Sharon's expectations of her children wouldn't cause them to do the same? Molly would need to be persuaded it was for real.

"...started?"

Molly startled, realizing Sharon had been speaking. "I'm sorry. What?"

"Shall we get started? We thought we could do a few shots in the family room as well as some outdoors. What do you think?"

"Some of each is what I would recommend," Molly agreed. "When I get the proofs to you, you'll have more to choose from."

"Fabulous!" Sharon said eagerly. She took Molly's arm, leading her toward the front porch. "You know, it's so hard to get everyone together for these things. What with everyone having work and school schedules, hobbies..." she trailed off. "Well, I'm sure you know how it is, having a family of your own."

"Yes," Molly answered, offering nothing more. "How many children do you have? Six?"

"Yes, that's right. Each is so unique and different from one another. Sometimes it's hard to comprehend that children can be born and raised by the same parents and be such opposites of one another." She laughed what Molly thought to be a beautiful sound.

"Tell me about it," Molly muttered, not completely aware she had spoken out loud.

"Are you close to your siblings?" Sharon smiled her radiant smile.

"We don't live close to one another, so we don't see each other much. Why don't we start in the family room since everyone is already in the house?" Molly asked, changing the subject.

"That would be wonderful."

Sharon led her into the house, making small talk all the way. Molly found herself swept up in her enthusiasm and zest for life. Her joy seemed contagious, and Molly felt herself relax.

Molly walked into the kitchen, appreciating the warm feeling in the air and the smell of apples and cinnamon wafting from the oven. She felt a twist of envy and forced herself to remember why she was here. As the kids wandered into the kitchen to meet her, she was even more surprised. She practically had to catch her jaw from hitting the floor as she tried not to stare. The children ranged in age from six to seventeen and sported everything from dresses to jeans and T-shirts, each one so individual, yet all dressed in black and white. One of the older boys sported several piercings and a tattoo, one of the older girls was in a miniskirt Molly was sure left part of her backside uncovered, and one of the younger boys even had a bowtie, at which she couldn't help but smile. Behind the one with the piercing and tattoos trailed the dad, dressed in black dress pants and a simple white shirt with a black jacket.

She could fully appreciate Sharon's statement of each of them being so different from one another.

As Molly began placing them in position, guiding their poses and placement of hands and tilting of heads, she was startled to realize that neither Sharon nor her husband required their jewelry-studded son to remove his jewelry or even cover his tattoo.

When Molly suggested a shot without them, Sharon replied with a confident, "No, that's okay. That's who he is, and that's okay with us. They only had one rule, black and white. The rest was up to them." Molly waited for the rest of something—anything—to be said, for surely there would be more. But nothing came. That was completely opposite from when she was a teenager. Maybe this *was* the real deal. Could it be?

As the shoot progressed, she watched them relate with one another: the older siblings caring for the younger, an unkind word here and there as they joked and laughed with one another, clearly having a ball. She watched with bitter envy as the jewel-studded son put his arm lovingly around one of the younger girls. And it continued the entire shoot, three hours in all. Molly kept waiting for the "aha moment" to arrive, proving it was all a fraud. But it never came.

As she wrapped it up, packing her equipment and hauling it out to her car, Sharon accompanied her.

"Molly, thank you so very much for doing this for us."

"My pleasure," she answered, truly meaning it. "The proofs should be ready in two weeks. When I get them back, I'll call to set up a time for you and your husband, as well as the rest of the family if you would like, to look them over."

"How about if you come for dinner on that day," Sharon said, clearly happy with the idea.

"Uhh, yeah, sure. That would be great," Molly answered, surprising herself. "I'll call you then."

She took her time driving home, enjoying the feel of the wind coming through the slightly open sunroof, the fresh smell of the late October air permeating the car. Some houses had Christmas lights up already, and though she thought it was too early, they were beautiful in the dusk.

As she pulled into her garage, her cell phone rang. Without looking at caller ID, she knew it would be John, wondering what time they were going to hang out.

Molly woke up and looked at the clock. It was too early to get up, but she wasn't feeling well and couldn't stay laying down. She sat up and realized she was still dressed in her jeans and T-shirt, her silky hair now a tangled mess. She sat for a moment trying to figure out what happened. She couldn't remember, her mind was a blank slate. And the harder she tried, the more panicked she became.

She decided to get up, so she slipped on an old oversized sweater, pulled her hair into a ponytail, and walked into the living room. She realized the door wasn't locked, and a shiver sliced through her. How could she not remember to lock the door? She was such an idiot.

As she turned the deadbolt, then got a glass of water and a couple of antacids, the evening began coming back to her in clips. She cringed with each one that revealed itself. Why did she do and say what she did? Poor John. She felt humiliated all over again and hoped she could avoid him for a while until he hopefully forgot about it. She didn't even know what to say to him. She looked at the digital clock on the end table just as it turned to read 4:03 a.m.

She set the now half-empty glass of water on the counter and sat down on the couch, tucking her knees to her chest, wrapping her sweater and her arms tightly around her legs, and resting her chin on her knees. A tear rolled down her cheek, hot against her cool skin. What had become of her? Were her parents right? How could that be? And what was she going to do about it if they were? Right now, she felt like she was on a train that was headed straight for a cliff, physically feeling the pain that was to come.

Her hands began to tremble, and she felt clammy. Her stomach lurched a bit, and she wondered for a moment if she should hightail it to the bathroom. Except her body wasn't capable of hightailing anywhere at the moment. She sat motionless, hoping the moment would pass. When it did, she chalked it up to simply being tired.

Molly stood up slowly, her legs wobbly beneath her. She made her way to her room, slipped out of her jeans, and climbed under the covers, sweater still in place. She took the envelope from Madison in her hand and looked at it without opening it, setting it down once again on her nightstand. Eventually she fell into a fitful sleep, waking to see it was 8:45. She needed to get up, shower, and go check in with Jo. And get a very, very strong cup of coffee on the way to calm her throbbing head and the occasional lingering nausea.

She kept herself busy throughout the day, trying hard to prevent thoughts of the past week from crowding their way in again. She drove to Jo's office and talked with her about a new direction she would like to take the column. Jo said she would give it some thought and get back to her. After talking business, they headed out for lunch at a little corner bistro, walking the two blocks from Jo's office. Jo asked the questions that Molly had been avoiding since the funeral, and

Molly met each one with a shrug or an elusive answer. She was relieved when Jo eventually gave up, and their conversation turned to more neutral ground.

Once seated at their table, Molly looked intently out the window. Jo tried to followed her gaze. Molly picked up her water glass, a slight tremor in her hand and her face pale, colorless.

"Are you feeling okay, Molly?"

"You know, I think I may be coming down with something. I didn't sleep well last night, and with the stress of the week or so, my body is rebelling."

"Your immune system is probably compromised. Why don't you take a few days off and rest up. Get some sleep. I'll cover the column for you."

"You sure?" Molly asked sheepishly.

"Of course I'm sure," she smiled and patted Molly's hand in a motherly fashion. "I need you to be healthy. Have you decided what you're going to do for the holidays yet? If you don't spend it with your brother and sister, why don't you come spend it with us?"

"That's really sweet, Jo. But I've already made plans with my sister," she lied, feeling instantly guilty. She seemed to be feeling guilty a lot lately. She hated to lie to Jo, but she was too tired to think up any other believable excuse.

Truth be told, spending the holidays with Jo's family, watching them in their Christmas joy—opening presents, laughing, having fun with one another—was not something Molly could deal with right now. She didn't know what she was going to do, but she did know she wasn't going to spend it at Jo's.

Molly ran some errands after leaving Jo and drove past John's house, knowing he was more than likely at work. Still, she felt the need to check. She wasn't sure what she'd do if he were home. She could go check how mad he was and bat her brown eyes again so he'd get over it. But how many times would that work?

She pulled up to the curb even though John's car was gone, then breathed a sigh of relief and hit the gas to leave. The risk of him unexpectedly coming home was too unnerving.

She drove home thinking about the contents of the mysterious envelope Madison had sneaked into her suitcase. It was still on her nightstand, twisted and bent from her hours of contemplation. It was time to open it.

Unlocking the house door, she went directly to the bedroom, sat on the edge of the bed, and ripped open the envelope before she had time to change her mind. Again.

The card, adorned with the most beautiful, rustic looking angel on the front, said simply, "You may be my little sister, but your heart is bigger than anyone else I know. Now it's time to be big enough to forgive your brother for tormenting you, and Dad for not stopping it. Be bigger than Max, Molly. Forgiving him doesn't make right what he did, it simply frees you to live a happier life. You're stronger than you think you are, and I'll be praying for you to funnel that strength into positive changes. Someday I hope you see yourself as I do—talented, beautiful, sweet, and gentle. And I'm sure the world would love to see you smile more." After which was drawn a bright happy smiley face. "Always your big sister, and always here for you. You're loved deeply, no matter how much you resist it. I love you, and there's nothing you can do about it. Maddie."

Molly smiled through the hot tears that fell from her thick black eyelashes. She could just picture Madison saying that to one of her clients in her shrink voice. However, those words spoken to her right now, created a strange mixture of relief that someone truly believed in her, and guilt at how many people she had let down. But forgive Max? That was a tall order, and one that would require prayer and strength that she knew she herself did not possess.

Chapter Six

Max walked through the door, hoisted his suitcase on the bed and began putting things away, still thinking about the past several days. He needed to get himself back to normal. He reached for the phone to call Mandi. He could always count on her to be there for him when he needed her. He knew she wanted more from him than he was willing to give, and sometimes he wondered if he was being unfair by not giving more.

He knew full well that he was keeping her on a string short enough to give her hope, yet long enough to give himself space. But he never allowed himself to dwell too deeply or to feel guilt. He convinced himself that, as long as he was straight with her, letting her know it wasn't serious and that they were not in a relationship, he was in the clear. As long as she knew the conditions, he had nothing to feel guilty about. But now and again, that irritating nagging in the pit of his stomach caused him to wonder.

When the phone continued to ring, eventually going to voicemail, he hung up without leaving a message. Her loss. He unpacked, grabbed the last pale ale from the refrigerator, stripped down to his boxers, and lay against the pillows on his bed. He flipped through the sports channels but found nothing of interest, nothing that led him to believe he would have any new business. He downed the rest of his beer, brushed his teeth, and fell into a fitful sleep.

Max reached his arm out from under the covers to turn off the alarm after two full minutes of the irritating beeping. He reluctantly poked his head out to remind himself he was the only one in the bed. Damn, it was cold in here! In one swift move, he leapt from the bed and wrapped himself in the plush black robe that hung over his door. He slid his feet into the warmth of his memory-foam slippers and made his way downstairs to pour a cup of coffee, already brewed, thanks to whoever invented the programmable coffeemaker that he had set the evening before.

He was eager to get to the office and see what all he had missed while he was gone, and to get back to familiar territory. *His* territory. His mind traveled a mile a minute in several different directions while he dressed and ate breakfast, until finally he dumped the rest of his oatmeal down the garbage disposal, grabbed his coffee off the counter, and headed out the door. He had a lot to catch up on from his absence, and it wasn't getting done here.

Somehow he managed to get stuck at nearly every red light, quickly understanding how and why road rage had become such an issue. Finally, he turned into the parking lot of the firm of which he had become partner two short years ago—Seamus Seamus & Forrester, PC. He pulled in neatly next to Paul's Cadillac, which looked like it had already been there for a while. Old man Seamus and his son Junior had taken him in as partner after he won a hugely respectable case for them, a case that brought in a significant amount of business from sports professionals, which was right in line with Max's personal interest.

He'd played football through college, and at one time he'd had dreams of playing professionally. Those dreams were cut short when he sustained a knee injury that he'd never fully recovered from. He had been looked over by one too many scouts when he finally realized that dream had to be put to rest. Being able to be part of the industry by representing the players was the next best thing.

"Maxwell!" Paul exclaimed when Max breezed through the door. "I thought I told you to take an extra day off to unpack and take care of business."

"Paul, do you know me at all?" Max scoffed.

"I do. Which is why I'm not at all surprised you're here." The old man grinned. "And I can't say I'm sorry to see you either." He gave Max a fatherly pat on the back and a half-hug as he pulled him close. "How are you doing?"

"Ready to get back to work. Lay it on me. Anything happen while I was gone?"

"Nothing we couldn't handle."

"You saying you don't need me?"

"Somehow we soldiered on," Paul teased.

"I'm going to hole up in my office, get the messages off my phone, maybe even return a few. Want to meet in your office for coffee in an hour or two so you can catch me up on all the gossip that's been going on around town?"

"Max, my man," Paul grinned, "you've got yourself a date."

"I don't date your kind. This is just coffee, Paul."

"You probably already had a date last night." He only half-teased.

"Nah," Max shrugged. "Didn't feel like sharing my own company with anyone else." He gave Paul a playful punch in the arm.

"Go on to your room," Paul chuckled. "It sure is good to have you back."

For the following hour and a half, Max listened to one voicemail after the other, jotting some down, deleting others without completely listening to the whole message. His cell phone vibrated in his coat pocket. He looked at the screen and saw it was Mandi.

"'Lo?" he answered, still jotting down a message.

"Hey there, Max. I saw I had a missed call from you but no voicemail."

"You know I don't leave voicemails."

"How did it go back in Minnesota?"

"Mandi, I can't talk right now. I just got in, and I have a lot of catching up to do."

"Oh, of course," she said.

He could sense the hurt in her voice, and he pushed the niggling guilt away. "Mandi, listen," he said gently, wondering how he could make her feel better. Damn, women were a pain sometimes. Their feelings got hurt so easily. His desk phone rang again and he felt torn between answering it and trying to finish his conversation with Mandi. If one could call it a conversation. "Mandi—"

"You know what, Max? Answer your other phone. I have to run; someone's at my door. You have a great day, okay?" And before he could fully say good-bye, the line went dead. He knew she was lying. There was no one at the door. But as soon as he answered his desk phone that continued to ring, he forgot all about Mandi.

At ten o'clock, Max gave a courtesy knock on Paul's open door. Paul looked up from the papers he was studying on his desk and immediately put them down when he saw Max.

"Let me call Junior and see if he can join us." He reached for the phone and hung up after a few moments without having said a word. "He must be running late. He finished up a trial late yesterday afternoon," Paul explained.

"I'll have to meet up with him when he gets in to hear about it. Anything good?"

"Eh, basically just a filler. Pro bono," he added.

"Pro bono—" Max snickered at the irony and saw Paul watching him quizzically. "Just something that happened at my parents' this past week," he explained. "It seems to be following me."

"Tell me about it." Paul got up and poured them both a cup of coffee from the carafe on the corner table. "My curiosity is piqued." He handed Max a cup of steaming black brew, then motioned him over to a seating area in front of a gas fireplace that was glowing warmly. "You've never talked about your parents much. How was the funeral? Most of all, how are you doing?" Paul took a sip of coffee and waited patiently for Max to answer.

"Not a whole lot to talk about."

"Oh? I don't think I buy that at all."

After a moment Max turned his attention from the fire back to Paul and said too quietly, "Smart man." Max stood and walked slowly over to the window, looking out at the mountains—majestic yet so cold, completely capped in pure white snow. Untouched. He noted the irony of how he viewed the mountains to how his heart felt. Cold and untouched. And once again, the guilt began prying loose the hinges.

He could feel Paul's eyes on his back as he waited for him to continue talking. "They've orchestrated a very strange will that I'm trying to come to terms with."

"Go on," Paul urged. "What kind of will?"

Max turned his attention away from the window to face the man he had so much respect and admiration for. The man he felt he knew even more than he had known his own father.

"There are a number of...hoops...shall we say for lack of a better term, that I need to jump through in order to get my inheritance. Kind of like a circus dog. A checklist that each of us has to complete."

"Sounds intriguing," Paul mused.

"Yeah, that's a good description," Max mumbled.

Max walked back to his chair and sat down. He leaned forward, elbows on his knees, looking down into the coffee cup that his hands circled around. "There are three items I need to complete. If I do it, there's a half-mil waiting for me to collect. Sounds like a bribe, if you ask me," he added.

"Depends on what those items are and what the motive is." Paul sat back in his chair, crossed one leg over the other, and studied him, waiting for Max to go on.

"Apparently I'm a screw-up and need to learn a lesson in humanity. Or humility," he added with a touch of sarcasm that he knew hadn't escaped Paul. If there was one thing Paul excelled at, it was intuition.

"That's a lesson we could all learn," Paul stated simply. "So what are they? These items."

"One is to help build a house from beginning to end for Habitat for Humanity."

"Hmm..." Paul contemplated.

"Hmm what?"

"Maybe they want you to learn good, hard, manual labor. And the meaning of a home. Not a house, but a home. Not many of us who have a home to go to each evening even give it a second thought. I know I usually don't." There was a moment of thoughtful silence. "What else?"

"I have to chair an AIDS fundraiser."

"Why AIDS?"

"Because my uncle died from HIV. Which, I might add, my parents never even told me about," he said defensively.

"Were you close to him?"

"Hell no."

"Then why would they?" Paul asked him matter-of-factly.

"Whose side are you on?" Had Max not known the old man as well as he did, he would have gotten angry.

"Yours, son. Always yours. I'm just trying to understand the terms and conditions and the motive behind them. In our line of work, we come to know very well there's always a motive. Good or bad, even when we can't find it. *Always* a motive," he stressed.

"They want me to use my brain and connections to put together a big gala or something." He saw Paul chuckle. "What's so funny?"

"Are you whining?"

Max shot him a dirty look and turned his attention back out the window to the safety of the mountains. The barren cold mountains that stood in stark contrast to the warmth of the office, fire blazing. And right now he preferred the cold, barren mountains.

"So do it."

"What?" Max turned and looked at him, wide-eyed.

"Do it." Paul repeated with more force. "What's the big deal? You'd be doing all of mankind a huge favor. Think of it as a pro bono project."

"That's what I was laughing about before when you mentioned Junior's pro bono trial. The timing was uncanny."

"If you ask me, we don't do nearly enough pro bono work in our profession."

"Tell me you're not getting soft on me."

"No, son. You'll find as you get older, things take on a whole different perspective. *Life* does," he added.

"Yeah, you're getting soft on me." Max chided him.

"Don't tell Junior. He'll have me committed to one of those old folks homes."

"The third thing I have to do..."

"There's more?" Paul interrupted.

"Yeah. I must have been a very bad boy," he chuckled, as did Paul. "I have to put in forty hours at a homeless shelter. That oughta be—" Max abruptly stopped talking as he remembered the part of the will where his dad said he had talked to his boss. How could he have forgotten that?

"You must think I'm an idiot, big guy," Max chuckled, shaking his head slowly.

"Why would I think that?" Paul asked, confusion evident.

"You can stop the act." Bitterness crept into Max's voice. "But you're good." Max shook his head again slowly.

"What act?" Paul was frowning. "What in God's name are you talking about?"

"I guess there's been too much going on in my mind that I forgot one very important detail in the will."

"What's that?"

Paul was either a great actor, he was quickly getting dementia, or he really didn't know. Max would like to believe the latter, but how could that be? That would mean his father was calling his bluff and lying for some reason.

"I know my father talked to you, Paul. Stop covering for him."

"I'm not covering anything for him. Yes, he talked to me. In fact, we met for lunch. And it was a good lunch. But I'm not sure what it is you think he told me."

"How about you come clean with me and tell me what he said then. Because at this point, I don't think I can handle it if my father was lying just to get me to do what he wanted me to do." The thought of that kind of betrayal and control stung Max.

"Settle down and stop jumping to conclusions, Maxwell." Paul stood, filled both their cups with the still steaming black brew, and sat back down, stretching both legs in front of him, crossing them at the ankles, looking now more like the lawyer than the friend. Max waited. "He called a while back—oh, hell, it must be about a year ago now or so—and asked if we could meet. We talked about you, what a fine job you're doing here at the firm, making partner, how proud of you he is...was."

"He really said that?" Max interrupted. "That he's proud of me?"

"Yes, he really did. Why does that surprise you so much?"

"Why didn't he ever tell me that?"

"When did you give him a chance, Max? When did you give him the time of day? You've been so caught up in trying to get ahead in the world of law. And for what? So you can get where I am? You already are."

"What else did my father say?"

"He told me that he and your mother were working on a project to try to right the wrongs they thought they'd done. He said you might not understand it, but they hoped you would someday. Or something to that effect," he added.

"He's right there," Max commented, more to himself than Paul.

"He wanted to ask me that if it ever came down to it—and that I would know when that time was, if it ever came at all—if I would support you and help you. Be able to understand and encourage flexibility with your work schedule and caseload. But he didn't give me details. It was just a pleasant, leisurely visit. But from what was said, Max, I got the distinct feeling that he and your mother loved you more than you ever realized. That they were more proud of you than you ever knew. He seemed one of the most grounded, well-intentioned, and genuinely good people I've ever met."

Max felt a sting of something unfamiliar, but he didn't know what it was. He hadn't known any of what Paul had just told him. He realized he had just assumed his parents would always be there, that he would never have to think about these things. He was ashamed to admit that by trying to be someone they could be proud of, he had missed the fact that they maybe already were.

For just a moment, he felt time had robbed him when his eyes were wide open. He wanted to think God had played a cruel joke on him, but that would mean he believed in God. And he didn't. Or did he? He didn't even know that right now. He just knew the unfamiliar feeling that had nagged him a moment ago had come back stronger, and it almost felt like pain. It was a pain he hadn't allowed himself to feel in a long time, and it wasn't something he wanted to feel. He had to stop it.

"So you didn't know about the so-called conditions?"

"No, I didn't. But I can't say it sounds unreasonable. It sounds like a father who loves his son and has the balls to show some tough love. The ones who don't are why we're in business. Because of the ones who feel the world owes them and that they're entitled to the whole world on a platter. The ones who don't take responsibility for their actions. It's always someone else's fault."

"If that's how you feel, why do you stay in the business?"

"Because there are also the ones who are falsely accused that deserve representation. There are the ones who simply made a dumb mistake, and I don't believe punishment is the answer. Learning the lesson is. Sometimes our clients are the victims of horrendous crimes while they were growing up, or in the name of love. Hell, often even victims of themselves. Those people need justice in the form of treatment and rehabilitation. Not condemnation, judgment, and punishment."

Paul paused a moment, standing in front of the large window, looking out at the mountains. Max knew Paul's love for the mountains ran as deep as his own, and Paul and his wife escaped to the mountains frequently, far enough so there was no cell phone service.

"I'm not talking about people who hurt children, murderers, rapists..." Paul clarified. "You'll notice I haven't taken one of those cases in decades."

Max did a mental run-through of all the cases he knew Paul had handled during his time there and the cases he had heard about prior to his being associated with the firm. And he couldn't remember a single one. "I told my sister I don't take those either. Don't think she believed me though. When did you stop taking those cases?" Max asked after some thought.

"When I felt like I was selling my soul to the devil. When it was simply about a win rather than justice." He turned to face Max. "When I stopped being able to sleep at night. Or look at myself in the mirror in the morning."

Max could feel the passion pulse through the old man that he felt for not only his job, but for the profession. He was more impressed with Paul now than he had ever been.

"What do you say you do the research on Habitat for Humanity, find out where and when the projects will be happening, and Junior and I will help. We'll make it a team project."

Max put his cup on the table where the coffee carafe was, then stood for a moment before he walked to the door. He leaned on the doorframe with his right hand, tucking his left in the pocket of his perfectly pressed pants. He looked down at the floor for a moment before he turned and looked at Paul who was still standing by the window, watching Max.

"Yeah, nice try. I don't know yet if I'm going to be the circus dog yet." And he walked out, stopping when he heard Paul's voice through the open door.

"Hey, Max?"

"Yeah?" he turned to look at him.

"Thanksgiving at my house? Connie will be hurt if you don't come. She loves you more than she does me," he teased.

"I can't think of anywhere else I'd rather be," Max grinned.

"Feel free to bring someone," Paul hinted.

Max thought briefly about Mandi. "Nah. It'll just be me."

But Paul noticed the hesitation. "If you change your mind, know it's okay. About bringing a guest that is, not changing your mind."

"Wouldn't dream of changing my mind. I want to see your beautiful wife."

The sound of Paul's laughter followed Max out the door.

Before Max was even back in his office, his mind was covering the huge trial he was to begin the following week. He mentally went through his opening, the exhibits, and his closing argument, examining them for how the prosecution might try to twist their case in order to win. He sat down and went through the stacks of papers, making sure each had been discovered. A discovery violation was the last thing he needed at this point.

He wished he had time to go to the gym before work to help him strategize. There was nothing like a good workout to get his heart pumping and his mind churning out ideas. To be at the top of his game. And that's sometimes what he felt like it was. A game. Who was going to be the winner and who would be the loser. And he hated to lose. Max did anything he had to in order not to lose. Losing was for losers, and Maxwell Forrester was not a loser.

The trial arrived before he knew it, but Max was more than ready and prepared. In fact, if he had to say so himself, he was on top of his game like never before. His opening statement went without a hitch, and throughout the trial he felt he had the jury eating out of the palm of his hand. And it felt good.

The morning of closing arguments, he studied his notes and played through his closing argument in his mind while he ate his breakfast—hearty steel-cut oats with berries, a piece of whole wheat toast, pomegranate juice, and coffee. His morning staple. His body wouldn't know what to do if he deviated from his routine breakfast. Once in a while he threw in a protein shake for good measure.

Max hoped the jury would come back with a verdict by the end of the day so he wouldn't have to wait over the weekend. Waiting wasn't something he did well. Besides, it seemed like a pretty open and shut case. If the jury had any brains at all, they would see the truth and straight through the prosecution's twisted tale of how the incident happened.

His client couldn't be held accountable for what he'd done. He had been under the influence of steroids, and everyone knows what steroids can make people do. Thanks to the media and the expectations of impossible-to-please fans, professional athletes were often forced into doing whatever they had to do to survive in the business. So no one could fault his client for that. And his witnesses had kicked ass on the stand the day before, and as far as he was concerned, the prosecution's witnesses were weak. They couldn't have won over a hill of ants, much less a jury. And Max believed, more than anything, that the winning card was the fact that his client had sworn off steroids, voicing his sincerest apologies, stating he was attending therapy for drug abuse...and he actually almost had Max convinced, he was that good.

Dressed in his black suit, the one that had brought him luck so many times before, not a black hair out of place, his blue eyes bright with anticipation of what was to come, he pulled into the parking lot and crossed to the door in long purposeful strides.

"Hey, Paul. How's it going?" he asked as he waltzed through the door.

"Never been better. Ready to knock 'em dead up there today?"

"Of course," Max answered confidently. "I don't know any other way."

Paul chuckled, "That's why you're a partner here. Don't forget it." But Max knew he was teasing. Paul wasn't in it for the win. That was Max and Junior's gig.

"Wouldn't dream of it." He patted the old man on the back. Max breezed into his office, made sure his briefcase was in order, and headed out the door for his short two-block walk to the courthouse. He enjoyed the walk—close enough to walk summer and winter, and far enough to walk off precourt jitters and postcourt wind-down.

Max walked past the security station in the courthouse, placed his hand in the scanner, and continued his journey to room 402, where he would be displaying his dynamic closing argument in a matter of moments. He felt the electricity of excitement surge throughout his entire being. He lived for these moments. The moments when he could shine and show the outcome of the hours he'd poured into a case. The hours of research, writing, reading case law, trying to find the tiniest of loopholes in cases or statutes to use to his advantage. He was known by others in his profession as a cutthroat attorney. Max saw it as simply skill on his part and jealousy on theirs.

He walked with a determined step, distracted briefly by a tall, slender, red-headed woman with a knockout red dress on. He completed a visual scan of her, head to foot, while continuing on to catch the elevator to the fourth floor. As he entered the courtroom, he was relieved to find he had arrived before his client, so he had time to display his things, get his visuals ready, and to mentally prepare.

The prosecution team arrived and took their side of the courtroom. The opposing attorney greeted him with an obligatory, "Good morning, Maxwell." He nodded in their direction, offering a distracted smile while he slid his hands into the pockets of his perfectly pressed black dress pants. Within five minutes his client, dressed in a pair of tan dress pants, a white silk button-up shirt, and a tan tweed sports coat, sauntered into the court room. He looked every part the wealthy athlete. Max realized he probably should have coached him a bit more on dress. He didn't want to negatively impact the jury. Especially in the eleventh hour. But it would have to be what it would be. The women of the jury could very well be positively impacted.

He smiled. He would be sure to play on that. His own perfectly straight, white-toothed smile, piercing blue eyes and black, perfectly combed hair had worked for him more times than he could possibly count. He was completely aware of the impact he had on women. One day he would settle down, but not anytime soon. He was having too much fun playing the field, enjoying the game while it lasted. The redhead in the lobby flashed through his mind. The life his parents had might have worked for them, but he didn't want that complication. The burden of knowing that everything he decided to do or not do would impact another…no. Things were simple right now. He could come and go whenever and wherever he pleased. Things could stay like this for a long time.

Max talked quietly with his client for a few moments, preparing him by filling him in on what the highlights of his closing argument would be. He stopped when the bailiff asked them all to rise as the judge walked in. He glanced at the prosecution as they all rose in respect for the judge, then sat back down at the bailiff's announcement that they may be seated.

Court proceeded as usual—preparatory matters were completed and the judge read the jury instructions as he had read them thousands of times before. The prosecutor rose to deliver his closing first, addressing the jury as though they were all friends and on the same side. Max watched the jurors' faces closely, trying to read what they were thinking as they listened to his opponent. Max leaned in to hear his client whisper something of interest a time or two, making sure to appear relaxed and confident, dazzling those in the jury who looked at him with his smile, as he took notes of what to add to his closing argument, capitalizing on the prosecutor's points.

Finally it was Max's turn to take the stage. He stood, straightened his tie, smoothed his suit jacket, and walked over to stand before the jury. Every move was deliberate.

"Ladies and gentlemen of the jury," he began, pausing for effect, looking at each member individually, "not only did my client not commit the preposterous acts the prosecution is trying to make you believe he did, but the evidence has told you it was literally impossible."

Max walked in front of the jury box, speaking as if he were having a personal conversation with each of them, making note of who was following his lead and who wasn't, pausing for emphasis when needed, startling them a time or two with a forceful word, a dramatic effect that had worked for him numerous times. He had learned that closing arguments weren't only about facts and evidence, but equally about theatrics and strategy. God it felt good to have so much power and to be back in his own controlled arena again.

He delivered a powerful punch for the concluding sentence and smiled inwardly at the noticeable impact it had on the jury. Then he took his place back at the table next to his client. The prosecutor stood for his one last chance to persuade the jury, to prove beyond a shadow of a doubt that the defendant was guilty. Max believed that was not only unlikely but impossible for him to do.

At least that's what the jury thought he believed. And that's all that mattered.

After both sides had finished, the jury filed out of the courtroom and into the jury deliberation room by means of the hallway that ran behind the courtroom. The court clerk notified counsel for both sides that they would be notified as soon as a verdict was in or if the jury had a question. At that point, after one final handshake with the prosecutor, Max instructed his client to remain in close proximity to the court and to keep his cell phone in his hand no matter what, so he could get a hold of him when he heard from the court clerk. Then he made his way out of the building.

Max headed toward his office, cell phone in hand, volume loud enough that there would be no chance to miss it, should it ring sooner than expected. He closed the door behind him but was too hyped up to sit at his desk. He paced, attempted to work on other files for a while, and finally resorted to the view from his window. The view that, no matter how many times he looked, he never tired of. The window encompassed a large part of the wall behind his desk. He stood there, gazing out at the city, watching the traffic below and marveling at how unpredictable life was; how one person's life could change forever while the rest of world marched on as if nothing had changed. He stayed still until his phone finally rang, letting him know that things were going to change again.

And in his direction, if the jury had any sense.

Chapter Seven

Madison was expertly and quickly getting everyone ready to leave the house so she could get them to school on time when Oliver took her hand, clinging tightly as though his life depended on it.

"Oliver, honey, let go. We're going to be late, and--" She stopped when she saw the seriousness in his wide eyes. "What's wrong?"

"I don't think I feel good. Maybe I should stay home."

Madison tried hard to stop the smile that threatened to escape. "You *think* you don't feel good? What are you feeling?" It was hard to imagine that in first grade something could be so bad that he didn't want to go to school. Madison asked a few questions, and Oliver reluctantly told her what was going on.

"Two boys are mad at me because they like the same girl."

"And?"

"Well, that girl is my best friend.

"Honey, I'm afraid I don't understand."

"Mom!" He said, exasperated, near tears. "They threatened to beat me up on the playground if I didn't back off."

"Back *off*?" Madison had folded him into a hug, smiled over his head, and said, "You have to go to school, sweetie, or they will do the same thing tomorrow and the next day. You have to show them you're not afraid of them." When on earth had first graders even started to notice each other that way?

"But I *am* afraid of them," he whimpered.

"Don't show them that, sweetie." She kneeled on one knee in front of him, placed her hands on his shoulders, looked directly in his eyes. "If they see that they can't bully you, then they won't try because it won't be so fun for them anymore." She kissed his forehead. "Deal?"

"Deal," he said, little more than a whimper, trying to make himself believe it was going to work that way.

It was nearly impossible for Madison to stay stern and not back down, the mamma bear in her wanted to protect her little cub from the tigers of the world. "I will watch you walk to the door, and when I pick you up, I will get there early and watch you walk to the car. Will that make you feel better?"

"Yeah." His voice was sad. "And maybe going to see Grandma and Grandpa this weekend will help. Grandma makes the best chocolate chip cookies."

Madison willed away the tears that sprang up, clouding her vision. She quickly looked away and reached for her sunglasses which she was wearing more frequently since being back home for moments exactly like this. She knew she had to have the conversation with the kids, and Phil was already irritated that she had put it off as long as she had. She just didn't have it in her to tear their world apart. The longer she could wait, the longer their world would remain fully intact. She knew it was crazy to even think that way, especially since she was a therapist and should know better, but the part that wanted to protect her children won over rationalization.

"Go on now, honey," she said gently, patting him on the bottom. "Hop in the car so we can go."

Zoey had been watching from the doorway and decided to put her two cents in. "Oliver, be a man and stand up to them."

"Zoey, I'm only six. That's not a man," he countered, sounding older than he was.

"Well, stop acting like a baby. If you're a baby, they'll treat ya like one." She flung her backpack over her shoulder with attitude and put a protective arm around her little brother. "Come on."

"And how is it you know all this when you're only nine?" Madison asked, hiding a smile through lingering tears.

"Cause I've been there, Mother. I was six three years ago."

"Oh," Madison stifled a giggle. "Silly me."

"You were a man, Zoey?" Oliver asked as if Zoey just confided to him the biggest secret ever told.

"No, stupid. I'm a girl." Zoey answered, sounding exasperated.

Madison listened to the two of them bantering back and forth and grinned at the camaraderie between her children despite their squabbles. That closeness was something she couldn't remember having with her own brother and sister for all too long. She hoped Zoey and Oliver would always be close and not become estranged from one another as she and her own siblings were.

"Come on, kiddos. We don't want to be late. Let's get going." After some playful teasing about who got to sit in the front, Zoey clearly taking advantage of lead in age, they both took their places in the backseat. Madison had never wavered over the fact that neither could sit in front until they were twelve years old. Zoey had argued with her more than once very dramatically about how it could be so dangerous in their big Durango. As if inside the confines of their vehicle, they would be safe from the evils of the world. Madison thought of that now as she wondered if her parents had felt fear within the confines of their own presumed-safe zone.

As soon as Oliver fastened himself in, he turned on the TV screen on the headrest of the seat in front of him and popped in his favorite movie.

"That one *again*, Ol?" Zoey scolded as she reached to turn it off.

"Mom!" Oliver complained, slapping Zoey's hand away.

Madison frowned. "Zoey, listen to your iPod and stop picking on your brother. You don't need to be worrying about anyone but yourself."

Zoey rolled her eyes in answer. "What*ever*."

"What*ever*?" Madison echoed, finding humor in the comment.

"Yes, what*ever*," Zoey said again. "You're too old to get it, Mom."

"Oh, I see. I am, am I?" Madison didn't find Zoey quite as funny this time. In fact, it outright stung. She wondered if that was really how her kids saw her. Old?

She dropped off the kids, watching Oliver walk to the door as promised. He hesitated briefly at the door as if finding the courage to muster forward, then disappeared. From there, Madison headed to the market to pick up some things for dinner that night. Normally, Natalia would do this, but she'd offered this morning since she'd be driving by the grocery store anyway.

After the grocery store she over to St. Thomas Catholic Church to pick up the garments there she was responsible for having laundered. It was a way she could serve at her church that fit neatly into her already too-full schedule. It was a rare evening anymore that she was not too exhausted to have a decent conversation with Phil. Their tenth wedding anniversary was coming up on New Year's Day, and guilt stabbed sharply as she realized that she was more overwhelmed about whether to make reservations for them somewhere than she was joyful about what they had done together in those ten years, the top of the list being Zoey and Oliver. She knew she would have to decide quickly, because anywhere worth staying required reservations months in advance, especially on New Year's.

Madison's appointment book was back-to-back today, as were most days. She felt fortunate to have a separate entrance for her office located on the west side of their home. She enjoyed having her office in her home, but she still needed a clear separation between work and home. And she certainly didn't want her patients walking through her home.

Madison followed the plush beige carpet to her office. Her degree hung proudly on the wall behind her desk. Greenery was displayed in every possible location. The skylight directly in the center of her ceiling let in enough sunlight so that a simple soft lamp in the corner of the room was sufficient lighting, giving the room a peaceful feeling. For her patients, as well as herself.

Being a therapist had always been her dream, and being able to work out of her home so she could be fully present for her children was a huge bonus. Madison felt so lucky she and Phil were on the same page when it came to parenting their children. Well, other than the times he told her she spoiled them way too much, especially when she had purchased that pony for Zoey's ninth birthday without consulting him first. He told her he would try to look at it as if she had only the best of intentions and did what she did because she was trying to be the best mom possible. But she knew she had gone too far without at least telling him about it first. She was just afraid he would have said no, and she didn't want to have that battle.

The knock on the door, indicating her first patient had arrived, brought her focus back to her job. By the time she answered the door, she had made a smooth, practiced mental transition, focusing entirely on the matter at hand. Her therapist mode was turned on like a light switch.

Before she knew it, it was time to wrap up her two o'clock session. It was a little after three, and time to go pick up the kids from school. Unless it was impossible for her to leave, Madison usually insisted on taking the kids to and from school herself. She loved having that time to spend with them, to transition to another part of the day together. Besides, she had promised Oliver she would be there before school was out so she could watch him walk from the building to the car. And that was one thing she had promised herself she would never do. Break a promise.

With the kids safely buckled in, Madison pulled away from the school.

"How was your day, you two?" she asked.

"Great. Made a new friend today," Zoey said matter-of-factly. "Her name is Lizzy, and she moved here from California."

"Well, that's wonderful, honey," Madison answered, looking at her daughter in her rearview mirror. "How was your day, Oliver?"

"Fine," he murmured, looking out the window.

"Anything you want to talk about?" she persisted.

"Uh-uh."

Madison looked at his sober demeanor in the backseat and decided to leave it alone. He would talk to her when he was ready. He always did. On his time. In fact, Oliver had done everything on his time, from the moment Madison went into labor with him.

Natalia had cookies fresh from the oven waiting for the kids. As if the scent wafted directly from the door to the car, Zoey had her seatbelt unbuckled before the car was in park and her door open as she made a beeline for the kitchen. Oliver trailed far behind her. Zoey grabbed a handful as she dashed by on her way to see her pony. Oliver, on the other hand, took one cookie and climbed up on the stool by the counter. Natalia poured him a glass of milk, mussed his hair, and left the room, leaving him with his mother.

"What's on your mind, buddy?"

"Nothin'."

"Nothing, huh? Are you sure?"

"Well...ya know those boys that were gonna beat me up?" He took a small bite of cookie as Madison watched him ponder a very heavy thought.

"Um-hm," she answered as she took a cookie herself and sat on the stool next to Oliver.

"Well, now they want to be my friend."

"You don't sound okay with that."

"Yeah, because if they're my friends, they will want to come to our house."

"And that's a problem?" Madison was confused. She had always loved having friends over to her house when she was a little girl.

"I kinda don't want them to see where I live."

Surprised, Madison asked the obvious. "Why, sweetie?"

"Because they don't have very much money. They might not like me because we're rich. Zoey says they just like me cause they found out we're rich." He said it matter-of-factly, throwing in an eye-roll, showing Madison that this was a big problem for him.

"Who said we're rich? Other than Zoey," she asked, curious more about his answer than an explanation at this point.

"I did."

"And what makes *you* think we're rich?" she questioned further.

"Duh, Mom." He answered like she was dense. "Just look at all the stuff we have."

Madison was speechless. She truly didn't know how to respond to his concerns. She hadn't thought of them as being rich. What they had and how they lived was all she knew. In later years, her own parents were much more frugal with her than she was with her own children, but they still had wealth, and she always knew it was there, even when her father made sure it wasn't readily available anymore. Life was still comfortable for her. She'd always had security. She had simply chosen not to be as frugal with Zoey and Oliver, hoping it would bring them security, not shame as it appeared to have for Oliver at this point.

They both fell silent. Oliver was now intent on licking the last chocolate chip in his cookie, and Madison was trying to understand his childhood dilemma. If that's what it could even be called. But to Oliver, she could tell it was a very real concern.

And then as if the conversation had never happened, Oliver jumped off his chair, calling over his shoulder, "I'll be in my room playing my video games."

The remainder of the day was a blur of activity as she finished up with her last client of the day and Natalia cared for the children. Madison helped with their homework while Natalia made dinner, then the evening routine with the children of baths, brushing teeth, and getting them settled in with a book or short movie, while Natalia cleaned up the dishes and the kitchen.

She was ready for Phil to be home. Even if conversation didn't come as it used to because they both fell into bed exhausted at the end of the day, she sometimes missed having his warm body to slide in next to, to hold her, to give her the comfort of knowing there was someone there for her no matter what, at the end of the day. That in itself gave her such relief. She absentmindedly thought about calling her parents before she got too tired to do the obligatory check for the week…and then she remembered that phone call would never be made again.

Madison was splashing cold water on her face when she heard the bedroom door creak open. Seconds later, Phil's arms circled her from behind. She felt herself stiffen, and knew Phil sensed it as well, as he drew back.

"Hi, honey," she smiled, eyes puffy from crying.

"Are the kids okay?" he asked, sudden concern clouding his eyes.

"Yes," she attempted to smile. "I was just thinking about Mom and Dad."

"Look, we've got to tell them tonight. This has gone on long enough."

"Phil, no—"

"Yes. I'm insisting on it. You're not protecting them, for Pete's sake. You're hurting them."

"I don't think I can."

"Well, you know what, Madison? This isn't about you." The anger in his voice startled her.

"Hey—that's not fair."

"No, what you're doing is not fair. To them. They have a right to know. How do you think they're going to feel when you tell them their grandparents died well over a week ago?"

"They don't need to know that part."

"Really?" Phil asked incredulously. "And what about the honesty thing you're always telling them is so important?"

"Not telling them adult information isn't being dishonest." She paused and took a deep breath, trying to regain her composure. "Phil, you just got home. Can we let this rest for tonight?"

"For tonight or for another week?" His voice sounded tired. "We're telling the kids tonight. I'll be right there beside you."

"Thanks for the support," she threw back at him.

"Madison, I know you're angry with me, but—"

"But you don't care."

"Yes, I do. But I care about my children as well. And they have a right to know what happened to their grandparents."

She met his eyes and stared, daring him to say something else. Anything. He just looked at her.

"Fine," she said quietly, voice tight. "Have it your way." She walked to the doorway. "Kids?" she called.

"Yeah, Mom?" They called back in unison.

"Come in here, please. Your father has something he wants to tell you."

"Madison—" Phil was standing right behind her.

She turned to face him, looking him square in the eye. "No, Phil. You think they need to know; you tell them. I'll be here to comfort them when their world falls apart."

Madison allowed the kids to stay home from school the following day, and she cancelled her appointments, claiming there was an illness in the family. And she wasn't far off. Both Zoey and Oliver had taken the news of their grandparents' death even harder than Madison had feared, and they both needed her undivided attention.

Phil, on the other hand, after a night of sleeping as far on his side of the bed as he could without falling off the edge, seemed only too eager to get out of the house in the morning. But she had to admit he'd delivered the heartbreaking news with such grace that it was almost comforting to Madison. However, she wasn't about to let him know that. Now or ever. She was still angry with him for forcing her hand when she told him she wasn't ready.

The day the kids went back to school, they left early enough to allow for breakfast at McDonald's, one of the kids' favorite places to go. Surprisingly, there were several kids already there, having a grand time in the PlayPlace. Madison cringed at what she knew was coming—the argument with Oliver about why he couldn't join them. As if on cue, he piped up.

"Momma, please can I play? Just today?"

"No, honey. You need to tell me what you want to eat," she said, trying to distract him.

"Pancakes. Like I always get. Please, Momma?" He begged, not backing down. "It would make me happy again," he offered as if he knew that would make all the difference.

"Oliver," she said, swallowing her frustration. "You know how I feel about the PlayPlace. Besides, you're too old for that."

"There's no germs in there. It's just kids like me, see? There's even a kid my age. Lookit!" He tugged her hand in an attempt to get her to look in the direction of the kids he wanted so badly to join.

"Oliverrrr, she said no." Zoey sounded more like a grown-up than his big sister. "There's probably boogers in there. That's just gross."

Madison noticed an elderly couple look at them and chuckle. She gave them an embarrassed smile, face flushing. "Zoey?" she said through a thin smile. "That's not appropriate talk." She took her by the hand and tried to lead her toward the counter.

"Well, you know it's true. You're the one who told us that," Zoey argued.

At this the elderly couple openly laughed, and the man said, "Out of the mouths of babes, huh?"

To which the woman added, smiling at Madison, "They do like to parrot what they hear, dear."

Madison felt her face get hot and flushed to the tops of her ears from embarrassment. She was not up for this right now.

"Kids," she said tightly, "we're getting breakfast without another word, and then we're leaving. Is that understood?"

To her relief, both kids followed her obediently to the counter so she could place their order.

When Madison returned home, she nearly walked right by Natalia who was in the kitchen. She startled when she saw her out of the corner of her eye. "Oh!" she laughed, her hand grasping at her chest. "You scared me half to death!"

Natalia continued wiping the countertops, moving to the refrigerator. "I'm sorry, Mrs. Shaw. I wasn't trying to hide," she explained.

"No need to be sorry." The two women exchanged familiar but respectfully distant smiles. Madison was so grateful for her and hoped Natalia knew how appreciated she was. Natalia had told Madison in the past that working for her and Phil was the best job she had ever had, but there still remained a distance between them. Madison not only kept in mind that Natalia was her employee, hired to care for the children and household tasks, but her hectic schedule didn't allow them much time to spend together, other than to discuss Natalia's duties. There just weren't enough hours in the day sometimes.

Madison stopped in the arched doorway that led from the kitchen to the family room, then turned back to look at Natalia.

"Natalia?"

"Yes, Mrs. Shaw?"

"Do you have a few moments?"

"Of course. Is there something you would like me to do?"

"Yes, actually there is. I would like you take a break and have a cup of tea with me in the sunroom." The sunroom was Madison's favorite spot. Phil had upgraded it nicely so she could enjoy it year round. Summer was her favorite time out there, watching the birds, the deer that made their way through the backyard, the flowers she had a gardener to care for regularly, but anytime, even late October as it was now, was beautiful.

"Is everything okay, Mrs. Shaw?"

"I just thought it would be nice for the two of us to spend some time together. As friends, not employee and employer. I don't really have friends," Madison added quietly. "Lots of acquaintances, but not friends."

"I would like that very much," Natalia answered, surprise in her voice.

"Well, that makes two of us. You sit down and relax. I'll get us some tea."

"Oh?" Natalia fidgeted with her pinky ring. "Are you okay, Mrs. Shaw?" she asked again.

"Yes," she smiled. "You go on in the sunroom and get comfortable. I'll be right in."

Natalia looked at Madison for a moment longer and then did as she was told. Within minutes, Madison joined her in the sunroom. She set a cup of steaming herbal tea and honey on the table beside Natalia, noticing her proper posture. Or was she tense? Is that the impression she gave Natalia? That she should be on guard?

Madison sat down in a wing chair to Natalia's left, tucked one leg under her, and gazed out at the beauty of the forest outside the large windows facing the south. There were two doves on a feeder, casting a peaceful mood to the moment. Madison thought about her parents, their will, and what was requested of her. She had to admit that what her parents thought of her stung. Did other people see her as a rich snob? Finally she spoke, still looking out the window.

"Natalia, do you know—I've realized I don't know anything about you."

"Mrs. Shaw?" Natalia asked, twisting her pinky ring again.

"I mean *really* know anything about you," she tried to clarify, seeing a combination of confusion and fear on Natalia's face. "I don't know your favorite color or your favorite author or, heck, even what kind of books you like to read. What kind of music do you listen to? Or even about your family. And what's more important than family? Nothing," she answered herself.

Madison watched as Natalia struggled with which question to answer first—or whether to answer at all.

Finally, eyes wide, Natalia asked, "But why would you be interested in those things?"

Madison sensed her uneasiness as Natalia shifted uncomfortably, and quickly rescued her from the moment. "Where do your parents live, Natalia? What do they do?"

Natalia smiled and visibly relaxed. "How nice of you to ask. They live in California. Not far from the border, actually. My dad works in a factory there, and my mom cleans houses. They both work very hard."

Madison noticed how she spoke of them with such fondness. "Are you close?"

"Oh, yes!" She smiled. "I don't know what I would ever do without them. They're such wonderful people." Natalia's face suddenly registered horror. "Oh! I'm so sorry, Mrs. Shaw. How inconsiderate of me so soon after you just lost your—I'm so sorry."

Madison thought Natalia was on the verge of melting into a puddle of tears as regret replaced the warmth that had just a moment ago glowed on Natalia's face.

She reached over and touched the young woman's shoulder. "You have nothing to be sorry about. I'm happy you're close to your parents. I would like to meet them sometime."

"I would like that," she said quietly, staring at the hot liquid in her cup.

They were both silent for a moment before Madison asked, "Natalia, do you think I'm a snob?"

"A snob?" she echoed. "Oh, no! You're a very nice lady. You're very good to me."

"I'm glad you feel that way," she answered warmly, smiling at Natalia. "You spend a lot of time with Zoey and Oliver."

"Yes. I love them very much." It was a simple statement in the form of a question. Madison realized Natalia was wondering where she was going with this. The poor woman probably thought her employer had lost her mind and was plumb crazy.

"Do you think they're spoiled?" Natalia's hesitation was instant. "Please be honest. I'm asking as a friend, not your employer."

"I know they are loved very much," she answered slowly, carefully.

"But do you think they're spoiled?"

"That's a hard question for me to answer."

"Just your opinion."

"They have much more than I ever had as a child growing up, but most kids do these days, I suppose."

"Were you poor?" Madison could have kicked herself for the insensitivity of her question, but it was out and too late to take it back.

"Yes, we were. But we were happier than any other family I knew."

The irony of that didn't escape Madison. Growing up, hers had been one of the wealthiest families on the block of the wealthy, and yet the walls of their home held unhappy hearts, kids who had everything yet wanted more. One kid who never felt like she belonged in that home, a boy who thought he ran the home, and herself, too busy socializing to be home. The two families seemed in such stark contrast to one another.

"How many brothers and sisters do you have?" Madison held her still warm cup between her hands, looking at the tea that was left in the bottom.

"An older sister and a younger brother," she answered with clear affection for them both.

The irony struck her yet once more. "Natalia? What are your parents like?" She now watched Natalia's expression, so warm and loving, a small smile playing on her lips.

"They are such strong, beautiful people. They love me and my brother and sister more than anything in the world, but boy, could they discipline with the best of them!" She laughed at the memories. "They continually gave of themselves. They made holidays so special. I remember Christmas Eve," her eyes were dreamy as her mind traveled back in time. "We all sat around the tree and read the Christmas story from the

Gospel of Luke." She looked at Madison and explained, "In the Bible."

"Yes, I'm aware of the Gospel of Luke." But not all too familiar with it, she thought sadly.

Natalia's longing gaze showed Madison that she was lost in her memories again. "Each of us would squabble over who got to read it that year. After that we got to open presents, one at a time. Then we got to play for a half hour or so before we went to my grandparents' house. Oh, how I loved going there," she said dreamily, completely lost in the memory. "The smells of my grandmother's cooking, the sparkling of the lights, my aunts, uncles, and cousins all laughing and crammed into the same room…" She laughed. "We were all dressed in our Christmas best. And we always went to midnight mass…."

Madison's heart pained with envy. How she would love to give Zoey and Oliver those memories. Thus far, Natalia's description of her childhood couldn't be more different from the one she had been giving her own children. But Zoey and Oliver were happy, weren't they? She had to ask the one person who knew them as well as she did. Perhaps more than Phil did.

"Do Zoey and Oliver seem happy to you, Natalia?"

"They seem fine, Mrs. Shaw." Again, her words slow and careful.

Fine. Madison wasn't sure she felt comfortable with that word but didn't want Natalia to feel cornered by her questioning what she meant.

They spent another half hour together, reminiscing about the kids, Natalia's family, and the uncertain plans for the upcoming holidays.

Their conversation haunted Madison throughout the following week. She paid attention to Zoey and

Oliver's behaviors closely, wondering if they seemed happy or just fine. *Fine* seemed a step down from happy. But she wasn't sure. She asked her patients how their week had gone, and if they answered "fine," she tried to read exactly what that meant to them. Was it a happy fine? Or a settle-for fine?

One evening when Phil came home from work and the tension had lifted just enough to reach out to him, she asked him. "Phil?"

"Um-hm?" He answered somewhat distractedly as he went through the mail.

"Can we talk for a minute?"

"Can it wait until the kids are in bed?"

"Sure. That's fine. They're brushing their teeth now." And then it hit her that there was that darn word again. *Fine.* And for her it wasn't a happy word, but a settle-for word. At least at that moment.

Finally, the kids had been given their hugs and kisses and were tucked into bed, each with their favorite stuffed animal snuggled closely beside them. Madison sat down next to Phil on the couch where he was now watching a ballgame. She took a deep breath.

"Phil, do you think the kids are spoiled?"

"That's an understatement," he laughed. Was that bitterness she heard?

"Really?" She was shocked not only at his answer, but by how quickly he answered. He hadn't even thought about it for the slightest moment.

"Yes, really." He looked at her with surprise of his own. "Why are you so surprised by my answer? If you don't want the answer, Maddie, don't ask the question."

"Well—I guess I expected you to think about it at least."

He took her hand in his own and stroked the back of it with his thumb. He looked into her eyes and said, "Honey, what other kids do you know that have everything Zoey and Oliver have? Whatever they want, they get. Hell, whatever they don't even know they want, they get."

"Being a mom is the most important thing in the world to me, Phil. I'm doing the best I can."

"There is such a thing as trying too hard, Maddie. They just need love. Giving them things is not love."

Madison felt her ugly side emerging and the words flew out before she could stop them. "And how would you know that?"

"What are you saying exactly?" His voice was hardly more than a whisper. She heard the tired exhale escape from his lips.

"You're never here, Phil. I'm here twenty-four-seven, because one of us has to be."

"Well, I must say I'm impressed you notice when I'm not here." He withdrew his hand from hers and bit his lower lip as if trying not to respond in a way he would regret.

"And what do you mean by that?" she needled.

He paused before answering. "Do you want the answer this time? To hell with it," he answered for her. "You're going to get the answer, whether you want it or not. I'll just throw caution to the wind and say it."

"Say what?" she dared him to continue.

"I'm not going to tell you only what you want to hear. I'm done with that."

"I've never asked you to tell me what I want to hear."

"No, not outright. But God help the person who doesn't agree with you. Or one who has an opinion different than yours." He stood up and walked across the room, then turned to face her again. "Madison, you don't notice anything around you except what you're doing for, and giving to, the kids. When is the last time you sat on the floor—or even at the kitchen table—and played a game with them? Doing something *with* them. Or the last time you went for a simple walk with them to explore nature."

"You know I hate bugs," she answered defensively.

"You're completely missing the point. And that's part of the problem." He paused for a moment. "Why do you think I'm gone so much, Maddie? There are plenty of people that work right along beside me, and they don't need to travel as much."

"I didn't know that." She followed him into the bedroom and looked at his back as he focused on something out the window.

"Exactly. You don't know anything that's staring you right in the face unless it's something you can do for, or give to, the kids." Phil let out a breath, turned and slowly walked over to where Madison sat completely still on the edge of the bed. He sat beside her. "You know I love them. In fact, not that this is a competition, but I love them every bit as much as you do."

"I doubt that. And *if* it's true, you have a funny way of showing it."

"Why? Because I don't buy them?"

She flinched as his words pierced her. "That's not fair." Her voice was quiet and tight.

"Isn't it Maddie?" He stood, walked across the room to his dresser, opened the drawer, and placed some socks and underwear on the bed. His shoulders slumped forward ever so slightly. He turned to face her. "You know what I don't think is fair? That you control everything the kids do, think, and have. It doesn't matter what they want to do or what I would like to do with them, because you always seem to know what's best and have a different plan. And your plan is the one that is followed. No one else is allowed to have one. I finally figured, what's the point? Why even try? I'm tired of being treated like a child in front of my own children."

"Is that what you think I do?" She struggled to meet his eyes, and when she did, she saw the answer openly displayed in his eyes. "Wow. What a depressing picture we've just painted of our lives."

"It's a canvas we can paint over and change, Madison. In fact, it's one that's begging to be changed."

"Now you sound like a shrink. That's my job." She watched as he took some sweaters out of his drawer, placing them on the bed, including the black and red sweater she loved so much. "I didn't know you had another business trip so soon."

"I don't."

"What are you doing?"

He stopped and looked at her, and she could see the sadness in his eyes, the weight on his shoulders. "Maddie, I'm going to give us both some space for a few days. I think we need it."

Panic rose in her chest. "You're leaving?" she blurted.

"Not leaving like you say it. Just giving us some breathing room."

"You're leaving," she repeated. "What, things get tough so you make your exit?"

"Madison—" He walked over and reached his hand out to touch her arm.

Madison jerked away and crossed the room. "Don't touch me right now," she whispered. A tear escaped, and she furiously brushed it away. She was not going to give him the satisfaction of seeing her cry. "And how do you propose I explain your absence to the kids?"

"Just tell them I had an unexpected business trip."

"I'm not going to lie to them for you."

"Only when it's convenient for you, is that it?"

"And what is that supposed to mean?"

"Think about it, Maddie."

She watched as he pulled his suitcase out from his closet and hoisted it onto the bed, placing his things inside and closing it up. Panic began to rise up again and she attempted to will it away.

"Phil, what has become of us?" she whispered, voice shaking.

"That's what we need space to figure out. And to figure out what we're going to do about it."

"Do I get a say in it?" she asked, anger rising to the surface again. Her emotions seemed to be all over the board, and she couldn't control them as she had worked so hard her entire life to do.

"Do you know you never even explained to me what was in your parents' will that had you in such emotional turmoil? That's important stuff. Sometimes it feels like all we are is roommates, and we don't even have a relationship anymore. Your life has become all about trying to be the perfect parent. Striving to be that perfect parent is suffocating the rest of your life, including you and me."

"Phil—"

He crossed the distance between them and gently put his finger on her lips. "No, Maddie. We're both too emotional and tired to have a rational discussion right now." She heard his voice catch. He circled his arms around her, kissed the top of her head, and reached to pick up his suitcase. "I'll have my cell phone on if you need me. Otherwise, let's take some time to breathe and pull ourselves back together. Give the kids a hug for me."

And she watched him walk out the door, sure her heart had never been so heavy, not even when she'd heard of her parents' death two short, long weeks ago.

Chapter Eight

Morning dawned, and as Molly yawned and stretched each limb, she realized she hadn't heard from John the previous day. She got up, haphazardly tied her gray jersey robe around her waist, and looked at her phone for verification that he hadn't called. Or if he had and she'd missed it. Seeing nothing, she decided he probably had a date that went too late.

After coffee, one cup laced with some Bailey's Irish Cream, and the fifteen hundred words she strove to write each morning, she sat back to admire the sun shining brightly through the kitchen window across the hall from her office. She marveled at the mountains, capped in light snow. Taos was so beautiful throughout the entire year. She had fallen in love with it from the moment she moved here.   She slipped into some warm running clothes and headed out for an overdue run, walking the first five minutes to warm her muscles. After her usual five-mile path, she walked the last half mile, then stretched. Her muscles were loudly complaining that she had not exercised them in far too long. It had been over a week, and now they were screaming at her.

As soon as Molly turned her key in the front door lock, she heard the music of her ringtone, "The House that Built Me," by Miranda Lambert. The irony of the song made it perfect for her, a bittersweet pang each time she heard it.

"Hello?"

"Hey there, kiddo."

"Hi John. I was just thinking of you this morning. Did you have a date last night?"

"Nope. Went out with a group from work. Was home by seven o'clock though. What did you do?"

Molly laughed. "What d'ya think I did?"

"Hmmm. Now I'm intrigued."

Molly could hear the smile in his voice. "Worked!" she laughed. "Just worked."

"And why are you out of breath now?" he asked with skepticism.

"I'm out of breath because I'm out of shape. I just got back from a run," she explained. "Eight o'clock?"

"Uh…"

"Tonight. Wanna come over at eight?" She was met with silence. "Going out again? You lawyers are a bunch of party animals."

"No, eight is fine."

"Yeah? You sure? Make it six thirty, and I'll make dinner if you bring a bottle of wine."

"Sure, okay. Sounds good," he relented.

"Gotta run, my friend. See ya at six thirty."

"I have a motions hearing today, so I'll be there as close to six thirty as I can, allowing for time to stop at the liquor store on my way. What do you want?"

"Seven Deadly Zins, if they have it. If not, use your judgment. I'm so not picky when it comes to wine."

"I'm aware."

"I can do without the sarcasm this early in the morning, wise guy. See ya later."

She hung up and called Jo to check in and to let her know she wouldn't be in until tomorrow.

"I've decided to stay home and work on my column and get some writing done on my book. My deadline to get it off to the publisher is approaching too fast. I need to buckle down and get some serious revisions done."

"Sounds like a plan. Can you take a break and meet for lunch?"

"Actually, would you be terribly disappointed if I took a rain check? I think I'm just going to write straight through today."

"Of course. I understand. Sounds like you're getting back to yourself, Molly. It's good to hear."

"It's good to feel. Trust me," she smiled into the phone.

As soon as they hung up, she jumped into a steaming hot shower, relaxing her muscles from the work they were forced to do on her run. The hand weights she had carried and the lunges she'd obsessed over after running had taken their toll, and the steaming shower felt like medicine. After sudsing and rinsing, she stood under the stream of water, letting it pulsate on her shoulders until it began turning cooler and her fingers were like prunes. She felt so good today and couldn't put her finger on why.

It wasn't until she was blow-drying her hair that she realized she hadn't had anything to drink last night. She wished her parents were able to know that she didn't need to drink after all. And the Bailey's in her coffee? Not any different than using creamer. They had been convinced she had a drinking problem, but last night she hadn't even drank a drop, and she'd done just fine. If she had a problem, she wouldn't have been able to do that, she rationalized.

Molly felt a mix of pride and relief, as if she had proven something to herself. Something bigger than she had even thought. And something she was more afraid of than she'd even realized.

She spent the rest of the morning drinking coffee and writing. Eventually she moved her laptop to the floor where she sprawled, changing positions in every which direction every hour or so until she took her first break of the day. She rose to her feet, groaning as she worked out the kinks. She made a peanut butter sandwich, grabbed an apple and a bottle of water from the fridge, and planted herself on the sofa. And that's where she stayed, moving only to tuck alternate legs under her as each fell asleep, until she noticed the sun had shifted considerably, casting shadows across the room. She was startled when she realized it was past five thirty. She stretched, put her computer back in her office, and began making dinner for John. She drained the last of the bottle of wine that sat on her counter into a glass to tide her over until John showed up with her very favorite. It was an evening to celebrate. A good day's work and the pleasure of having proved her parents wrong about their assumption.

John hadn't arrived yet by six thirty-five, so Molly poured herself a small glass of cinnamon schnapps and started the gas fireplace. Then she sat, staring at the dancing flames, deep in thought, until the doorbell rang.

"Oh, man! It smells so good in—" He looked at the glass in her hand. "You started without me?"

"I didn't know what time you were going to show up."

"Are you sure that's it?"

"Of course I'm sure. What else would it be?" She spouted, irritation spilling over. "If I didn't know better, I'd think my mom and dad got to you."

"All I meant was—"

Molly waved her hand in dismissal. "No worries." She felt John's eyes on her every move as she made the finishing touches to dinner. She began to wish for an escape from the heat of his eyes burning a hole through her.

"What have you decided about your inheritance?"

"How do you know about that?" She turned to face him, accusation laced her words.

"You told me about it the other night."

John's tone made her squirm slightly. "Oh yeah. I forgot," she lied, her face feeling hot with embarrassment as she tried fruitlessly to remember. *Darn! What is going on with you, Molly?* she scolded herself.

"Actually, I haven't decided yet."

"Why not?"

"No reason." She took another drink from her glass, draining the last of it.

"There *is* a reason, Moll. Something is stopping you. Want to talk about it?"

"Nope." She heard John exhale with exasperation.

"It's going to be one of those nights, huh?"

"One of what nights?" She turned to look at him, belligerence taking root.

"Nothing."

"Look, I'm sorry John. I just don't want to talk about it. Not tonight." Her eyes pleaded with him to understand and just leave it alone for tonight, but then she decided she did owe him an explanation of some sort. He was the one who was always there for her. She leaned against the counter, looking at him as he sat facing her from one of the stools on the other side.

"Taking their dog sounds easy enough, but I don't know if I have time. I mean…well…" Her voice trailed off as she didn't want to finish the rest of what she knew was the truth holding her back. "Mentoring an adult in the literacy program, teaching them to read so they can experience the beauty of words—that sounds doable. But the twelve-step program? I am not an alcoholic, John. You know that as well as I do. It's absurd that they even suggested that." She turned and opened the oven, taking out the vegetable casserole for herself and the stuffed chicken breast for John.

"Did you bring the wine?" Molly interrupted herself as she burst out laughing. "How was that for timing?"

"Hysterical," he answered dryly, but smiling nonetheless. "Of course I brought the wine. I told you I would." She watched as he walked over and pulled the bottle out of his trench coat pocket.

"Can you open it and pour us a glass? You know where the corkscrew is.

"I'll pour you a glass. I'm sticking with water. Or Pepsi, if you have one."

"I do. It's in the fridge. Why aren't you drinking?"

"Quit pouting," he laughed. "I have an early morning and just don't feel like it tonight."

"More for me," she teased, though she was secretly disappointed. She accepted the glass he now handed her. "I love this one. It is by far my favorite."

Molly set the table, lit a candle for the center, and they sat down, giving thanks for their food before they dug in.

"No eating in front of the TV tonight?" John asked.

"Are you disappointed?"

"Surprised, but not disappointed," he answered as he got up to get them both a napkin. "Did you have a rough day today?

"No, why would you ask that? In fact, it was a super productive day."

"Just wondering what drove you to get cinnamon schnapps? I've never seen you drink that before."

"My car," she answered, taking a bite of her casserole.

"Molly, sarcasm aside. Just for a while. Think you can handle that?"

"I'll do my best," she teased.

The rest of dinner consisted of casual conversation, each sharing the highlights of their day. He drained the rest of his Pepsi.

Want another soda?" she asked as she poured more wine in her glass.

"Water would be great."

"Whoa!" She drew back dramatically. "Hitting the hard stuff now, huh?" She chuckled lightly and filled his glass with ice and water from the purifier. They made their way to the living room, leaving the dishes sit. "What do you want to watch?"

"Is that a trick question?"

"No. It's me being considerate. I can be considerate sometimes, you know."

"Maybe we could leave the television off for a minute. I'd like to talk."

"We talked while we were eating," she bantered.

John watched her take another drink and turn on the TV. "Molly, just for a minute."

She sensed the seriousness of his voice, mentally rolled her eyes, and looked at him, waiting for him to say whatever it was he needed to say. "Well?"

"You're not making this easy."

"Since when has our conversation been anything but easy? That's always been the best and most unusual part of our friendship. And why dating didn't work," she added.

"About that..."

Molly felt her stomach do a quick somersault and took a quick drink. "What about it?" She looked at him, trying her hardest to hide her discomfort, knowing it was rare that she could hide anything from John. He knew her too well.

"I've been thinking..."

"Sounds scary," she quickly interjected, hoping humor would delay what she feared was coming.

"Don't be glib. I think...I think we should give it another try."

She heard his voice quiver ever so slightly, typical when he was nervous about something, and she watched him lick his lips. "Tell me you're not serious," she said, more than just a little hopeful.

"As a heart attack. Molly." He quietly continued, "You and I are more compatible than most people who have been married for decades. We're best friends. We have fun together. Most of the time."

"Most of the time?"

"Interesting that that's the part you choose to question."

Molly drained her glass, the discomfort of the moment making her squirm. "John, I thought we'd talked about this. More than once, actually."

"We have. But I've changed my mind."

"Why?"

"Because I love you. More than just a mere friend," he explained. "Because we work together, and you know we do. I want us to be together." He got up and moved over next to her on the sofa. "Tell me we can give it a shot." He reached up and tucked her hair behind her ear.

"Dry spell in your dating life, huh?" She teased halfheartedly, trying to make light of the moment. If she were to be completely honest with herself, she thought she wanted him, too, but things seemed fuzzy right now. She couldn't make sense of what was happening.

And before she could figure out what was happening, she was in his arms. He picked her up and carried her like she weighed nothing at all, depositing her gently on her bed. Somewhere in the back of her mind, she knew it was wrong, but that knowledge was overpowered by what was actually happening. And before she could give that voice in the back of her mind any further attention, it was too late.

Molly felt a slight movement next to her. Her immediate reaction was confusion. A dream? Until the memories came back, slowly at first, then the floodgates opened. She folded her arm over her eyes as a wave of regret surged through her chest and pounding head. Maybe if she could just go back to sleep, she would wake up to a different scenario. But she knew that was only wishful thinking. What in the hell had she done? She almost groaned out loud but stopped herself so as not to wake up John, whom she thought was still sleeping.

She was surprised when John leaned toward her, his face hovering above her as he looked at her with an expression that tore her heart wide open. A combination of love and intense pain. She couldn't hide what she was feeling; her eyes betrayed her. And she knew John well enough to know she had just crushed his heart. Just that one brief look into her eyes, and she knew he could see her heart and everything she did—and didn't—hold there.

She watched him slowly sit up and swing his legs over the edge of the bed, his back to her. He sat for a moment as if he were going to say something, then simply stood without a word and slipped into his pants.

"John?" she asked weakly.

"I have to get to work."

"Do you want some breakfast?"

"No thanks."

"Are you sure? I should probably get up anyway."

"Actually, you should probably go back to sleep. I'll let myself out and lock up.

"You sure?" she asked so quietly she wasn't even sure he heard her.

"I said I would."

She flinched at the edge she heard in his words. "John…"

He stood, inhaled, followed by a long exhale as he ran his hand through his short hair. Then he turned to face her as she sat on the edge of the bed.

"Look, Molly. I'm not sure what last night was to you. And, frankly, I probably don't want to know. I thought I made my intentions pretty clear. Obviously, I was mistaken." He looked deep into her eyes for a moment before forcing himself to proceed. "I think it's time to move in our own directions."

"What? What are you saying?"

"I think you know what I'm saying."

"We've discussed this before, and we decided friendship is the best place to be for us."

"Actually, *you* decided that, Molly. I simply agreed to be able to keep you in my life. I need to move on, and you being in my life doesn't allow room for that."

Molly got up, put her hand on the wall briefly for balance, then slipped on her robe, pulling it tight around her. She imagined her hair was a mess but didn't have the energy or interest to think about it right now, much less care about it. Her dissolving friendship with John and her throbbing head were all she could think about.

"I see. So we have to be what you want us to be or nothing at all? I'm failing to see the fairness in that."

"It's not about being fair." He crossed the room to stand in front of her, reaching out to brush a strand of wild hair back from her face. "It's about not being able to get on with my life because I keep hoping something will change your mind. It's about being so damn in love with you, I can't even see straight. It's about the pain I feel when you talk about a date with another man."

"You go on dates, too," she countered. "And I haven't been on a date in forever." She knew she was sounding desperate and defensive, but she didn't care.

"I tell you I do. A couple of times I have. But it never went past a drink or dinner," he explained.

"So you're just taking away your friendship without even discussing it with me? How exactly is that fair?"

"Babe, you'll figure things out. You've been using me for your safety net. It's time you get some legs strong enough to stand on your own and carry you through the mud and muck of life. As long as you have me to carry you through, you'll never do it on your own."

"Friends are supposed to be able to depend on each other, but apparently not in your world." Her sarcasm had a nasty tone. She knew her words were like darts being thrown right at his heart.

"I understand you're angry. And in a selfish way, I'm flattered." He ran his fingers through his hair again, his eyes shining moist.

"Flattered? How nice for you," she said, sounding defeated despite the sarcasm consuming each word.

"I can't keep hoping anymore, Molly. And as long as I'm around you as close as we are, that's all I do. It's tearing me up inside."

"You'll get over me. In that way. Just give it time," she pleaded.

"I've been giving it nothing *but* time," he said gently, reaching out to wipe a tear from her cheek as his own threatened to erupt. "This isn't all I want. I want more in my life than just waiting for these feelings to pass. *That's* what isn't fair. To me. Maybe I'm being arrogant, but I think I deserve more."

"You do," she agreed, surprised at her words. "Maybe I can some day. I need time."

"You're trying to buy time and make up for what you feel was a mistake that should have never happened last night." He kissed the top of her head, the same head that now felt like it was going to explode with ferocious pain. "Go back to bed, get some more sleep." He smiled down at Molly, gave her a hug that lingered a moment longer than usual, then disappeared around the corner.

Molly lay in bed, crying silently so John wouldn't hear her. Hot hears from a broken heart of losing her best friend, and from the pain in her head. She felt a wave of nausea ride through her stomach. She lay still until it passed and pretended to be asleep when she felt John's presence standing in the doorway, then heard his footsteps retreat from the room before he left her life.

When she heard the front door close, she wept until she didn't have a single tear left. She rolled over and stared out at the bleak, gray sky as it spit rain against the window. To hell with sleeping. As if she could anyway.

She got up and walked barefoot and naked into the kitchen. The wine left in the bottle from last night caught her attention, as did the house key beside it that had once belonged to John. The finality of that drew a few more tears she didn't know she had. A wave of hopelessness and abandonment surged through her core. Molly looked at the wine bottle, hesitated, then bypassed it to reach in the cupboard above it where the stronger whiskey was. The whiskey she usually didn't drink but kept on hand for unexpected company. But right now her own company qualified in her book as unexpected.

Chapter Nine

Max threw every ounce of strength he had into his work as he tried to keep his mind from traveling in a thousand different directions. When he was at his desk with an open case file in front of him, he ended up staring out the window instead. In court, he would look at the judge but not see him. Instead he was thinking of his parents, the life they'd shared, the life he'd kept so separate from theirs. He thought about their will, their last evening on this earth before they met their fate. What had they been thinking at that last moment? He thought about past conversations he'd had with his father, his father meeting with Paul, and his own most recent conversation with Paul.

It went on and on in a vicious circle, twirling its way into a near tornado within the confines of his mind. What *didn't* cross his mind more than a time or two, however, was the inheritance. And on the rare occasion he did think of it, he didn't think of in terms of money but as something he had to do. The conditions that had been written out for him were far more about his pride than about the dollars involved.

After a week of not much more than working and doing mental gymnastics, turning and twisting every thought in every possible direction, he decided he needed to get out of his own head for a while. He was bordering on driving himself beyond return.

The day before Thanksgiving, he picked up his phone and called Mandi, disappointed to hear she was busy and couldn't see him. And surprised to find himself more than a little jealous. The fact that he was jealous at all was an uncomfortable surprise to him. It irritated him, and it just gave his mind one more thing to think about. As if he needed anything else.

Max was actually grateful that he would be spending the holiday tomorrow with Paul, Connie, Junior, and his wife, Suzanne. He wondered what Molly and Madison would be doing, but he wasn't curious enough to call and find out. Their lives had been separate for so many years—his parents' passing wasn't going to change that now. Even if he did have any hopes of it happening, they were all too set in their ways and busy with their own lives. He certainly wouldn't mind getting to know his niece and nephew though. Max had never pursued it because he knew Phil wasn't fond of him. In fact, that was an understatement.

Max finished work early and decided to call it a day. He poked his head into Paul's office to assure him he would be there at one o'clock sharp the following day. "To see your wife," he teased Paul.

"Will you be bringing a guest?"

"What do you think?" Paul laughed, and Max walked out with a "See you tomorrow" thrown over his shoulder.

He stopped off at the gym on his way home, working up a sweat like never before. He worked off anxieties, thoughts that were unwelcome and persistent, as well as those that were pleasant and fleeting. He worked off stress from being behind at work due to not being able to focus, his family situation, and even Mandi. By the time he was done, he had no energy left whatsoever except to take a shower.

Skin red and tingling from scrubbing and the hottest water he could stand, he felt renewed energy and felt a little life back in his blood. He decided to stop at his favorite corner sports bar for a drink and to maybe catch a bit of a game. He walked in, said an obligatory greeting to those he knew, and found a place at the bar directly in front of a football game, teams unknown at that point. But at least it was a game. He ordered a beer, tipped the bartender well, and settled in to watch the game.

He hadn't been watching for more than ten minutes when he heard a familiar voice behind him. "Hi, Max."

Max swiveled around on his barstool and looked appreciatively at Mandi, who was dressed in a pair of jeans and a dazzling white sweater, her blond hair loose and wavy.

"Hey, Blondie," he said. "Whatcha drinking? Can I buy you one?"

"Diet Coke. But no, thank you. I'm actually sitting over there," she pointed in the direction of a man with sharply chiseled features, watching her closely.

Max looked in the man's direction, smiled, stood, and gave Mandi a long, close hug that suggested the intimacy they had shared, watching the man's expression, giving him a wink for final measure.

"I know what you're doing, Max," she said in his ear as he hugged her. "It's not going to work."

"I think it is," he pulled back and looked at her, victory in his eyes. "In fact, I think it worked very well."

"Max, you have no right."

"I know I don't. But right or not, I want you with me."

"And I want you to figure out what it is you want. Because, frankly, my friend, you don't even know what that is."

"I know I want you to come with me to Paul and Connie's for Thanksgiving tomorrow." The minute the words were out the surprise registered on his face. Max knew by the twinkle in Mandi's green eyes that she was enjoying his surprise.

"What if I have plans?"

"Cancel them."

"You think you're that special that I would cancel any plans I have simply because you want me to do something with you?"

"Yup, as a matter of fact, I do." He smiled, playing with her.

"I have to get back to my date." She hesitated a beat, her green eyes glimmering with the life and mischief that he enjoyed so much about her. And with that, he watched her make her way back to the man waiting for her, whose eyes were on Max as if to let him know who had the victory.

The remainder of his time at the bar, Max made a point of turning from the game to glance at them, enjoying watching the man squirm. After nursing his beer, he stood, looked around, and took a detour that led him past Mandi's table. He stopped for a moment to shake the man's hand and introduce himself, then he turned to Mandi. "Pick you up at noon tomorrow? You know how Paul and Connie like to eat on time."

"Have a nice evening alone, Max," she said, her discomfort evident.

Max held her with his eyes, making sure her date knew that despite the fact he was out with Mandi tonight, he was nonetheless the outsider here. Max was pleased that his tactics appeared to have the desired effect. He knew Mandi well enough to know she would be going home shortly. Alone.

His phone rang at just past midnight, and he smiled when he looked at caller ID. "Hey, Blondie," he answered, his voice husky.

"Max, why did you invite me to go with you tomorrow? Spending Thanksgiving together? That doesn't sound like you."

"I'm hurt."

"You've got to have an ulterior motive. Jealousy is not your thing."

"Wasn't."

"What?"

"*Wasn't* my thing."

"So did you ask just because I was with someone else and you wanted to win?"

"Win what?"

"I don't know. That's what I'm trying to figure out. Usually it's about winning with you."

"That has been the case, yes."

"Has been or *is*?"

"Mandi, don't make things so complicated. I want you to go with me or I wouldn't have asked."

"I'll let you know tomorrow."

"Do you have a better offer?" He attempted to sound disinterested to masquerade the fact that he was stung by her lack of interest.

"I said, I will let you know tomorrow. If I can and the offer is still open, then it's a plan. Good night, Max."

Max held the phone in his hand long after it went dead. Mandi had avoided him before, but this was the first time she had ever actually rejected him. He'd always had the upper hand, and this was unfamiliar territory. He couldn't fall asleep. Thoughts of Mandi, trying to figure out his feelings for her, and if she would go with him, pervaded every corner of his mind. He flipped on the TV to a late night news show and finally fell asleep by the end of the broadcast.

As soon as he woke up, Max checked his phone to see if there was a message from Mandi. Seeing none, he got out of bed slowly, wincing with painful pleasure a time or two as his sore muscles reminded him of his workout the night before.

A cup of coffee in hand, he opened the front door to get the newspaper. He was shocked to find Mandi standing there, holding it out for him. He couldn't decide what he felt—relief, shock, or self-consciousness. Realizing it was Mandi, self-consciousness was the first to go, quickly replaced by pleasure.

"Hey, Blondie. Come on in." He stepped aside, holding the door open for her.

"Is it safe?"

"Is that what you came to find out?"

"No. You've never made it a secret that I'm not the only woman in your life. I just don't want to have it staring me in the face."

"It?" he asked, amused.

"Take that as you will."

"Come on." He motioned for her to come in. "Want a cup of coffee?"

"Thought you'd never ask."

He poured her a cup of what looked like steaming mud and handed it to her at the counter where she was now perched on a stool. She looked in her cup and wrinkled her nose.

"So did you come to criticize my coffee or to tell me you're going to go with me today? Or are you going to make me beg?" Max asked.

"About that...before I decide, I want to be sure you weren't drunk when you asked."

"I nursed one beer the entire time I was there."

"I noticed."

"So you were watching," he stated simply, pleased.

"What's behind this Max? Don't play with me."

"But you're so fun to play with," he winked, reaching to circle his arm around her waist.

"You know what I mean," she swatted at his hand that was now on her leg.

He pulled back, sighed, and leaned against the countertop. "Can't we just let it be what it will be?"

"And what is that exactly?" His silence invited her to continue. She exhaled, exasperation obvious. "I'm too tired for your games, Max."

"Are you whining?"

"Quit teasing me," she warned, anger sparking in her eyes. "Especially right now." She kept a steady gaze on him, making him squirm. "I don't get it," she finally continued. "I finally decide to move on and find someone who thinks I'm enough. Just me. And then...there's something about you that seems different. Are you? Or am I just hoping?"

"I don't know what it is," he admitted, finally looking at her seriously. "Yes, it's different, but I don't know for sure what it is, either. Can we just leave it at that and see where it goes?"

Mandi sat quietly, looking at him, absorbing his words. Finally she stood. "I'll see you at noon. And Max?" she said over her shoulder as she began to walk toward the door, "Don't make more of this than what it is."

He smiled as she closed the door behind her.

Max and Mandi arrived at twelve thirty. Paul looked at Max after Mandi stepped past him, and he raised his brows at Max, showing his approval. Max knew they made a striking couple—he in his pressed jeans and tweed jacket over a black turtleneck, and Mandi in a pair of gray slacks and an emerald green sweater, her blond hair in a single French braid, her green eyes glowing bright, matching her sweater.

After introductions were complete, the men made their way to the family room, a warm fire crackling in the fireplace and a football game on TV, while Mandi followed Connie into the kitchen with the treasures she'd brought. Max's eyes followed her, and she grinned at him. The holiday aromas of turkey, cinnamon, and apples wafted through the house, and Max felt a peacefulness he hadn't felt in a long time. If ever.

"Are you always this happy on Thanksgiving or is there more to that silly grin on your face?" Paul asked. Junior laughed.

"Is that a trick question?" Max teased.

"She's quite a looker," Junior added.

"Indeed, she is."

"Where did you meet?" he asked.

"I've known Mandi for a long time."

"Is it serious?" Paul asked, surprised.

"No. I don't know."

"Which is it?" Paul asked, amused. "No, or I don't know?"

"It hasn't been, but who knows. A day at a time."

"Now those are some wise words, young man. Just don't drag your feet too long. The good ones get snapped up fast."

Max felt like a child who just pleased his father. And it felt good.

Dinner went equally as well. They talked about how the football teams were doing and their ratings. Max genuinely shocked to find Mandi was so knowledgeable. As long as he'd known her, he never knew she kept up on sports.

"So have you made a decision about the Habitat for Humanity project yet?" Paul asked.

Max shook his head in the negative. "Haven't had time."

"Well, I asked Junior already, and he said he would be willing to help."

Junior rolled his eyes at Max. "Yeah. Thanks, big guy."

Max watched Mandi raise her wine glass daintily to her lips and her eyebrows in curiosity. "What's this about?"

He began to explain the surface details, but his phone rang. He wasn't going to answer it until he looked at the incoming number and saw Madison's name appear on the screen. He'd only just recently programmed it in.

"Madison?" And then there was silence on Max's end as the rest of them watched his expression change every few seconds. Finally he spoke.

"Where is she?" More speaking from the other end of the line before he answered. "I'll take the next flight out and meet you there."

When he hung up, he saw all eyes on him expectantly. Paul asked the question.

"Is everything okay, son?"

"I sure hope so," he answered, his voice tight with concern. "My little sister is in the hospital. She overdosed last night."

Chapter Ten

Madison sat with Molly. The silence in the room was deafening. Madison marveled at how silence could seem so loud in the room, yet the activity level right outside Molly's room felt so far away it was silent and in slow motion. She watched the others wandering around, and her heart cracked as she noticed that the similarities between them and Molly were more obvious than the differences. Molly had been eerily quiet. Even more than she normally was. She didn't even seem to notice her surroundings until Madison stood.

"Where are you going?" Molly whispered without looking up.

"To see if your brother is here yet."

"That should be a good time." Even in her malaise, the sarcasm surfaced.

"Molly, he's worried sick about you."

"I'm sure."

"I'm sorry, but I don't think you have the right to expect us not to care. Just because you've convinced yourself we—or anyone else, for that matter—never have, doesn't mean we didn't and don't."

"When did you become the expert on my loving brother?"

"Probably about the time you decided to let that chip on your shoulder and your sarcasm chase everyone away. But you know what, Moll? We're not going anywhere. Not this time." Her words were quiet and firm, laced with anger. "I agree that Max hasn't been good to you, to say the least, but people can change. Give him that chance."

"I've given him enough chances. And if sticking up for him is what you're here to do, then you can go ahead and leave. I didn't ask you to come."

"I don't care whether you asked me to or not. I'm here because I want to be, and there's nothing you can do about it." Two tears escaped Molly's eyes and trailed down each side of her face, disappearing into the pillow.

"I'm sorry," she whispered. "I know I'm being a brat. I just want it all to go away."

"All *what* to go away? Help me to understand," she pleaded.

"The pain, the emotional turmoil, the humiliation. All of it."

A sickening feeling landed in the pit of Madison's stomach. "Molly, tell me this wasn't intentional." Madison watched for a hopeful sign but was met with a stoic stare. "Molly..." Madison felt pinpricks of fear crawl over her skin.

"I can't tell you anything, Madison. Because I don't know."

"You don't know if you wanted to die?"

"I don't think I wanted to die. I just want to feel something other than what I do. God, Madison," she said, tears running freely now. "I'm just so tired." Her voice sounded like a weak child's. "How did I even get here?"

Madison felt a wave of relief as she saw a sudden flash of life back in Molly's eyes. Granted, it was in the form of fear, but at least it was life. Molly reached for the call button on her bed to summon a nurse, pushing it before Madison could stop her.

"Molly, you don't need a nurse. I'm right here."

A nurse rounded the corner, pushing the curtain back to peer at Molly. "What is it, dear?" she asked

Molly, her emotionless tone belying her term of endearment.

"How did I get here? What happened? Where was I? Why can't I remember?"

Molly's eyes were wide, her voice in a panic as she tried to sit up. Her actions pushed the nurse into a fresh mode. One ready to call for backup if need be.

"Molly, I need you to calm down," she spoke with years of experience in de-escalating what she sensed was happening.

"I can't calm down," Molly shot back, her anger rising.

Max stood in the doorway to her room, looking at the nurse and Madison with unspoken questions. The nurse was too busy with Molly to notice him, and Madison didn't have an answer to give him.

Max went to her side. "Sis…"

"Get away from me," she spat as she jerked away from Max. "You're probably loving this."

"Molly—"

"For God's sake, I'm not crazy!" The irony of her own words struck through the air. Molly lay back in her bed, defeated, silent tears coursing down her cheeks. "Please just get out. All of you."

Madison crossed the room to her side, took her hand in her own, tried to reassure her. "Honey—"

"Madison, please," she whimpered. "Leave."

Madison felt a weight on her shoulders as she turned to leave, wishing beyond anything she had ever felt that she could remove this burden from Molly. She had reached the door, Max a step in front of her, when Molly's weak voice called her name again. She turned to look at Molly, who was calming from the sedative the nurse had given her.

"How did I get here?"

"A woman went to check on you and—well, she found you."

"Oh my God..." Molly groaned, remembering some more. "Jo," she whispered.

"Yes, I believe that's what her name was. How do you know her?"

"She's my boss for the column I write at the paper. She must think I'm really a piece of work."

Madison saw the first sign of color in Molly's cheeks. "I would say the only thing she's thinking right now is how glad she is that you're alive. She hasn't been allowed to come in to see you, but she's been calling."

"Probably to fire me."

"You have an inside connection to an attorney if she's wanting to do that," Max said as he poked his head back into the room. Madison held her breath, not knowing what to expect from Molly. She was immensely relieved when she saw the faintest glimmer of light in Molly's eyes, if only for the briefest of moments. It was the first time Madison could remember that the sound of Max's voice didn't set her sister off.

As she and Max turned once more to leave the room, the doctor strode in. His timing couldn't have been more perfect. Madison didn't want to leave Molly alone, and she knew Max was burning with questions as much as she was, and Molly wasn't open for them to ask.

"I'm Dr. Wiley," he smiled, shaking Max's hand first, then Madison's. After introductions, he sat on the edge of Molly's bed. "How are you feeling, young lady?"

"Never better."

Dr. Wiley smiled knowingly. "Molly, we're going to keep you for another night. After that, I strongly recommend you go to a rehab facility. We have—"

"Not only no, but hell no." Her voice was low and even.

"As I was saying," he continued, seemingly unfazed by her response, "we have some very reputable ones in the area. There are three in Taos alone."

"I'm not going to rehab. Rehab is for addicts. I'm not an addict."

"No?" His eyebrows raised slightly as he looked at her for clarification.

"No." She stared him in the eye, challenging him. "I made a stupid mistake. Everyone makes mistakes."

"A mistake that almost cost you your life is rather serious, don't you think?"

"I'm still here, aren't I?"

"Yes, you are. But you might not be so lucky next time."

"There won't be a next time."

Madison wasn't convinced, nor was she sure Molly was, beneath her facade.

"A social worker is scheduled to come visit with you later this evening. Would you just talk with her?"

"Sure." Madison looked at Max and saw her own surprise mirrored on his face that Molly had agreed so willingly. She'd expected Molly to fight against it; she was relieved that she hadn't. But both she and Max understood better when Molly followed up with her motive. "If I do that, I get out of here, right?"

Dr. Wiley stood, giving no indication that he heard her. "She will be here about seven o'clock. After dinner."

"I'm not hungry."

Dr. Wiley smiled, patted her shoulder in a fatherly manner. Molly's posture visibly tensed up.

"Maybe you will be later. If not, that's okay, too. No one is going to force feed you." At that Madison saw her relax beneath his hand, the struggle eased. Dr. Wiley walked to the door, a slight nod for Max and Madison to follow him. Molly turned her head to look out the window.

"Your sister is a very lucky girl," he began after they were out of Molly's hearing range. "I would like you both to do whatever you have to in order to convince her how important it would be for her to enter a rehab clinic."

"What if we can't do that?" Madison asked. "You've seen how difficult she can be."

"No more difficult than any other alcoholic, Mrs. Shaw," he explained. "In fact, I would say she's doing quite well, considering. But that being said, I believe she needs more help than she can get from family and friends."

"I don't even know if Molly has any friends," Madison stated, seeing surprise register on Dr. Wiley's face. What must he be thinking about them right now?

"A support network is critical. A support network of peers who are or have been where she's at. A rehab facility would be a good start to an imperative lifelong change."

"We'll see what we can do," Max extended his hand to the man.

"I'll be back in tomorrow before she's released, so I'll see you both then." And after a last brief handshake with each of them, he was off, leaving them looking at one another for a moment before they walked back into the room to find Molly facing away, staring at the wall where she stayed focused for a long while.

The social worker showed up at seven o'clock sharp, expertly scanning the room. Her eyes lingered for just a moment on Molly's tray of food that had scarcely been touched. Introductions were once again made with Max and Madison. Madison giggled, uncharacteristic for her, when she learned the woman's name. She quickly explained when she saw the woman look at her with obvious interest.

"Martha, I'm just amused because we're covering about every "M" name in the book." The woman continued to look at her, clearly confused. "My parents liked "M" names as you can tell, and my brother's girlfriend of the month fits right in, and now you," Madison explained further, now feeling somewhat foolish. She hadn't, however, missed the dagger Max shot her at her reference to Mandi.

Martha chuckled. "Happy to be a part of the family."

She pulled a chair beside the one Molly was now sitting in with arms wrapped around her knees that were tucked against her chest.

"Hi Molly. As you've heard," she grinned, looking at Madison, "I'm Martha."

Martha looked up at Madison and Max. "Could you two give me some time alone with Molly? Perhaps go grab a cup of coffee." she suggested.

"Of course," they said in unison. Madison was eager to get some air and space and assumed Max was equally so. They needed to figure out what was going on and what was going to happen next.

Madison took Max up on his offer to go to a restaurant a couple of blocks away. They walked to his car in silence. A silence that continued until they reached the restaurant and were seated.

"Did you leave the kids with the nanny?"

Max probably didn't have a hidden meaning behind his question, but it hit a raw nerve anyway.

"No, they're with their father. It's good for all of them to be alone together." She felt her back stiffen, her words sounding sharper than she intended.

"I agree," Max put up his hands in surrender. "No need to get defensive."

"I'm sorry," she looked at her water glass and then at him. "Your question just rubbed my nose in something that has been an unpleasant discovery lately."

"Sounds interesting."

"Trust me, it's not. Eye-opening maybe. But not interesting." Madison felt Max's eyes on her and looked back up. "Don't judge me, Max."

"Why do you automatically assume I'm judging you?"

"Now who's getting defensive?" She looked back down at her water glass, pushing the ice down with her index finger. "You're a lawyer. You like to think you have things all figured out."

Madison sipped a cup of hot chamomile tea and Max sipped his coffee while they waited for their food. They made small talk, catching each other up on things that didn't really matter, neither digging too deep or offering too much. Madison knew she was holding back and had a strong sense that Max was doing the same thing. She thought it sad that each felt the need to guard the lives they lived apart from one another.

Their waitress was a cute, petite, dark-haired bombshell who would have caught any man's eye, but Madison noticed she hadn't even gotten a second glance from her brother. She wasn't sure if she should be amused or concerned.

Their food finally arrived and they ate in silence, Madison more interested in pushing her food around her plate with her fork than eating. "Don't play with your food," Max said, sounding a lot like their father.

Madison glanced at him, a bittersweet smile tugging at one corner of her mouth.

They resumed making small talk, mostly discussing work, an area she knew each was mutually comfortable with. Madison made casual mention of Phil and the kids and even how she and Natalia had finally gotten to be friends after being under the same roof for so long.

Max mentioned Mandi, and Madison raised her eyebrows in interest.

"I don't know where it's going yet, so don't ask," he said before she could ask.

"Man! You get so defensive! I was only thinking that it could get confusing adding yet another "M" name to this family. Pretty soon we'll have the whole list of names beginning with M covered."

She watched as Max laughed despite himself, but he quickly added, "She's not 'in this family,' as you put it. Yet."

But Madison could sense the difference in her brother as he spoke of her. Mandi made him happy, and that made her happy. She had just told Molly a couple of hours ago that people can change. She hoped Max was proving her right.

Molly decided almost as soon as Martha began talking with her that she liked the woman. She had a grandmotherly feel to her, from the old, comfortable looking burgundy and gray wool sweater to the long gray braid that rested at the nape of her neck and midway down her back. Martha offered her pieces of her own life, and it made Molly feel even more comfortable. For the first time in a very long time, she didn't feel like she was under the spotlight of interrogation. After half an hour of pleasantries and superficial talk, Martha got to what Molly assumed was the meat of their meeting.

"Molly, what happened?"

Molly put her head against the back of her chair and wrapped her arms around her legs a little tighter. Her bare feet peeked out from beneath a light blanket. "I don't even know where to begin. Or how," she said quietly.

"How about with what happened yesterday?"

Molly remained silent, lost in the maze of her own thoughts, staring at the floor. Was that a pattern in the tile or was the floor dirty? She didn't really care, but she didn't want to think about anything that had happened yesterday.

"Molly?"

She turned her head to look at Martha, then back down at the floor before leaning her head against the chair again, closed her eyes, and whispered, "I don't know."

"I think you do," Martha replied quietly. Her voice was so gentle that Molly wanted to take refuge in her presence. To hide. "What's the one thing that stands out in your mind?"

"There isn't one thing. Everything feels jumbled up." She sighed a sound of defeat. "I feel like such a complete idiot."

"Why?"

"For being weak. I'm not a weak person," she added stubbornly.

"Everyone is at one time or another. And there's nothing wrong with that."

"This moment of weakness is going to define who I am to other people."

"Which people?"

"Jo. Madison..." Silence. "John," she whispered his name. "And even Max." Her voice was such a low whisper it was barely audible.

"Who's John?"

"My best friend. *Was* my best friend. I managed to screw that up."

"And how do you think you screwed that up?"

Molly managed a small smile. It sounded odd to hear Martha say those words. But it was a comfortable odd. Over the next half hour, intermingled with long moments of silence, through which Martha waited patiently, Molly filled Martha in about John, how their friendship happened, how they could talk for hours about everything, anything, or nothing at all, how they tried dating but decided it wasn't right. Or rather, how Molly had decided that on her own, according to John the other evening.

"Do you love him?"

"Of course I do. He's my best friend."

"Some people think it's important that their partner is their best friend."

"It didn't work for us." Her attention went back to the floor and those stupid specks.

"Was alcohol an important part of your friendship with John?"

"What do you mean?" she asked, disinterestedly.

"When you attempted dating one another, were you drinking at the time?"

"A glass of wine or two, yeah. What's that got to do with anything?" Molly waited for an accusation that much to her surprise and relief, didn't come.

"What do you remember from yesterday?"

Molly looked at the wall across from them, pulling her long hair into a haphazard ponytail. Finally she faced Martha. She may as well just get this over with so she could go to bed. Or better yet, home. But that was highly unlikely since Dr. Wiley hadn't exactly agreed to that. As much as she liked Martha, she was tired. And her darn hands wouldn't stop trembling. It was all making her agitated and irritable.

"The night before, I made dinner for John. After dinner he wanted to talk."

She saw Martha watching her trembling hands as she reached for the water glass on the table beside her.

"Are you feeling okay, Molly?"

"Yes. No! My damn hands won't stay still." Molly could feel Martha's patient gaze, watching as Molly took the blanket and let it fall to the floor. A moment ago it had been a source of security, and now it irritated her. "It's hot as hell in here, and I feel like I'm going to throw up."

"You're feeling the symptoms of withdrawal."

"No, I'm not. This has happened before, and I've never been hospitalized like this before. It's this dumb place," she insisted.

"It has nothing to do with being so bad off one time that you had to be hospitalized." That unnerving calmness again. "It's your body's way of craving more alcohol. That's what withdrawal is. And it can be very dangerous."

"Call it what you want," she replied. All she knew was that she wanted it to end. It was miserable. "Besides, how would you know what this is? Because that's what the books taught you? Well, what do the books know?"

"I've helped countless others go through exactly what you're going through now. And," she added softly, "I've been there. Right where you are."

"I doubt it," she said, tiny droplets of sweat beading on her forehead.

"You will get through this, Molly. You will get to the other side where you feel human again. Where you can think clearly. But it will take work. Hard work."

"Screw that."

"I don't see where you really have much of a choice, do you? Unless, of course, you want to stay feeling as you do now."

Fear rose up in Molly's chest. She wanted this to be over, not the threat of staying in this miserable place. For the first time, she felt the urge to fight to overcome this misery, no matter what she had to do. But as soon as she felt the spark, it died again.

"Molly, when did you start drinking? That night at dinner or earlier in the day?"

"Why?"

"Because that's why you're here. I'm trying to find out when it started. And what started it."

"Before John got to my house, I had a drink. Then I had a glass of wine when he got there."

"One?"

"One or two."

Martha smiled a sad smile, looking as if she knew a secret Molly didn't. It unnerved Molly. She wanted to know the secret.

"And then?"

"He wanted to talk; he told me he was in love with me and that he wanted to give us another try. That he couldn't keep things as they were because it was too painful for him. I gave in, but as soon as I woke up, I knew that I had made a huge mistake." She reached for her water glass, then decided her stomach wouldn't be able to keep it down. Not even one small sip. And yet she was so thirsty she could barely speak.

Martha handed her a cup with some ice chips. "Here. This might help." Molly reached a pale, shaking hand to take the plastic cup. "Why do you think you made a huge mistake, as you called it?"

She gingerly took one ice chip in her mouth. "Because it gave him false hope. But...I don't know...things just seem so fuzzy. Not clear."

"Go on," she encouraged gently.

"He must have known what was going on in my head. That's how it always was with us. We knew what the other was thinking." She paused a moment and looked at Martha who was watching her trembling hands and the beads of sweat on her forehead. She could even feel them on the nape of her neck. Loose strands of hair were sticking to the perspiration.

Molly stood up quickly, grabbing onto the chair as her balance faltered. She steadied herself, let go, and paced the length of the room, disappearing into the bathroom then reappearing.

"When will this stop?" she asked, words laced in anger. Frustration. "It reeks in here. I need a shower." She began to get undressed and began running the water. Martha sat outside the bathroom door, keeping Molly within sight. She leaned over, braced her arms on the wall of the shower, hung her head, not sure if her stomach was going to turn over and up or if she dared to move.

Finally she emerged, a towel wrapped around her thin figure and another around her hair. Her hands still trembled but had calmed considerably from what they had been.

"How do you feel?"

"A little better." And as she realized she sounded better to her own ears, relief swept through her. She slipped on the hospital-issued white robe, scratchy from too much starch, and sat back down, her hair still in a towel.

"Do you feel up to continuing our conversation?" "I'm really tired. I just want to go to bed."

"Do you want something to help you sleep?"

"Yes, please."

Martha went to get a nurse, meeting Max and Madison in the hallway. She explained to them that Molly was in bed, and it would be best if they could check in with her tomorrow.

"I'm going to suggest she stay a couple days longer. She's too fragile to be leaving tomorrow," Martha explained.

"What time should we be in tomorrow?" Madison asked, concerned.

"Why don't you call in the morning. I'll be staying with her through the night, so I'll be here in the morning." Martha handed Madison a business card with her number as well as the floor's main line.

They shook hands and the siblings departed. Madison stopped and looked back toward Molly's room, hesitating briefly.

"Come on, sis," Max coaxed, taking her arm. "There's nothing you can do here right now. You heard the lady."

"I suppose so," she answered reluctantly, following her brother. "Max, what if we've contributed to this?"

"Don't even go there, Madison. I'm not taking responsibility for Molly's behavior. She's been self-destructive most of her life. You know that. Think back. Is there anything Molly has started that she hasn't quit? Or at the very least begged Mom and Dad to let her quit? She's always playing victim to life's circumstances, trying to hide behind something or other, whether it was her room, her friends, her writing, or alcohol."

"You sound so cold," she stopped, stared at Max. "You don't feel the least bit guilty for being so mean to her?"

"Yes, Madison, I do." His steps slowed, and he exhaled slowly, sounding as exhausted as she felt.

"You do?" she echoed.

"Yes, I do. There, I said it. Are you happy? But that being said, I will not take responsibility for her behavior now. She's responsible for that all on her own."

"You just said—"

"You don't need to remind me what I said." He began walking away .

"How can you be so...so cold?"

"I'm a lawyer, remember?" He showed the faintest hint of a smile. "Madison, I'm just saying, don't make this about me or you or anyone else. You are not responsible for how someone else behaves. Molly is an adult who is responsible for her own choices and her own behavior."

"Are you trying to steal my job, little brother? You sound like Dr. Phil. He's *my* mentor," she laughed, silently wondering how in the world she could even be laughing right now. Maybe she was going stark-raving crazy. They walked a moment in silence before Madison became serious again. "Max, for being a therapist, sometimes I feel like a total idiot when it comes to the people I should know best. My own family." Max didn't even know the half of it and she wasn't about to tell him. What she and Phil were going through wasn't relevant to anything that was happening here. "I feel clueless and that's so unnerving."

"Maybe it's because you're too close to look at it from the proper perspective. Love is blind, isn't that what they say? Your problem is that your heart's too big. Even as a kid—when I broke my arm it didn't bother you, but you couldn't handle it when my heart was broken from my first girlfriend dumping me. Still a mistake on her part."

"And...there's my arrogant brother back," she laughed. "You were scaring me for a minute. I thought you were an imposter. My brother isn't known for his touchy-feely sentiments."

Madison slipped her arm through Max's as he walked her to her car before going to his own. They had agreed that he would leave on Sunday and she would stay with Molly until she was discharged and they had a plan in place. Pausing at her car door, she leaned over and gave him a hug, finding comfort when he squeezed her back. Despite Molly's state of affairs, she and Max were finding their way through it together. For the first time she could remember, they were really being there for each other. It made her sad that it had taken something so serious for that to happen, but grateful nonetheless.

Molly lay in bed, eyes closed, trying to make sense of what was happening. Martha had mumbled something about slipping out to get a cup of coffee and to walk out the kinks that had invaded her body, but Molly had tuned out the rest and fallen into a blissful sleep. She had slept better than she had expected, though she knew the sleeping pill helped considerably. Despite sweating through her hospital gown twice, waking with a headache she swore was going to split her skull wide open, and muscle twitches Molly had vaguely been aware of during the course of the night, the night was uneventful.

She was awake, yet lying with her eyes closed when she heard Martha walk into the room. She contemplated briefly whether she wanted to let Martha think she was sleeping or open her eyes to reveal that she was awake. She allowed a sliver of light to find its way through her eyelids as she looked at Martha.

Martha smiled at her. "How are you feeling?"

"Like I got hit by a truck," she groaned. "But I think I'm going to make it."

Martha chuckled. "That sounds about right."

"What time did you leave last night?"

"I didn't."

"You stayed all night?" Molly asked, confused.

"I did," she smiled.

"Do you always do that?"

"Not always," Martha smiled again.

"Why are we up so early?" Molly complained. "What time is it?"

"It's not so early. It's ten o'clock."

"Oh, man," she groaned again.

"Time to rise and shine. We have work to do."

Molly's eyebrows raised, her eyes widened. "Are you kidding me?"

"Not even a little. Hop on up, take a shower, comb your hair, and brush your teeth. I'll be back in an hour."

"I thought you were such a nice woman," Molly said with a touch of sarcasm. "And here you are—a drill sergeant."

Martha laughed, a happy, joyous sound that hurt Molly's head. She wished she could feel happy and joyous right now. Molly looked at Martha with envy as she began to leave the room.

"Martha?"

The woman turned to look at Molly as though she had all the time in the world. "Yes, dear?"

"I'm scared." Her voice was little more than a whisper.

Martha went back to Molly's side and sat on the edge of the bed. "Of what?"

"I don't know what happened. I don't think I meant to drink that much. And the pills...I mean...I don't wanna die." Her eyes pleaded with the woman to believe her. "I was drinking. A lot. And I felt something change inside of me. I knew it wasn't good, but I just didn't have the energy to stop. I was so tired."

"I know. I understand."

"How can you possibly know?" She looked away from Martha.

"Because, my dear child, I was you once, a long time ago. But not long enough ago that I don't remember. I was exactly where you are now."

Molly's eyes opened wide. "You?"

"Yes, me. I didn't want to admit I had a problem. I was young and successful, on my way to the top of the company I worked for. A group of us went out a lot after work hours, and then I stopped. I began going home and drinking alone. And since I wasn't without a job, hadn't lost a marriage, never had a DUI—you get the picture—I didn't see how it was a problem. I just needed a little release. And I wasn't hurting anyone."

Molly watched her carefully, hanging onto every word.

"That is, until I hurt myself. If I hadn't been drinking, it wouldn't have happened. That's when I realized alcohol was a problem for me. When I drank, I became someone I didn't like very well. When I woke up sick, I vowed to myself that was it. No more. But that lasted until I felt better and I needed to relax. Which usually wasn't longer than later that day."

"Martha, you're describing my life," Molly whispered, a tear trailing down her pale cheek.

"And that of so many others," she explained. "See, child, you're really not that unique. We all have similar stories."

"We?"

"We who cannot and should not drink alcohol."

"You seem so happy, Martha."

"I am. Very happy," she smiled.

"I wanna be happy again." Martha waited for her to continue. "You know, when I wake up in the morning, I get so disgusted when I look at myself in the mirror. I hate that I'm so weak."

"Yes, I do know. I was there. And that's what we're going to tackle. You're going to look at that beautiful face of yours in the mirror again one day and see it for what it is. Intelligent. Strong. Beautiful." Martha stood and began walking to the door. "Get up, take a shower, and put on some clothes. We're going to a meeting at noon."

"A meeting?"

"Yes. Don't worry. I'll go with you."

Molly trusted Martha and would do anything she asked of her right now. And if she said they were going to a meeting, Molly was going with her to a meeting. In fact, now that she was feeling like she was able to function again, minimal as it was, it was enough to make her reconsider Dr. Wiley's suggestion. Something needed to change. And for the first time, she didn't think she could do it alone. Alone hadn't worked very well for her in the past. Maybe it was time to try something else.

By the time Martha came back to the room, Molly had made her decision. And as she looked at Martha, she couldn't remember the last time she'd believed in someone so much. If ever.

"Martha, I need help."

"That's the smartest thing you will have ever said in your entire life."

"Please help me before I change my mind."

Martha stepped out of the room and came back in with Dr. Wiley, paperwork in hand, and by the time Madison returned to Molly's room, the process was completed and Molly was on her way to the life she had always longed for and would never have known existed had she not met Martha. And *how* she met Martha— well, she wasn't sure she was grateful for that, but she would take it. At least at this very moment she had a glimmer of hope that she hadn't had in a long time.

Martha helped Molly get checked into her new home for the several weeks, insisting Madison leave once she saw where it was her sister was going to be. Molly's legs were shaking as they somehow carried her up the stairs to the front door. She heard Madison and Martha talking at the bottom of the stairs, but wasn't able to focus on what they were saying. Her mind was traveling a mile a minute. She thought she heard Madison say something. She turned and saw her taking long strides to her car, head down.

"Martha?"

"She'll be fine. Right now, you just need to worry about yourself. You have a lot of hard work to do, and it's going to take everything you've got."

As soon as they walked through the front door, a woman met them and showed them to her room. She rifled through Molly's things Madison had gathered from the house for her at the hospital, before she knew she would be going to rehab. When the woman removed some things out of the bag she felt the sting of her space being invaded, and tears began to fall. She wanted to turn and run, but she felt a hand firmly on her elbow, leading her to a room with chairs set in a circle, smoke swirling through the air. And it was there she sat motionless, feeling dazed and confused for the next hour, absorbing every word spoken, until she heard a voice that sounded eerily like her own, yet so far away.

"Hi, my name is Molly. And I'm an alcoholic."

Chapter Eleven

As luck would have it, Phil had to leave for an annual out-of-state convention the day Madison returned home. She took advantage of the continued time apart to reconnect with the kids and to spend some enjoyable girl time with Natalia. It didn't escape her that she felt secretly relieved not to have to face the elephant in the room that their issues were. She knew they would need to be dealt with sooner or later, but she was more than okay with it having to be later.

By the time the day arrived that he was to return home, however, she had spent a considerable amount of time reevaluating not only their marriage, but her life with and without Phil. She replayed instances in her mind, some like a needle stuck on an old vinyl album, playing the same words over and over again. She heard the words she'd said and the ones she hadn't but were in her mind nonetheless, and she felt ashamed. When had she become so self-centered and self-important? Had she always been that way? Life seemed to have happened without her conscious awareness of choices she had made—things she'd done without considering Phil or even inviting him into the equation. As if that were her right and in her power anyway.

She thought of the conversations she'd had with Natalia over the past month, and how even though she admired the simpler life Natalia had growing up, she still hadn't done anything to change what she knew needed to be changed. It was just easier to remain at the status quo. But status quo didn't help anyone be anything other than the same. And as much as she knew that, she took the path of least resistance.

She wondered when she had gotten to be so controlling and overpowering, wondering how far back it had been such a part of how she behaved. The need to control and be *in* control left no room for Phil to be a husband or a father.

She realized that not only had she not done a single thing toward beginning her tasks from her parents' will—or even taken the time to decide whether she was going to or not—but she hadn't even discussed it with Phil yet. Guilt cut deep, making scars she was sure would last a very long time. But it was time to heal. However long that would take, and whatever steps it would take—it was time.

Instead of taking the kids with her as she usually did when she picked Phil up from the airport, Madison arranged to have Natalia stay with the kids. She spent an hour getting dressed up in a pair of well-fitted jeans, a black, low-cut sweater, and black boots. Her hair and makeup were done to perfection for her husband only, the first time since she could remember.

Natalia whistled behind her as she left the house, and she laughed. She felt good. She just hoped it wasn't too late. Time alone with her husband was long overdue, not to mention the talk she'd put off far too long. Before Phil had taken his leave for them to think things through…in fact, long before then.

He was coming in on a later flight, and despite it being dark, she spotted Phil instantly as she pulled up to the passenger pickup area. He looked tired and worn. Again, guilt stabbed at her as she wondered how much of that exhaustion was her doing. When had she stopped appreciating him as a husband, a man, and her best friend? When had she stopped noticing him?

She saw the recognition in his face when he saw the car, but he hadn't fully seen her yet. She saw him glance in the backseat, knowing he was expecting to see the kids. When he didn't see them, she saw his eyes go from concern to confusion in a matter of seconds until he opened the door and saw her.

Madison stepped out of the car and hugged her husband, feeling the warmth of his body. The driver behind them honked his horn, urging them to hurry along, but she didn't even give it a second thought. She was paying attention to nothing other than what she saw in his eyes.

"Welcome home," she said softly. "I'll drive."

Phil smiled and tossed his luggage in the back of the SUV and got in the passenger's side.

"Where are we going?" he asked as she took a detour from the road that led to their house. "And where are the kids?"

"They're home with Natalia," she answered, glancing at him and hoping she wouldn't see disappointment.

"I'm intrigued." She saw him look out the side window, then the front, and then at her. "Where are you taking me?"

"You'll see."

"Madison—"

"Phil, don't worry. I know you're tired, and I promise you won't need to expend an ounce of energy. Trust me. I promise I'll make it worth your while."

She heard him chuckle softly. "The last time I heard that was—"

Was that sadness she heard in his voice? Was she too late? Desperation crept in, undermining her confidence.

"Yeah, I know. A very long time ago."

He didn't respond, and fear kept her from looking over at him. They continued on in silence until she could see the sign up ahead and hope surged once again.

"Here we are." She pulled into a parking space and turned off the ignition. She looked over at Phil and saw the recognition that crossed his face. She watched closely, a combination of fear and hope nearly paralyzing her.

"This is where we spent our wedding night," he said, so quietly she could hardly hear him.

"Phil, I'm sorry." She spoke just as quietly, hoping he would understand the weight of those words. She was sorry for so much. For what she had done, as well as what she hadn't and should have. "I have so much to say, and there's so much I want to hear. *Really hear*," she reiterated.

She watched as he exhaled slowly, resting his head against the headrest, and fear seized her. She was too late after all. Tears burned the back of her eyelids. Pain crushed her heart, and she felt like she couldn't breathe. She slowly put her hand on the keys, still in the ignition, and began to start the car. His warm hand covered hers, stopping her.

She sat motionless for a moment, afraid to move, until she worked up the courage to look at him, surprised to see his eyes shining with tears in the glow of the moonlight that slanted through the windshield.

"No kids tonight, huh?"

"Are you disappointed?" she asked, afraid to hear the answer.

"I love our kids—"

Madison was so certain what was coming next, she nearly missed what he did say.

"But, no, I'm not disappointed. I'm delighted."

It took a moment to register. Her head snapped around to look at him. She needed to see that she'd heard him correctly. "What?"

"I love my wife. And I've missed her more than you know."

"About as much as I've missed my husband," she smiled through her tears.

When Phil and Madison got home, Natalia was in the kitchen cleaning up after dropping the kids off at school. Madison smiled at her and laughed when Natalia winked knowingly.

"Mrs. Shaw, it's written all over your face," she whispered in Madison's ear when they hugged. And Madison could do nothing but grin.

Madison had been speaking with Molly daily and couldn't believe the changes she heard in her voice from call to call. It was like her sister was transforming from a caterpillar to a butterfly before her very eyes. Last time they'd talked, Molly had actually said something nice about Max, and Madison knew a miracle had happened. She'd never thought she'd hear anything like it in her lifetime.

So Madison decided to enlist Phil's help in planning a Christmas gathering at the farmhouse. She called Molly while Phil called Max, each sighing with relief when they learned they both agreed to be there.

Now, as she and Phil sat on the couch the evening following his return home, cuddling in front of the fire, Madison turned to Phil and said, "So I've been thinking..."

"Uh-oh," he teased.

"I would like to look into sponsoring a child from a third-world country. Africa perhaps. Maybe we could sponsor one Zoey's age and one Oliver's age and get the kids involved with corresponding with them."

He pulled away enough to be able to look into her eyes. "That, my gorgeous wife, is one of the best ideas you have ever had."

"I wish I could take credit for it, but I can't."

"Oh?"

"Yeah…About that will I never told you about…"

She held his hand and turned sideways on the sofa, facing him, lifting one foot onto the sofa cushion, the side of her knee resting against the back of the sofa, the other planted on the floor. She held his hand in her own and began at the beginning. Back to when she walked into the kitchen her mother once cherished, complete with the yellow Asiatic Lily that resembled her mother, the conversations with Molly and Max, the meeting with Stephen.

She watched Phil closely as he absorbed every word, hoping to get a feel for what he was thinking as she spoke. After a moment of silence he brushed a solitary tear that crept down her cheek, his thumb lingering against the heat of her flushed skin.

"I have an idea, too," he said quietly.

"Yeah?"

"Yeah. And it's a doozy."

She laughed, enjoying the long-lost closeness they shared once again. "A doozy?" She repeated.

"Why don't we ask Natalia if she wants to help."

"Yeah?"

"Yeah," he mirrored her response.

"How about not as the nanny, but as part of our family."

"Now that, Mrs. Shaw, is the third fabulous idea you had tonight."

"Third? Well, now I'm curious. What was the second?"

"The the second was agreeing to my idea." He ducked her playful punch aimed at his arm, pulling her instead into an embrace. An embrace she hoped to never take for granted again.

Christmas was getting closer, and before she even realized it, Madison had fallen into her old habit of being so caught up in planning, doing, and making sure everyone had more than they needed. It wasn't until Phil suggested they take a few moments to research some child sponsorship organizations that she realized old habits die hard. Phil was eager to have the children each choose a child to sponsor. His gentle reminder made her grateful all over again that she had such an amazing husband. He had so easily persuaded her into taking on the challenge of the tasks set forth by her parents.

"Madison," he'd said, "weigh it out. There are innumerable benefits if you do it, none if you don't. What's the harm? And when have you ever backed down from a challenge?" And he was so right.

As she put aside what she was currently doing to sit beside him at the table, laptop in front of them, Phil said, "I would like to suggest that this year for Christmas, Zoey and Oliver get one gift each..." He looked at Madison and laughed. "Don't look at me like I have two heads, honey. This is going to be harder for you than it will be for them. Trust me."

"The problem is what to do with all the gifts I already purchased," she groaned.

"I know you. You keep every single receipt. Return them." He took her hand in his own. "Now as I was saying, they each get one gift. *And*," he smiled, "they choose any child they would like to sponsor and share lives with. They could write letters; we could help them read about the country their friend lives in. You know, like what they eat, how they live, what they do. Maybe we could even take the kids to meet them someday."

She watched him as he told her his dream for their children that year for Christmas, knowing he was expecting resistance from her at the very least. If not a flat-out, resounding no.

"I think that's the best idea anyone in this family has had in a very long time." She looked at him and laughed. "Now you're looking at me like *I* have two heads."

"I'm just waiting for the second one to come out of hiding. It's there somewhere," he joked, eyes lit up.

"Shut up," she laughed, playfully punching him in the arm.

"So violent!" he teased. "But you hit like a girl."

It wasn't long before they were on the floor wrestling, laughing, and soon two little bodies jumped in laughing, joining in on the fun. Madison thought this was by far the best moment of her life before she stopped thinking anything at all to simply enjoy this moment.

The next morning after getting the kids off to school, instead of hiding out in her office trying to fill every moment with something constructive until her first appointment arrived, Madison sought out Natalia to join her for a cup of tea. Madison had come to enjoy, and even count on, the time she was able to spend with Natalia.

Since the heart-to-heart conversation they had shared about Madison's fears and questions about the kids, she'd come to treasure Natalia's insight and company. The more she learned about Natalia's childhood and about who she was today, the more respect and admiration she had for her. Natalia's childhood was one of trial and tribulation with racial discrimination, parents who struggled for the next dollar in order to feed and clothe their children, chores each evening and weekend, being teased for the out-of-style clothes they wore to school, and even for smelling of onions from their father working in the onion fields.

But the trials they had endured only made them stronger and more cohesive as a family. They shared bedrooms, had one small bathroom, and oftentimes they took in more as they opened their doors to family and friends who were struggling and who were even less fortunate than they were. They laughed, they loved, they learned to do without, and only rely on each other and God. Faith was a lifeline for each of them, individually and as a family unit. And they were happy. They weren't wealthy, but they were rich.

Madison cried as Natalia recounted painful memories, laughed at the funny stories, and longed for the simplicity of which she spoke. She shared with Natalia the terms of her parents' will, and Natalia thought it was such a splendid idea and she asked to participate, if only in a small way, with Madison, Phil, and the kids, the delight clearly shining in her eyes. And she told Madison how honored she was when Madison asked her to be included in researching child sponsorship agencies and to be present when Zoey and Oliver chose a child to befriend.

By the time they were done talking, Madison realized they had gone clear through her first morning appointment, since the woman scheduled had never shown. She felt a surge of excitement to begin her two requirements named in the will. What had begun as an unrealistic and unfair requirement was turning into a fun challenge. And Madison loved to conquer a challenge.

She wasn't all that different from her brother after all, she thought.

Chapter Twelve

Madison and Max both showed up for the rehab facilitated family meeting the week prior to Molly leaving their care. While she took comfort in Madison's presence, she had resisted Max's and blatantly refused to see him at first. After she had finally relented, Madison left the two of them alone while she went and spoke with some of the staff. Molly's posture relaxed as she watched her, which was the opening her brother had used to get into her world.

"Why do you work so hard to keep me out?" he asked her.

"You've never tried too hard to be let in."

"Molly—you scared the crap out of me." His voice was quiet, subdued.

She continued watching Madison laugh with Joe across the room. "Nahh," she had answered while not taking her eyes off of her sister for fear of what she would see in Max. "You're still full of crap."

"You're not going to make this easy, are you?"

"And that surprises you?" She finally looked at him, not sure what she felt when she did, if anything at all. But at least it wasn't hatred or contempt, and for that she was relieved.

"I'd like you to give me a chance."

"A chance at what?"

She looked carefully into his eyes, trying to see what she was sure would be there—arrogance, evil— but she couldn't seem to find it. Instead she saw what looked like pleading, maybe even sadness. But was that even possible for Max?

"A chance to change. People can change, you know."

"Yes, people can. I guess I've just never placed you in that category before." A smile tugged at the corner of her mouth.

She saw her brother visibly relax a bit, exhaling. "Whew. For a minute I thought I was SOL."

"I still wouldn't say you're not." She saw him tense again and realized she was enjoying the bantering more than she cared to admit. In a good way this time, however, rather than in anger. "Max," she held his gaze, "I believe we can heal and get a brother-sister relationship back. Or just get one to begin with, since I'm not sure we ever had one. But it's going to take some time."

"How much time? Because it's ticking away. The way I figure it—"

"Man, you're such a lawyer," she shook her head.

"And who's this, Molly?" she heard a voice above her and looked up to see her favorite therapist. "Would this be Max?"

"Uh-oh," Max groaned. "I'm sure you haven't heard many good things about me."

"Actually," he said, "I haven't heard anything at all. Good things, that is," he added, his smile a contrast to his statement. "Why don't we go talk for a while? Just the three of us."

Molly looked at her brother, certain he was going to find an excuse to leave. She was shocked when he agreed. Perhaps a bit reluctantly, but he agreed. Molly felt a ray of hope mixed with fear. It reminded her of finger painting when she was a little girl and the yellow would mix with the black. She met Madison's eyes from across the room, watching as Madison quickly excused herself from whatever story Joe happened to be telling her.

The therapist stopped her from following them. "Why don't I talk to Max and Molly alone first." Madison's eyebrows raised in question and the shock registered on her face.

Some time later, the therapist, followed by Max and Molly, emerged from the same hallway they had disappeared from. Madison watched them closely. In fact, it looked to Molly like she was holding her breath. She watched as Madison's lower jaw all but fell open when Max gave her an awkward hug, and laughed aloud at her sister's shock when she didn't slug her brother, but rather hugged him back.

As Max turned to leave, a step behind Madison, he suddenly stopped, waited a beat, and turned toward Molly. His eyes stayed on hers for an uncomfortable moment too long. "Molly," he said so quietly she could hardly hear, "I really am sorry, sis."

Madison stopped dead in her tracks and turned, her eyes two huge blue pools of wonder, which was the only thing that made Molly believe he actually said what she thought she'd heard. "Yeah," she whispered. "Me too."

They still had a long way to go, but it was a start in the right direction.

Molly's breath caught as she approached her front door. First day back—she felt like a stranger breaking into the home she used to feel so secure in. The keys clinked quietly in her fingers. She was jittery from the unknown. Treatment, in its controlled environment, had been so safe. Here she was on her own, in a world that was anything but controlled and safe. In fact, exactly the opposite.

Finally getting the key inserted, she opened the door slowly, then stood still in the doorway, taking in her surroundings as if seeing them for the first time. She knew she should call Jo to check in, not only to see if she still had a job, but because the woman had crossed over from being her employer and friend to the woman who had literally saved her life. How do you thank someone for that? And would Jo even want to hear from her? She felt her stomach do a small somersault. First things first. She needed to call Madison, who made her promise to call her every day.

Molly delayed calling Jo while she emptied every drop of wine and liquor out, watching it swirl down the drain. The smell of it made her a bit nauseous, but truth be told, she wished she could have just one glass, just to prove she was normal.

Such a glutton for punishment, she thought. She had learned so much in treatment and had received so much strength, yet she still felt so weak. She felt like a baby learning to walk, her legs wobbly beneath her. The irony of her parents' request based on a suspicion they had, and the timing of this life-changing episode she had just gone through hadn't gone unnoticed. In fact it was a little eerie. Almost like her parents had willed something to happen that would make Molly realize the seriousness of her self-destructive behavior. Or simply to prove they were right. Whichever it was, it had worked, and it amused her.

Finally she decided to bite the bullet and call Jo. The phone rang four, then five times, and Molly was beginning to think she would get off easy and just be able to leave a voicemail, when Jo answered.

Molly's voice caught in her throat. "Hi, Jo."

Jo couldn't have been more understanding. She offered for Molly to take whatever time she needed to get better, but Molly insisted she *was* better and wanted to stay busy. She only wanted the time to attend whatever meetings she needed to keep from drinking, whether that be daily or more than one a day.

The counselors had taught her to take one day at a time, and no more. Whatever helped her get through that one day, or even that one moment, without drinking was the goal. And Molly had learned that looking at it in such small, bite-size morsels was much easier to commit to than thinking never again, which put her in a tailspin of anxiety.

Hanging up from Jo, she opened the cabinet for a glass and saw a bottle tucked in the very back of the cabinet, hidden from everyone but herself. She reached for the bottle, looked at it as a friend from long ago that she no longer wished to be friends with, and crossed the floor to the sink. As she watched the last of the golden liquid swirl down the drain, looking almost beautiful, she thought about the exchange with Jo just a moment ago.

"Jo? What made you come to my house?"

"You didn't show up for breakfast like we had planned, and you weren't answering your phone. You *always* answer your phone."

"I don't know how to thank you. You saved my life," she whispered, holding back tears that threatened to erupt, unable to stop the few that escaped.

"Molly," Jo said, her voice wavering slightly, "you scared me to death. Don't ever do that again. Come to me, call me, day or night. Time isn't an issue. Is that clear?"

"Crystal."

Molly smiled, eyes shining bright with unshed tears. Jo was such a treasure, and she realized that now more than ever.

She threw the last bottle away, scoured out the sink with lemon juice, and took the trash bag to the garbage can that sat beside the house. Then she put on her running shoes and headed out the door to get some much needed exercise. Her therapist had told her that now wasn't the time to let her exercise habits falter.

Molly thought about calling John but changed her mind. She knew he had spoken with Maddie at the hospital before she'd gone into rehab, because he'd shown up to check on her. He'd told Maddie that when he had called Molly later that day after he left her house, she'd answered and tried to carry an intelligent conversation, but was unable to. He'd attempted to stop over after work but Molly wouldn't let him in, and finally he'd given up and left. But when he couldn't reach her the next morning, he'd called Jo who had told him Molly had been admitted at the hospital. Madison had told him it probably wasn't a good idea to see her at the time, and that even if she thought it was, the hospital wouldn't allow it anyway. So he asked her to let Molly know he was there, and then he'd left.

Molly remembered his knocking on her door that night, but at the time she hadn't cared. In some selfish way, she had wanted to punish him, to make him feel the hurt that she was feeling. It wasn't fair for her to have to go through it alone, she'd decided. So even though she'd known it wasn't right, she also hadn't cared. She just drank some more to make it go away.

She picked up the phone and began punching in his number, but hung up before she finished, the embarrassment and humiliation more than she could tolerate right now. Facing him would be way too awkward. She knew she needed to apologize to him, but she just wasn't ready.

As she sat there contemplating whether she should call, her phone rang. She looked at the incoming number, saw that it was John, and silenced the ringer. She decided it was best not to face the issue tonight. She turned off her phone so the temptation to answer if he called again wasn't an issue. She needed time to process the whole situation. And while she knew he would probably worry again if she didn't answer, the fact that she didn't want to deal with it right now outweighed what she *should* do.

Suddenly she felt more like her brother than not like him. She got up and paced the floor, feeling agitated. Nervous. She picked up her cranberry spritzer and went into her office to write. She was going to work on her novel. Once she began writing, she was usually better able to block out everything else, placing herself into the lives of her characters.

Molly got up to stretch and was amazed when she realized almost three hours had passed. She was equally amazed by the amount of material she had written. Writing this late when she had been drinking wasn't even possible. The alcohol took away any motivation or ability to think clearly enough to write a coherent sentence, much less a scene. Pleased, and with renewed strength in her sobriety, she undressed, crawled beneath her warm, flannel sheets, and fell into a peaceful sleep.

Max checked in with Madison frequently on Molly's condition and progress, figuring he wouldn't push Molly by over-intruding or calling her too much. He didn't want to risk reversing the progress they had made, and he certainly didn't want their rocky relationship to give her another excuse to relapse.

Especially since Madison said she was doing so well. He was trusting Madison's professional advice to give Molly space, and really, it was advice he was all too happy to follow. Instead, he threw himself into his work and spent more time with Mandi. He was beginning to enjoy that more than he could ever remember enjoying a woman's company before. Paul had asked him again about the Habitat for Humanity project, wondering what Max was so afraid of.

"Even if you decide not to follow through with the rest, this is something I think you, me, and Junior should do. For us," he'd said.

Finally Max relented—if nothing else, to get Paul off of his back. Although he couldn't deny that a part of him was looking forward to it, and he didn't know why. He did know he felt a need to do something with his life that made a difference in this world, and that was a new feeling for him. One he didn't quite know what to do with. His parents' death and Molly's close call were giving him cause to pause and reflect on his own life—what he had done so far and what he hadn't but should have done. Regret was a hell of a place to live, and he was discovering he had his share of regrets.

So today was the first day he, Paul, and Junior were to start building the home for their project, and they were meeting at the worksite in just a little while. He drove along the freeway, the radio turned up loudly. The sky was a vibrant red off to the east, signaling a possible front moving in. Suddenly he felt the need to pause and admire the morning. Seizing the moment, he pulled off at the next exit, found a road with not a car in sight, turned the radio off, and just sat there in stillness and silence, drinking in the beauty of the early morning sky, the peacefulness.

For the first time he could ever remember, he didn't have to work at shutting down his thoughts. And he couldn't remember the last time he had ever taken the time to just be—to *be* without feeling the need to produce, whether thought or action. And it felt good. It couldn't just be a coincidence that he felt this strong sense of peace at that moment. He stayed silent and still, absorbing the beauty of the mountains in the not too far distance, the white caps thick with snow, until his mind began to wander. He reluctantly started his car and made his way to the meeting place.

He spotted Paul and Junior instantly at the jobsite, feeling a brotherhood with them that he had never felt with other men. They were all wearing jeans, flannel shirts beneath unzipped hooded jackets, and work boots. He couldn't remember ever seeing Paul in anything other than his suit or dress slacks and a sweater. Seeing him dressed as he was for the manual labor that awaited them gave Max an even greater respect for the man. He found himself hoping that someday he could be even half the man Paul was…and that thought was followed by a stab of guilt.

Why had he never thought that way about his own father? His father had been a powerful man, but as Max looked back in time, he couldn't remember his father holding an influential or prominent place in his life. Was it because his dad wasn't available to him or because he wasn't available for his father? He used to feel bitterness that his father hadn't been there for him, but as the last couple of months had unfolded, the line of distinction seemed less clear. He wasn't sure he'd ever given his father a chance to be a father. Guilt needled deeper as he imagined the pain he must have caused his dad.

He knew how much Paul enjoyed spending time with Junior, working together side by side. Junior's life was such a crucial part of Paul's life. Had Max robbed his own father of that? Suddenly he wished his father could be standing there with them, the four of them participating in this project together.

And then, from somewhere he couldn't explain, he felt his father's presence with them. And that presence appeared again as Paul slammed the hammer down on the first nail, driving it deep into the wood, as the resentment and anger he'd harbored for so long released and transformed into something almost beautiful. That feeling of another presence made itself known several times throughout that day as the men worked, focusing on accomplishing the tasks they'd set out to do, stopping at intervals long enough to laugh, joke, and have fun with one another. The others working on the project quickly became part of their group, bringing a new dimension to Max's day. He found himself opening up to others in ways he had never allowed to happen before. This day truly was a miracle that he could feel happening. And it felt good.

Chapter Thirteen

Phil, Madison, Zoey, Oliver, and Natalia decided to drive to the farmhouse two days earlier than Max and Molly so they could have some time alone together, to cut down a tree, get Vivian's Christmas decorations out of storage, and prepare the house for their Christmas together. This would be the first time the three would be together for Christmas since they were kids and all living at home. Madison wasn't sure if what she was feeling was nervousness or anticipation. Perhaps a little of both.

As soon as the car stopped, Zoey bolted out the door and ran for the front door, looking for Grandpa and Grandma. Madison's heart broke as she watched her daughter stop mid-run, remembering they were gone. Madison and Phil watched her for a few moments as she stood still, and then Oliver ran up beside her, worried about his sister. Zoey turned to them, huge tears sliding down her cheeks.

"I think it was a mistake not to have them here for the funeral," Madison said quietly, not quite sure if she was talking to herself or to Phil.

"We can't change what has already happened, babe, so no beating yourself up. We just need to work with what we have now."

"I know. My decision just wasn't fair to them. In trying to protect them, I've created nothing but confusion. I've just prolonged the necessity of dealing with it."

"They'll both be fine," he assured, wrapping his arm around her shoulders. They watched as Zoey put a protective arm around Oliver. "Let's go in the house and get settled in so we can go pick up a tree, shall we?" he smiled warmly at Madison, giving her a slight nudge.

"Yeah. It's too cold to stand out here." She shivered.

They were just getting over a brutal cold snap, finally beginning to thaw before the next weather system would inevitably settle upon them in typical Minnesota fashion.

Natalia entertained the kids and put together a light dinner while Madison and Phil carried in the bags, placing everything in the appropriate rooms. After they finished eating, Madison and Natalia drove to the supermarket in town to pick up groceries for the meals they would make together. They both planned to enlist Zoey's help so one day she would have the skills to entertain. Oliver's too, if he wanted. But Madison didn't think he'd pass up the opportunity to be his daddy's helper. Oliver loved spending time with Phil so much that Madison sometimes worried Oliver would try to fold himself into Phil's suitcase to go with him on his business trips.

While the two women were gone, Phil was charged with searching for the ornaments and the lights and putting them in the family room where they would be decorating the tree once Max and Molly arrived the following evening.

When they were all reunited back at the house at dusk, they piled into the car once more and found a tree farm. Dressed in layers upon layers of woolen warm clothes, to include hats, scarves, and gloves, and armed with flashlights, they set out to find the perfect tree.

In past years, Madison usually paid for a tree to be delivered to them. They'd roughed it one year by going to the tree lot to pick one that was bundled and ready to go. When the tree would finally be up, blue and white lights on just so, she would finish decorating it after the kids were in bed. She would strategically place blue and silver bulbs, bows, and pine cones between the branches. Phil and the children would carefully place the star on the top of the tree the following morning.

But Natalia had told her how her family used to choose a tree together. Then her father would string the lights, and she and her siblings made popcorn garlands and paper chains. Most of their ornaments were handmade items they had made in school. She told Madison that she and her brothers and sisters would have such fun seeing their art projects from years past hanging on the tree, and they loved the way their parents took such pride in them. Natalia said her parents would often see her sitting on the floor in front of the tree, committing each ornament to memory.

Madison had watched Natalia's eyes glisten with joy as she told the story and decided that's what she wanted to do with Oliver and Zoey that year. Along with Max and Molly, of course. Provided she could coax them into participating. She felt a new energy to make Christmas this year a time for her family that was better than anything they had ever known.

As they trampled through the tree farm, the crisp snow crunching beneath their boots as the kids found the deepest spots they could, they each pointed out the trees they liked. Oliver wanted one that looked like it came straight from the set of the *Charlie Brown Christmas*. Zoey wanted the biggest, tallest tree on the entire farm. Madison naturally wanted the most perfectly formed one—old habits die hard—and Phil and Natalia chose the same one. It was smaller than Zoey's, so it at least fit on top of the SUV, not perfect so Madison would overcome her need for perfection, but not as scrawny and sad-looking as the one Oliver had his heart set on.

Oliver's face looked as sad as his chosen tree at the idea of not being able to rescue it. And it was Phil who backed down and agreed to cut Oliver's tree as well since Oliver had so sadly stated, "But Daddy, no one else will want it either. How would you feel if you were that tree?"

As they dragged the trees back to the parking lot, Oliver proudly hauling his own with Zoey's help, Natalia had the kids looking for shapes in the stars, pointing out some of the constellations. Before long, the trees were lying down beside them as they made snow angels, laughing and acting as though they were all children. Madison couldn't remember ever seeing her kids so free and happy. In fact, she couldn't remember seeing any of them this happy. Including herself. This was a memory she would cherish forever.

She lay for a moment in the snow after making her angel. Looking up at the sky, she whispered, "Thanks, Mom and Dad."

Oliver came and jumped on her, followed by Zoey, and the snowball fight was on, eventually all ending in a giant heap of gloves, boots, snow, and fun, until Phil mentioned hot chocolate, and that was all it took for them to race for the car. Madison brought up the rear, absorbing every drop of the moment, every move each one made, watching as they made shadows with their flashlights until they reached the car.

Later that night, after hot chocolate with extra marshmallows, Madison got the kids into bed, tucking the covers tightly around them like they said Grandma used to do. She read them a bedtime story, but both were sleeping before she finished. As she stood to leave, she realized Phil was watching from the bedroom door.

"What are you smiling at?" she whispered.

"You."

"Me?" She asked, sashaying toward him.

"Yes, you," he whispered, looking down at her with tenderness. "I don't think I've ever seen you so happy as you have been today."

She leaned against him, and he folded his arms around her. "Phil, I think my parents knew exactly what they were doing."

"Parents always do," he teased, slipping an arm around her and leading her from the room and down the stairs to see that Natalia had retired for the night. "Tired?" he asked her.

"Not really."

"Good," he smiled. "Because I was thinking it would be nice to build a roaring fire and snuggle." He looked at her, eyes filled with mischief.

"Snuggle?"

"Um-hm," he smiled coyly.

"I couldn't think of anything better," she laughed.

Madison and Phil awoke to the smell of bacon wafting through the air and the beautiful sound of the kids laughing downstairs. Madison pulled her robe around her, slipped on her warm slippers, and padded downstairs, peeking around the kitchen doorway to see Zoey and Oliver each perched on a stool in front of the counter as they helped Natalia form cinnamon rolls and carefully place each one in the pan. She stood silently watching, basking in the glow from the day before, especially the evening at the tree farm.

Oliver caught sight of her and yelled, "Mom!" and ran to give her a hug. She kneeled down and pulled him in a tight embrace, putting one hand on the floor in back of her as he nearly knocked her over.

"Me and Nat are making cinnamon rolls, and we're letting Oliver help," Zoey said, all too grown up, white puffs of flour on her cheeks and chin.

"Oh, is that how it is," Madison replied, stifling a laugh as she noticed the flour in Oliver's hair.

"Mom, that's not true," Oliver piped up. "Me and Natalia are letting Zoey help *us*, huh, Nat?"

"Looks to me like you're all in this...mess...together," Madison said, stopping the budding argument. The two women grinned at each other.

"There's coffee on and ready, Madison."

Madison poured herself a cup, deeply inhaling the heavenly aroma of the freshly ground beans. She refilled Natalia's cup. "Mmm...Natalia, this coffee is so fabulous. Exactly what I needed."

"Your mother has so many flavors of coffee in the pantry. This is the cinnamon vanilla."

"It's perfect," she purred, smiling.

"What time are the others arriving?"

"Sometime this afternoon, I believe. I told them we could pick them up at the airport, but both of them insisted on renting a car. Seems like a waste."

Natalia quietly smiled. "I see you and Mr. Shaw got the tree up and ready for decorating."

"We did." Madison leaned against the counter with a silly grin on her face. Natalia laughed. Madison laughed at the expression on the kids' faces as they tried to figure out what was so funny. She couldn't resist giving each a hug.

"We thought Max and Phil could string the lights while the rest of us make the popcorn garland and paper chains. What do you think, Nat?"

"Fun!" The kids exclaimed in unison.

"Maybe I should help Daddy and Uncle Max with the lights since I'm a man, too," Oliver said.

"Well, little man," Madison answered, "I think the girls need a man's help on the important project of making the decorations."

"Okay," he said, sounding torn. "But you'll have to explain that to Dad and Uncle Max, so they're not too disappointed."

"I'll do my best," she said in all the seriousness she could muster.

"Do your best for what?" Phil asked as he entered the kitchen, heading straight for the coffeepot and shooting her a mischievous grin.

"Explaining to you and Uncle Max that the girls are in need of Oliver's help making the ornaments for the tree while you guys hang the lights."

"Oh! Well..." he said, pretending to be thinking hard. "I guess we can try to make do, but we'll have to steal you from the girls if we need you, little dude."

"Okay, Daddy. That sounds fair."

"What do you guys say we head down to the pond after breakfast and check out the ice? I hear your mother used to be quite the skater in her day."

"You were?" Zoey asked, eyes wide with disbelief.

"Well..." Madison grinned. "I could hold my own, I guess."

"Is that why Grandma has so many ice skates in the garage?"

"Yup," Madison laughed as she remembered her mother picking up skates of every size every time they were on sale. "Just in case we have company and they want to skate," her mother had explained.

Both kids scrambled off their stools, dashing for the garage to find the skates.

"Whoa!" Phil called behind them. "Are you two forgetting something?"

"What?" they both said, oblivious to anything other than the ice skates.

"How about eating and getting dressed?"

"Oh," Zoey laughed, followed by Oliver, trying to be like his big sister.

When they arrived at the pond, Phil started a fire in the fire pit, and Natalia and Madison helped the kids get their skates on, followed by their own. As soon as they slid onto the ice, Oliver's feet came out from under him. Zoey's quickly followed. Madison helped them back on their feet, as Natalia struggled to stay upright herself. Phil stayed and tended the fire, getting the hotdogs and marshmallows ready, as well as the thermos of hot cocoa they'd brought with them.

After some time on the ice, Madison made her way over to Phil. For the next little while, they stood with arms entwined, watching Natalia with the kids. Madison wasn't sure she would ever get rid of the smile lines that were being etched into her face, but she didn't care. This had been the best Christmas, hands down, that she could ever remember. And Christmas hadn't even officially arrived yet.

A shiver of fear raced down her spine. Fear that her life was too good to be true. Fear because life was so fragile and could end in a millisecond, as it had for her parents. It had the potential to take all of this away faster than she had found it. She didn't want to take a single second for granted. She wanted to drink in every drop of this beautiful life she had discovered and continued to find new every moment.

They consumed every hotdog, half of the marshmallows, and every drop of the hot cocoa, then they made their way back to the house to see if Molly or Max had arrived yet. Snow began to fall softly, and Oliver tried to catch flakes on his tongue while Zoey tried to see if she could prove her teacher wrong by finding two snowflakes that were identical in shape and size.

"Mom! I think I found them!" she squealed with delight. But when they dissolved before she could show Madison, her interest in searching for any more dissolved as well. Natalia placed a comforting arm around her. Oliver put his mittened hand in her other one, and Phil and Madison brought up the rear, keeping all of them in their sight.

Molly's car was parked in front of the house, but Max hadn't arrived yet. As they walked up the snow-covered path, Molly opened the front door and came out onto the porch, arms crossed in front of her, shivering.

"Well, well, well..." Madison smiled. "You do own a pair of shoes."

"Only because my feet would freeze to the porch if I didn't have them on. I'd forgotten how cold it gets here!" she laughed.

"Are you my Aunt Molly?" Oliver asked, staring up at her.

"Of course she is, dum-dum." Zoey retorted. "She sure isn't Uncle Max."

"Kids." Phil intervened. "Zoey, Oliver hasn't seen Molly for several years, so it would be unlikely that he would remember her, don't you think?"

"Well, Dad," Zoey explained, sounding more like nineteen than nine, "there are only two people coming—Uncle Max and Aunt Molly. He has to know that if it's not Uncle Max, it's Aunt Molly."

"Just because that makes sense to you doesn't necessarily mean it does to everyone else, Ms. Hotshot," he teased, swatting her bottom and urging her to get up the stairs and into the house.

Smoke curled up from the chimney. "And you even started a fire." Madison climbed the stairs and hugged her sister.

"I certainly hope so. Otherwise the house is on fire."

"Very funny," Madison said, scrunching her nose.

By the time they were out of their snowy clothes and Madison and Natalia had them thrown in the dryer, Max's car came up the driveway.

"Uncle Max!" Oliver exclaimed, watching the car until it came to a stop.

"Oliver," Zoey chided, "there's no way you can remember him. You haven't seen him since you were a baby."

"I do too remember him!" Oliver exclaimed. "Besides, if it's not Aunt Molly, it has to be Uncle Max," he mimicked her.

As Max walked into the entryway, brushing the snow off of his coat, Oliver simply stood and stared.

"Zoey was right," he said, disappointed.

"About what, little man?" Max ruffled Oliver's hair.

"I don't remember you."

"Well, I wouldn't think so. You were just a baby when I saw you last. And babies don't remember a whole lot." Max laughed, and Oliver sulked away to stand by his dad. Madison watched the exchange before crossing the floor to her brother and giving him a hug. She felt Phil's presence behind her as he reached his hand out to Max.

"Max? Good to see you, man."

"Likewise."

The two men eyed each other for a moment until Molly came into the kitchen. "Oh, it's you."

Madison saw Molly smile when she turned away from Max. Her little sister hadn't lost her spunk.

"Glad you made it, little brother. I was just about to begin worrying because of the snow. Are the roads getting bad?"

"No, and you worry too much."

"Mandi didn't come?"

"You sound disappointed. I'm not enough?" he grinned.

"Oh, you're definitely enough. Maybe too much," Molly teased.

"Jeez, kid! Lighten up. I just got here!" He looked at Madison and answered her previous question, "Mandi will be coming up on Christmas morning. I thought it would be a good idea for it to be just us to begin with."

"Yeah, good idea. You wouldn't want to scare her off before you have her hooked." Madison teased. Max smiled mischievously, and Madison added, "Oh my stars! You're the one who's hooked, aren't you?"

Looking at the silly grin that stayed on Max's face and his continued silence, she said, "I never thought I would see the day when my little brother finally found *the one*."

"Hey, sis," he finally said, the grin still in place. "Help me take my things up to my room, would you? I need to talk to you."

Madison looked at Phil and raised her eyebrows, curiosity consuming her. Phil simply smiled at her and nodded for her to go. She looked at the kids, busy helping Molly and Natalia prepare something for dinner.

Max picked up his suitcase, and Madison folded his coat over her arm and followed him up the stairs. When they reached his room, she laid his coat on the bed and sat in the chair in the corner of the room, crossing one leg over the other, eagerly waiting for him to talk. When he remained silent, she didn't think she could wait a minute longer.

"Well?"

"Sis..." he hesitated. "This is so weird. Three months ago, who would have ever thought I would be having a heart-to-heart with my big sister."

"Never in my wildest dreams would I have imagined the changes that have occurred in any of us over the past few months. And I have a feeling it's all just beginning. But tell me what's on your mind, because I'm going crazy waiting."

"I think I'm going to ask Mandi to marry me," he blurted.

Madison was speechless and felt like she couldn't breathe for a moment.

"This is the part where you're supposed to say something," he added. "Preferably something positive, like 'I think that's great, Maxwell,'" he said, mimicking the sound of her voice.

"I'm not sure what to say," she finally said. "Of course, I think it's great! But marriage is a commitment and isn't something to be taken lightly. What brought this on? I mean, have you thought about it?" Her eyes were wide, her face serious. "And when did this all happen? What do you mean you're *thinking* about it? You better *know* before you ask."

He sat on the edge of the bed, facing her. "I don't know what happened. It's like...all of a sudden...I saw her out with someone else, and it occurred to me. She's everything I have ever wanted. What have I been waiting for? For her to move on and find someone else? She's beautiful, sweet, smart, funny.... We have so much fun together...she gets me. And I know damn well that's no easy thing."

"Do you love her?"

"I do."

"And this isn't just an impulsive decision?"

"Quick but not impulsive, if that makes sense."

"Does she feel the same way?"

"I think so. But we'll be finding out soon enough. I bought a ring and want to give it to her on Christmas Day." He reached in his coat pocket, pulled out a little black box, and opened it. Madison inhaled sharply as she saw the most exquisite John Atencio set sparkling diamond she had ever seen.

"Oh, wow!" she gasped. "Max, that is absolutely stunning."

He laughed nervously. "Let's hope Mandi thinks so."

Madison looked at her brother with tears in her eyes. She went to sit beside him, enveloping him in an enormous hug. "I am so proud of you, little brother. And so happy."

She pulled back, wiped her tears with the back of her hand, and laughed. "This has got to account for the weirdest couple of months ever! In a good way," she added quickly. "But weird, nonetheless."

"Mom and Dad's accident—and Molly's stunt—made me realize how quickly life can end. I don't want to grow old alone, and I don't want my life to end without having really experienced it." She saw a sparkle in his eyes, revealing an excitement for life that was contagious. "I see my boss Paul and his wife, and Junior and his wife, and even you and Phil…and I want that."

He was rambling, but she remained quiet, allowing him to continue. His words kept coming as if it were out of his control to stop them. "Building this house for Habitat for Humanity with Paul and Junior, working side by side with so many people who have so many other things they could be doing but are helping someone else instead. Planning the fundraiser for AIDS research—"

"When did you decide to do that?" she interrupted, eyes wide.

"Mandi and I are doing it together. It's something we decided a few weeks ago," he explained. "I like feeling that I'm using my organizational and legal skills for something…beneficial. And Mandi working on it with me, Maddie"—he paused and looked at her, wide-eyed—"It just feels so…different. Like part of me doesn't even recognize myself anymore.

"Well, I gotta admit, Max, I'm not sure *I* recognize you anymore. It's kind of freaking me out."

"You!" He exclaimed. "Imagine how I feel. I look in the mirror expecting to see someone else looking back at me. I don't know what's happening." He paused again, and Madison smiled, encouraging him to continue. So he did.

"And this thing with Molly. I mean, how did Mom and Dad know about that? It's like they're up there, wherever "there" is—I'm not sold on the whole heaven, hell, or even God thing yet—but it's like they're orchestrating all these changes from the other side. It's creepy and awesome at the same time."

He looked at her as she sat motionless, still silent. "Say something," he said, somewhat breathless from talking so quickly.

"I was waiting for you to give me the chance," she laughed. "I totally agree with you. There have been so many odd things happening in my life over the past couple of months. I mean, for starters, look at us. Did you ever in a million years dream we would all be having Christmas together? Have you ever seen Molly so alive and willing to share her life?

"I've even gotten to know the kids' nanny in a whole new way. She's a friend, like nothing I have ever had with anyone else. Max, she's worked for us for several years. And we're friends only now? And I haven't even technically begun my to-do list from the folks yet." Her voice carried emotion and amazement.

"Natalia no longer works *for* us, but *with* us. That's such a huge difference. She has taught me so much about life, love, and what's important in the life of a child. I'm the one with the degree, but she's the one teaching me. And more than I ever learned in school, that's for sure. And all this happened because Mom and Dad brought to my attention how I was living, and the fact that it wasn't as perfect for everyone, including myself, as I thought I was making it. They're speaking to me from the other side. I swear! The difference is, though, that I definitely believe there is a God, a heaven, and a hell. How else would you explain all this? Coincidence? No way," she exclaimed.

She finally stopped, realizing she had been pacing the floor as she carried on. She looked at Max and they both began laughing. Laughing like they hadn't done in decades, if ever, together. She saw Molly poke her head in the room, Zoey and Oliver in tow.

"What, pray tell, is going on in here?" Molly asked, grinning.

Zoey and Oliver ran over and jumped up on Max's bed, one sitting on either side of him, Oliver on his haunches.

"Dinner anyone?" Natalia's voice came up from the bottom of the stairs. "That's if anyone is even hungry," she called.

"Are you guys going to answer me?" Molly insisted, still grinning. "I'm feeling a little like the odd man out."

"Aunt Molly, you're silly," Oliver laughed. "You're not a man, you're a girl."

"Okay, then, I'm feeling like the odd *girl* out," she corrected herself. Lily came around the corner and jumped up on the bed, licking Oliver's face, and Oliver squealed in delight.

"What the hell?" Max asked, looking at the dog. "What's that?"

"It's called a dog."

"No shit, Sherlock. But where did it come from?"

"I gave birth to it," Molly laughed. "What do you think?"

Madison laughed as she watched Lily play with the kids on the bed. "You said you were going to take Mom and Dad's dog, but I didn't realize you had her already."

"That's why I was a little later than I thought I would be. I stopped by Stephen's to pick her up so the kids could spend some time with her."

"And it was a darn good thing you did. I think they missed her," she grinned.

"Yeah," Molly said, smiling as she watched them. "I think the little pup and I are going to get along just fine."

"Moll," Max explained above all the noise, "you and I need to take a little walk later. I'll fill you in on what was going on before the little rat came in the room."

"Deal," Molly said. "And she's not a rat. She's a cute white Maltese. Let's go eat. I'm starving."

"Me too!" both kids hollered and raced for the stairs.

"Walk!" Madison yelled behind them, laughing.

Chapter Fourteen

After a fun-filled dinner with enough food to feed the city and enough laughter to fill the North Pole, Madison told Natalia to go enjoy herself and Madison would clean up.

"Are you sure, Maddie?"

"I'm more than sure. Now scoot." She smiled. "Go have fun with the others, curl up and read a book, or take a nap."

Natalia gave her a hug, a smile that melted Madison's heart, and went upstairs.

"Come on, little sis," Max said. "Let's go for a walk. And for God's sake, wear boots. Or at least the shoes I saw you actually own."

"We haven't even left the house yet and you're already bossing me? This sounds like a fun walk," she grinned.

Madison stopped them before they could leave the room. "Wait for me. Clean up can wait. Let's go down by the pond." Her suggestion was met with four eyes looking at her like she'd lost her mind.

"What?"

"It's cold out there."

"And snowing," Max added.

"Come on," Madison pleaded. "There's enough coats and boots around here to clothe an army. The moonlight reflecting off the snow makes it plenty light to see the path to the pond."

The kids came running into the room, squealing in unison, "We wanna go too!"

"See?" Madison said, proving her point. "Even the kids are brave enough to go. You're not going to be shown up by two kids, are you?" She watched Max and Molly look at each other before Molly rolled her eyes. "You just couldn't let my brother and me be alone for a minute, could you?"

"Not alone, no. Murders have happened in less time than that." She ducked to miss the wadded-up napkin Max through at her. "Is that a yes?"

Neither answered her, but when they began bundling up, she knew she'd won. She swatted the kids lightly on the rear end and sent them to climb into their snowsuits and boots. "Phil," she called into the living room where he was watching TV. "We're going down to the pond. Do you want to come with?"

"Nope."

"Even want to think about it?" Max called.

"Nope," he called back. "But thanks for asking."

"Wimp!" Max called back.

The kids bounded out the door with energy the others envied.

Madison was the first to speak. "Well, Max?"

"Well what?"

"Come on, don't play dumb. Tell Molly."

"Yeah, Molly would like to know the big secret," Molly agreed.

They all paused to look for the owl who had just made his presence known, and then Max began unfolding his news to Molly, while Madison watched their interactions with one another, still in awe that the two were able to have a human civilized conversation.

Max walked, hands in his pockets, and looked up. Madison and Molly followed his gaze, looking up at the twinkling of the stars in the cold night sky.

The bonfire pit remained as they had left it earlier in the day. The sticks used for roasting marshmallows were leaning up against the picnic table, marshmallow remains frozen on the pointed ends. The ashes from the earlier fire were now covered with a light layer of freshly fallen snow. A solitary piece of wood remained, jutting through the white.

Madison inhaled slowly and deeply, as if trying to breathe in every memory she could. Max took one of the roasting sticks, studied the end, then stuck it through the snow, prying it into the frozen ground, working the remaining lingering marshmallow into the earth. Molly sat silently on a bench at the picnic table, staring at the frozen pond nearby. They had spent countless hours on that pond, the three of them. Sometimes Madison had even come out here before school in the morning, circling and dipping gracefully on her ice skates, big green pompoms tied to her laces.

Zoey and Oliver treaded gingerly onto the ice until they had their footing, then both grinned ear to ear and ran, sliding and giggling, stopping abruptly and falling forward when they met with the snow. Madison laughed and looked back at Molly and Max.

"Gee, guys. The mood sure has turned somber in a matter of minutes." She looked at Zoey and Oliver with envy as they now lay making snow angels in the drifts of snow. "Mom and Dad would never believe the three of us are actually here," she said.

"And acting civilized."

"Yeah," Molly agreed. "Some of us are."

Madison smiled as she watched Molly duck to miss the snowball Max hurled at her.

"So Max, when do I get to have a conversation alone with Mandi?"

Max's eyebrows knit together. "How 'bout never."

"What are you afraid of?" Molly asked innocently.

Max said nothing, just glared at her, and Madison smiled. So it would take some time to get *all* the wrinkles out, she thought. But they had come so far, she could still hardly believe it.

Max scooped the snow out of the fire pit and began gathering wood, strategically placing it in the pit. He turned to see Madison watching him, an amused smile on her face.

"What?" The gruffness in his tone surprised her.

"Whoa! What was that about?"

"Nothing."

"Really? Because it sure sounded like something."

"You know..." he paused before continuing. "Mom and Dad would have loved to have seen this. To have been here. Here we are, finally—communicating—and they aren't even here to witness it."

"This isn't one of your cases. No witnesses necessary," she teased lightly.

"Madison..." She watched him shift uncomfortably. "Why did they make you the executor of their estate?

"I'm not sure. Maybe just because I'm the oldest? Why is that such a hang-up for you?"

"Just curious. Since I'm the one with the legal experience, it would just seem logical that I would have been the one."

"We've already had this discussion, Max. Maybe that's exactly why they didn't. Maybe they didn't want this to turn into just another estate being settled. This was about so much more than that. Besides, you're not an estate attorney." She tried to explain as delicately as she could, so she didn't step on his toes in the process. "It wasn't a legal process to them. That's what they had Stephen for."

"Even if that's the case, I'm still the son. I should have been the executor."

"That's a bit chauvinistic even for you, don't you think?" Madison looked at him in disbelief.

"I think it's pretty typical of something he would say," Molly interjected.

"Moll, shut up," Max shot her a look.

"Just sayin'."

"Not only am I the oldest," Madison continued, "but I lived the closest and had the most contact with them over the last several years." She looked at Max who was looking at the pond, but appeared to be staring right past the kids without even seeing them. "It's strange to think we're orphans." Madison wrapped her arms around herself her, looking at the pond just as Oliver pushed Zoey.

"Oliver!" she called out. "Stop that!" Oliver turned and looked at her, then averted his eyes from her at being caught.

"I wish we could have just one more day with them. Just one day as a family," Madison said. She wrapped her arms a little tighter, feeling the chill in the air pierce her heart, the pain weighing her down like an anchor on the old fishing boat her father used to have. A tear slid down her cheek and she quickly brushed it away. She felt Max's arm around her shoulders, and she leaned her head on his shoulder.

"I'm sorry, Maddie. It's just something I've been wondering and just had to ask. Again."

She pulled away and looked at him dramatically. "Will wonders never cease. Did I just hear you apologize?"

"I thought I did, too, but realized I must be hallucinating," Molly chimed in. "No alcohol needed."

Max lightly cuffed the back of her head. "Smart ass. Don't come to expect hearing it again."

Madison laughed. "How about we put away the nostalgia for a while and have fun planning your wedding?"

"How about I plan my own wedding?" Max retorted. "Besides, I thought we came out here to tell Molly the news, not to take a walk down memory lane. What a buzz kill." "You're the one who started it," Molly chuckled, blinking away a lingering tear that threatened to freeze on her eyelash. Max talked about Mandi, warning them that they better be nice to her and threatened them if they told Mandi anything bad about him.

"So in other words we can't talk about you at all? Because there would be nothing left to say." Molly teased and Max threw another packed snowball at her, narrowly missing her.

The kids burst through the door first, running through the kitchen, snow falling from their boots and mittens to the floor. Phil met them, turning them instantly around with one move back to the door. He planted a kiss on Madison's cherry red cheek.

"Brrr. You're frozen."

"Not anymore," she looked into his eyes. "In fact, it's rather warm in here."

"Get a room," Max scoffed. "You two are sick."

"You're just jealous," she laughed. "Besides, we have one." She looked at him coyly, "In fact it's right next to yours."

"I prove my point," Max said triumphantly. "You're sick."

Madison laughed at her brother. She suspected that what was happening between them was exactly what their parents had aimed for. It was as if she and her siblings had become internal shape shifters. She wished their parents were here, able to see the transformations taking place. That they would be able to experience the joy in something so remarkable, caused by something they had orchestrated.

Madison left the rest of them as they settled in to watch *How the Grinch Stole Christmas* on DVD, and went to clean up the dishes that remained untouched since before they had walked to the pond. She looked out as she passed the big bay window in the kitchen and saw the snow was falling in heavier, bigger flakes, the white of the snow making it appear to be dusk rather than nightfall.

She had insisted that Natalia relax and let her do the cleanup, and now she was getting a taste of the real life of mom and wife—the dirty, non-glamorous parts that she had never had to deal with, thanks to Natalia. She couldn't help but wonder if having Natalia with her since the kids were born had really been a blessing, or if she was simply spoiled? She thought about all the times she had taken advantage of Natalia's hard work and was sad to realize it was more often than not. Had she ever even given it a second thought? She couldn't remember.

She looked down at her hands in the hot soapy dishwater. No dishes remained, but the water was cleansing her soul as well as her hands. She marveled at the fact that her mother had never had a dishwasher but had chosen to do dishes by hand. Something unheard of in today's world. Her mother had even baked her own bread for as long as she could remember. And Madison had never truly appreciated any of it.

Instead she'd thought her mother was crazy and old-fashioned. They'd had plenty of money for the pleasures in life, yet her mother had chosen not to take advantage of so many. And Madison was only just beginning to truly understand why. The simplicity of it was soothing to her very core. It was therapy that people paid thousands of dollars to find, and it was in giving up things that she realized it could be found.

She looked up and gazed out the window in front of her, watching the huge white flakes fall so gently it was almost mesmerizing.

When her fingers had become wrinkled as prunes, Madison drained the dishwater, watching the water swirl down the drain. She dried her hands and hung the dishtowel, then she made her way to the family room where Phil and the kids were now quietly reading a book in front of the fire. Natalia was curled up under a blanket in the corner of the sofa, her own book open in front of her as she stared into the fire, a small smile filled with contentment on her lips. Madison went and sat down beside her, covering up with a portion of the blanket that trailed beside Natalia. The two women sat silently watching the fire, enjoying the warm presence of the friendship that blanketed them.

"The peace that I feel here," Natalia murmured, "it's like nothing I've felt for a very long time."

"I feel it too," Madison answered, smiling, her voice close to a whisper. The reflection of the firelight danced in her eyes. "The absence of anything resembling something other than what is right here, right now. Pure simplicity."

They sat for a while longer, listening to the fire licking the newly placed logs Phil had just added, staying huddled beneath the warm fleece blanket. They both startled when they heard the front door open and felt a cold breeze ripple through the room. Max and Molly were back from a quick trip outside so Molly could look at Max's BMW he was renting. They were talking and laughing loudly.

Madison looked at Natalia and explained, "You know, before my parents died, you would never have seen them not on each other's last nerve. Much less actually talking and laughing."

A shadow crossed her face as her eyes became sad. "It's just too bad it took their death to make that happen. What they wouldn't give to be able to see this. They gave their lives, but are not able to see the reward."

Natalia put her hand on Madison's arm. "I have a feeling they know, Maddie."

"I hope so."

"Well, who's up for decorating a tree?" Max's voice boomed in the quiet of the room, sending the kids squealing with delight.

Phil popped the corn for the popcorn chain, and Natalia, Madison, and Molly got the glue and red, green, and white construction paper, already cut into perfectly sized strips, set them on the table and gathered with the kids to see who could make the longest chain. Natalia and Oliver were a team, Molly and Zoey, and Madison was left to fend for herself. Max retreated to the privacy of his bedroom, phone in hand, already punching in numbers before he reached the first step.

Phil had just finished popping the corn and had placed it on the porch to cool when Max returned to the kitchen.

"What's that goofy grin you have plastered on your face?" Phil teased him.

"Must be from seeing you, man," Max chuckled.

"Careful. Madison will get jealous. Want to help with getting the lights on the tree? I need someone to get the bottom branches."

"Well, aren't you just the wise guy. Come on, I'll show you how it's done."

"Oh, you will, huh? It's on, big guy. Show me how it's done." He laughed and tossed a string of lights to Max, who began to lasso them onto the tree. Madison watched from the kitchen and rolled her eyes, jerking her head in their direction for Molly to watch.

"Why do men always feel the need to compete?" she asked. "Don't answer that," she quickly added. "Rhetorical question with no valid answer."

"I was thinking more along the lines of why they feel the need to be such dorks," Molly grimaced. "We should be videotaping them and putting it on YouTube."

"Ha!" Madison blurted and laughed out loud. The men turned to look at her like she had lost her mind, and she laughed harder. The kids squealed with delight at being part of the inside joke.

They stayed up until midnight decorating the tree, listening to some old Christmas albums they had found in the basement, and drinking hot apple cider with cinnamon sticks. When the last of the decorations were made and on the tree, they all sat down on the floor in front of the tree while Phil had the honor of plugging in the lights. Madison watched the reflection of the brightly colored lights dance in the kids' eyes as they beamed. No blue and white this year. It was, by unanimous decision, multicolored all the way.

Maddie's heart skipped a beat as Phil winked at her. He still has that electrifying effect, she thought, and they shared a smile as though they were the only two in the room.

"And again, get a room!" Max scowled.

"Quit being a voyeur!" Madison shot back, laughing.

Madison stayed up as the rest retired for the night. She sat down by the tree alone, her legs covered by the forest-green fleece blanket she had shared with Natalia. She stared at the tree, reliving the fun they had

had making the ornaments and stringing them on the tree. She looked at the fire, dancing and sparking with renewed life from the freshly placed log she had added just moments before. She looked around the room, seeming to notice things for the first time. The quilt with its perfect stitching that hung on the wall. Had that always been there? She vaguely remembered her mother saying something about making it in a quilting class she had taken. Had it meant something special? She couldn't remember. She had been so busy with her own life that her mother's hadn't left a lasting impression.

She looked to her right at the family photo wall, seeing pictures that had been there for years and years, some fading in color as her memory seemed to be doing. But somehow, it felt like she was seeing them for the first time. With new eyes. Their school pictures still hung in order of each grade they had mastered, their senior pictures being the last in the lineup. There were pictures of all three of them when they had graduated from college, too. She smiled as she noticed her hairstyles as the years passed and what she'd chosen to wear for pictures each year. She suddenly remembered vividly the orange-and-lime-green outfit she'd insisted on wearing for her third-grade pictures— and for a week straight, much to her mother's dismay. It was her "teenager suit," she'd insisted. She wondered how she would handle it if she were in her mother's shoes and it was Zoey insisting on such a thing. Would she allow it?

Madison heard the creak of a floorboard above her. She held her breath until she was certain whomever it was had gone back to bed. She wanted to be alone with her memories.

She looked back at the wall that held the photos, people suspended in time, and noticed the plaque that hung above all of the pictures, right next to a large wedding picture of her parents. "All because two people fell in love," it said. Her heart ached as she read it. She got up and walked over for a closer look. She looked at her mother in the picture and noticed how beautiful she had been, admired her fine, delicate features. Had she ever really noticed that when she was alive? She knew Max looked like their mother, but had she ever really noticed their features? And what about her hands. She looked at her mother's hands in the photo and then at her own, trying hard to find some resemblance. Seeing none, she walked slowly back to the sofa and covered back up with the blanket. A tear slid down her cheek as she looked at the fire, now down to the last of the embers, a less vibrant orange hue, but still so beautiful.

A voice behind her made her jump. "Want some company?"

"Hi, sweetie," she smiled at Molly. "Are you offering?"

"I am." Molly came and sat beside Madison, tugging part of the blanket over her lap and leaning against her sister. "I'm so glad to have you in my cheering section."

"I'm happy to be there. That you're actually allowing me to be," she clarified. Neither said anything for a moment, then Madison added, "I'm glad you went to treatment, Molly."

"Me too." She rested her head on Madison's shoulder.

"Are you happy?"

"Happier than I've been in a long time. Possibly ever."

"Have you talked to John?"

Molly was quiet for a moment. "No."

"You know he's worried about you. He's called me a few times to check how you're doing."

"Is it worry or is it guilt?"

"Guilt?"

"I don't need him feeling guilty, thinking it was his decision to end our friendship that caused me to drink myself into oblivion."

"Was it?"

"No."

"How can you be so sure?"

"I overdosed because I'm an alcoholic, Maddie. It has nothing to do with what anyone else has said or done. I'm learning so much about what makes me tick. Why I do the things I do. Why..." she hesitated a moment, "why I'm such a nutcase. I have a valid, very real reason. It's called being crazy. Can you say that?" she chuckled.

"Does being your sister help my case?" Madison teased.

"No freeloading." They sat in silence, each lost in her own thoughts. "I've learned I can't even blame Max for my behavior. I mean, sure, he was an ass. But he didn't cause me to do anything I did." She nestled closer into Maddie's side. "Did you begin any of your inheritance goals?"

"Funny you should ask. Phil and I decided to make that one of the kids' Christmas gifts this year. We did the research on child sponsorship programs. There are so many good ones, but we've finally decided on one."

"So how is that a Christmas gift for the kids?" Molly asked, lifting her head to look at her sister.

"Because they are going to choose who, and from which country, they would like to help, get to know, and hopefully visit someday."

"What an amazing idea!" Molly exclaimed. "How in the world did you ever come up with that idea?"

"I didn't. My fabulous husband did." Madison smiled warmly.

"What's the deal with you guys, anyway? Haven't you been married long enough for the honeymoon to be over?" she teased.

"It was. But Molly, these last couple of months have been so amazing. Things are better with us now than they ever have been. I'm not even sure what or how it all happened." Her voice trailed off.

"Oh man." Molly groaned and rolled her eyes. "You guys make marriage hard to live up to."

"You *are* being sarcastic, right?"

"Now when have you ever known me to be sarcastic?"

"Like right now?" They both laughed. "I guess we know you started on the road to your inheritance. In a backdoor sort of way."

Molly chuckled dryly. "Yup. I'm actually off to a running start, huh? I'm taking Mom and Dad's dog home-" She sat up and looked around. "Speaking of which, where is she?"

Madison called the dog's name, and the little white ball of fur jumped up on her lap.

"Hey, wrong Momma," Molly teased, scooping up Lily and settling her onto her own lap. "Anyway, I've been tending to my alcohol problem I didn't even know I had until Mom and Dad set a curse on me by bringing it to my attention…and I have a meeting with the adult literacy program coordinator for my area right after the new year."

"You don't ever do things halfway, do you?"

"Not my style." She elbowed her sister gently. "So what else have you done? You only have one other thing. You can't let Max get his done before you. And so far he's working on two out of three, too."

"No pressure, right?" Madison smiled, the glowing embers shining in her eyes. "Maybe he won't do the third. Sure, he's changed, but still...." She looked at Molly petting Lily. "Natalia has asked to participate with us, so that has been a treat."

"Where did you find her, by the way? She's amazing."

"Indeed, she is," Madison replied fondly. "She has become family to us, and she's taught me a lot over the past couple of months."

"About what?"

"Living," Madison said matter-of-factly. "Just about life." She stared at what remained in the fireplace, which wasn't much. "Did you ever think you'd see the day in this lifetime that our brother would be content with just one woman?"

"Just because he's getting married doesn't mean he'll be content," Molly retorted. "But he'd better be."

Madison chuckled. "He's changed more than I ever thought he would, don't you think?"

"Oh, yeah," she said dramatically.

Madison laughed quietly. "You've changed, too, though. Not just Max. In fact, I can't decide which of us has changed the most."

Molly rested her head back on her big sister's shoulder. "Maybe it's my writer's imagination, but it almost feels like Mom and Dad are spiritually connected to us, rewriting our lives by writing a play, and we're the cast of characters."

"And quite the cast of characters we are!" Madison laughed. "Do you think you'll ever get a steady job. Or a *real* job, as Max calls it?"

"I have a *real* job," she mimicked Madison and sat upright, frustration taking root. "Maddie, for crying out loud! I'm a regular contributor for a widely read column, I've published four books...Uggg!" She let her head fall back against the sofa cushion, covered her face with her hands for a moment before going on. "I just get so frustrated with the lack of acceptance from you guys. Have you even read my books?" She looked at Madison. "Know what? Don't even answer that."

"Molly--"

"No, don't," she stopped her, voice filled with frustration. "What I do may not be as widely accepted or what people would think of as normal, namely Max—and even you, by the sounds of things—but it more than pays my bills, I love what I do, and it's who I am. I create. Characters, settings, plots, word combinations, photos..."

Madison didn't know what to say as shame crept up on her. "I'm sorry," she whispered, glancing at Molly out of the corner of her eye, in time to see a tear streak down her cheek.

"Wanna know what I found?"

"I don't know, do I?" Madison asked lightly, trying to lighten the intensity of the moment.

"I was in Mom and Dad's room looking at Mom's clothes in her closet. I always loved the way she smelled. Like cherries or apple blossoms." She got a dreamy look in her eyes for just a moment. "There was a box on the floor on Dad's side of the closet so I peeked."

"You mean snooped?"

"Maddie, I'm being serious. Besides it's not snooping when we have to go through it anyway. I just got to it first and I'm glad I did."

"What was in the box?" Madison looked at her sister gently.

"All of my work. Articles I've written, my books, newspaper articles from interviews--" She choked back a sob.

"Why didn't you tell me this earlier?"

"I needed to process it. You know--try figure out what it meant."

"It meant they were proud of you, sweetie." She wrapped her arm around Molly and held her close. "Oh, honey, I wish you could have known that so long ago."

The two sisters stayed up and talked until two in the morning. Finally, Madison yawned and decided to turn in. She stood, bent over to give Molly a hug and a peck on her cheek, and headed for the stairs. Molly scooped up the blanket, gathered Lily from the floor, and moved to the big chair closer to the tree. She tucked her legs beneath her, and Lily snuggled against Molly's neck, burying her face in her hair.

Chapter Fifteen

Despite being up so late the night before and her body that was kinked from sleeping in the chair with Lily, Molly got up early and dressed in layers from head to toe. In her warm running gear, she could be a model for Under Armour attire. Her Adidas running shoes, though, looked oddly out of place. She slipped her iPod into the media pocket of her jacket, set her ear buds firmly in place, and headed out the door.

She cherished the time alone with nature and no human interaction whatsoever, not even in her music. No voices, no communication, just the instrumental songs she had downloaded on her iPod and the sounds of nature.

The new layer of snow glistened in the sunlight. The sky was a brilliant blue, not a cloud to be seen. The air was so cold it felt like she was breathing in ice crystals. She watched the vapor coming from every exhale. Little critters had left their paw prints in the snow, and she even crossed some deer tracks.

A black squirrel scampered in front of her, a sharp contrast to the pure white of the snow that blanketed the earth around her. She had always loved black squirrels. Max used to tease her that it was because they were so odd and out of place in the rest of the gray squirrel community, and that's why she could relate to them. He used to tell her that she was at odds with the majority of the human population. She grinned now as she remembered his relentless teasing and how they used to fight. He still had a tendency to get under her skin, but her new life had shown her how to deal with stressors better.

And Max had definitely been a stressor in her life at one time. The snowplow had gone through earlier in the morning, so she stayed on the plowed road, careful not to slip where the snow had melted, creating invisible icy patches. "Black ice," her father used to call it.

Running, she felt such an immense freedom, pure exhilaration, from the very core of her being. She felt more centered than she ever had—her heart was truly happy, a happiness and peacefulness she hadn't known for a very long time. If ever.

Snippets of conversation from her twelve-step meetings played through her mind like her own internal affirmation tape. She reflected on her new ability to communicate with her brother, the warmth and acceptance she already felt from Lily.... It was all so amazing.

And yet, deep within, she still felt the threat of possibly drinking again; the "what if" actually caused more concern than she wanted to admit. She often wondered if someday she would be able to drink like a normal person. If she could enjoy one glass of wine and stop. Or even be able to stop without finishing a glass. But from what she heard from other people, that would never happen, and it was something she would have to learn to deal with.

And yet, she played with the hope of being able to have a glass of wine while she wrote, or while watching TV in the evenings. Or at lunch with Jo.

As she thought of it now, she could feel the peace slip ever so slightly, and anxiety began to grip her chest, squeezing, stealing her joy, her breath, as she ran just a little bit faster.

She remembered her new mantra—*a day at a time; a moment at a time*—and her breaths became more steady, her anxiety slipped away, and peace seeped back to soothe her. Her breathing becoming even once again. The power of a thought run wild amazed her—it could change a person's physical being. Even the most subtle thought could accumulate momentum, gaining strength as it snowballed, and create an avalanche that would bury her peace before she knew what happened.

Feeling at ease once again, back in control, she simply tuned in to the soft melodic notes of the guitar streaming quietly through her ear buds. She noticed things she never used to notice. A vibrant male cardinal sitting in a pine tree, two doves in another, the fresh winter country air, and an occasional dog barking in the distance. True gifts. She felt so blessed.

She wondered where her mom and dad were. Were they able to see their children at the farmhouse? Could they hear their conversations and even their laughter together?

She felt sorrow as she wondered if her parents had felt anything when they died. Was there pain? She hoped the pain was taken from them before they could feel anything. Why hadn't she given them more of a chance instead of closing herself off from them—the people who would have given anything to help her. Instead she'd avoided them. And all for what? she wondered. To prove the independence she used to strive so hard for? Except now she knew it was pure selfishness. She had acted like a self-centered brat.

She wanted to believe they could see her now. To see the changes she felt happening in her life because of their love that didn't die when they did. The love they had made had certainly survived them. True, pure love. The purest love of that between a parent and a child.

Before she knew it, she had run full circle and was back to the driveway. She walked to the porch, allowing her heart rate to slow before stretching her muscles. She took one last cleansing breath of the cold, clean air, and opened the door to squealing kids and laughing adults. She felt like she had come home.

Zoey ran to meet her, gushing with excitement, "Uncle Max's girlfriend is coming today!"

Molly looked at Max with surprise. "I thought she was coming tomorrow."

"We thought today would be nice so she can be with us tonight. You know—break her in." He grinned. "And with the price of changing flights last minute," he groaned, letting them know the hit to his pocketbook was painful, "you better be nice. Do I have your permission to have a guest?"

"Only if I can have a talk with her and tell her what the real Maxwell Forrester is like."

"Keep your distance from her, sis. I know where you sleep," he said, mischief dancing in his eyes. "I'm not above putting a spider in your bed."

"Do it and die."

Madison allowed the kids to stay in their pajamas late into the morning as they ate cereal and toast for breakfast, playing with Lily between bites. Molly and Natalia had insisted on cooking the meal, which freed her up considerably for the better part of the day.

After Molly showered and changed, she and Natalia ran their plan by Madison of what they planned to make for Christmas Eve dinner—prime rib, clam chowder, garden burgers for the vegetarians in the group, roasted potatoes, butternut squash, glazed carrots, and a variety of pies, one of which was sure to be pecan. That had been a favorite during their years of growing up. There would also be a cranberry-cherry pie, which Natalia had told Madison was her favorite from her childhood. Madison was delighted to leave the cooking to them so she could play board games with the kids. Phil and Max, of course, snuck quietly into the family room to watch football.

Madison heard a car outside, and Max entered the kitchen, headed for the front door. Madison, Zoey, Oliver, and Molly watched through the window as he walked over to Mandi's car and wrapped his arms around her.

When they kissed, Zoey squealed and Oliver wrinkled up his nose.

"Eww, gross!" he exclaimed.

Madison held her breath, hoping the couple would keep it G-rated, yet she was unable to tear herself away.

Natalia laughed. "I think they can see you through the window just as well as you can see them. You all should just take a picture. Give them some privacy, for Pete's sake."

"Who's Pete?" Oliver asked. Madison saw his big sister shoot him a quick look of irritation before she stared back out the window.

"She's beautiful!" Zoey exclaimed, clearly as impressed as a nine-year-old could be.

Madison and Molly quickly agreed. Mandi's blond, bouncing curls cascaded below a pink hat, and a pink cashmere sweater hung just below her hips. Black leggings completed the outfit, revealing impeccable self-care.

They watched the two lovebirds embrace again, hold hands and talk, both laughing, as he picked up her bags with one hand and led her into the house.

As soon as the front door opened, all the guilty parties spying through the window just moments before scurried quickly back to their original activities as though they hadn't been aware of a thing.

Max walked in and looked at all of them in disbelief, scolding them, "Don't you guys try to pretend you weren't just all glued to the window hoping to catch a glimpse of God only knows what."

"What on earth do you mean?" Madison asked innocently.

He laughed and rolled his eyes. "You guys are despicable."

The rest of Christmas went by much too quickly in a flurry of activity and getting to know each other. On a few occasions, old personalities resurfaced and conflicted. Each time, Madison held her breath in hopes that it wouldn't escalate, relieved when each of those moments passed without any casualties or fallout. They were making more deposits than withdrawals in their new family relationship account, and it showed.

They talked openly about the inheritance and their journeys to earn their share. Mandi and Natalia showed intense interest as they listened, stating wistfully that they wished they could have known the amazing people who had loved their children so much that they gave them the gift of true character and the possibility to change the world.

When Max proposed to Mandi, getting down on one knee and being the gentleman Madison and Molly had never known him to be, Mandi was speechless, her emerald eyes glimmering.

She finally clapped her hands together, whispered, "Oh, yes," and cried as Carrie Underwood sang "O Holy Night" on the stereo in the background.

The two of them retreated to the family room while the rest of the group gathered around the old worn kitchen table with Phil's computer so Zoey and Oliver could look at the children available for sponsorship. Both kids were thrilled with their soon-to-be new friends, and couldn't wait to go back to school and tell all of their friends. Oliver chose a six-year-old boy from Tanzania, and Zoey a nine-year-old girl from Guatemala. Both begged for someone to help them write their first letter immediately.

As they wrote their letters, Zoey in her own handwriting and Oliver dictating to Molly as she wrote, Madison watched them, her heart spilling with love and pride. She looked at the old farm table—each scratch, dent, and secret engraving adding character to the place that held so many family dinners and conversations.

It was at this table that Phil had asked her father for her hand in marriage, and it was where she had told them of Zoey's impending birth. This wasn't just a table. This was a part of them. Of their history. Of the way she wished things could be again, only with present players in this game of life included.

She wished she had come to share the news at this table of Oliver's conception as well, but she had been in a rush and chose to call them instead. She thought about the talks her mother had had with her at this table when Madison came home from a night out with friends. The family meetings her father sporadically called to check in with everyone. And the endless circles of holding hands around the table as they said grace before meals, Max usually squeezing Molly's hand so tight she would cry. She remembered the time Molly had kicked Max so hard under the table that he was the one who cried.

She remembered the checked red and white tablecloth onto which her mother had spent hours and hours embroidering the names of people who had shared a meal with them at this table. A different color of thread for each year.

She walked to the hutch where the treasured heirloom used to be kept. Madison's eyes stung with unshed tears as she saw the tablecloth carefully in place, the needle tucked into the fabric, a name partially completed. Her mother hadn't been able to finish that name before her life had been finished.

Madison ran her hand softly along the well-used fabric, touching each slightly raised, embroidered name. She felt a hand gently touch her shoulder and turned to see Molly standing behind her, her large brown eyes brimming with memories.

"I remember Mom working on that, the very same evening after company would leave," she whispered. "She wouldn't even wait until the next day."

Madison sniffed. "Yeah, I remember that too."

She pulled the cloth from its resting place and turned to look at Molly, smiling through her tears. "I think we have two new family members who need to autograph this so we can stitch them into our family. What do you say?"

Molly put an arm around her sister, leaning into her. "Great idea."

By the time they were all packed and ready to head for their respective homes, they had forged new, stronger bonds than they had even hoped for when they had started out. They vowed to keep in touch, to call one another at least once a week.

As each one of the three left, each turned one final time to look at the house. Madison wondered if they, too, were trying to burn into memory every event that had happened over the last couple of days, wanting to never forget. Max, however, she noticed was less sentimental and eager to move on with his life and making Mandi a part of it.

Chapter Sixteen

Molly was still to touch base with Madison at a minimum of every other day. At least for the time being. Madison said she would reassess the contact arrangement when she was more secure in Molly's safety. And Molly didn't argue. On the contrary. She was flattered that Madison cared that much.

As the weeks and months passed, Molly's confidence grew stronger and her legs more stable beneath her, allowing her required calls to Madison to be cut down to twice a week with the exception that one of those was over the weekend. Even with the new plan in place, they called each other frequently, missing their conversations if too much time lapsed between calls. Natalia flew in to stay with Molly for an occasional weekend and became like a sister to Molly and Madison.

Lily adjusted to her new home in no time at all. Molly couldn't imagine her life without her anymore— or why she had resisted taking her to begin with. Each time she walked through the door, she was greeted by Lily's enthusiasm at her being home. Lily would jump up on her or be right under foot, waiting for Molly to sit down so she could jump up on her lap to shower her with dog kisses.

Molly began her time with the adult literacy program and was assigned a thirty-year-old man. As fate would have it, his name was Michael. She laughed when he introduced himself. Michael's eyebrows arched quizzically, and she quickly explained the draw of "M" names in her family.

They met at the library once a week for two hours, occasionally making it a treat by meeting at a coffee shop. After awhile, they began to spend the better part of their time together sharing personal stories. Molly kept hers a little more guarded, not yet ready to let anyone in too close.

Michael, however, was refreshingly open and honest, and his rugged attractiveness did not go unnoticed by Molly. He told her about his ten-year-old daughter, Sara, with a woman he had briefly dated. He explained that, although the relationship had been a mistake, his daughter was the joy of his life.

He admitted to Molly that he had always been embarrassed by not knowing how to read and he was desperately afraid that Sara would find out. He kept that secret close to the vest and prayed that every day would be another day without her finding out. He knew that the disappointment he would inevitably see in her eyes would kill him.

He had managed to get manual labor jobs, mostly in the construction trade, that allowed him to work without reading. At least he could read a blueprint, which helped make him more employable, and on the occasion he did have to read something, he asked his sister to help him. She was the only one who knew his secret, other than his parents. And they had taken his secret to the grave.

Molly listened to him, realizing how good her childhood had been in comparison. How she had wasted away the time she could have made count with her parents. She missed them so much—sometimes the ache was so raw that she feared she would split wide open, laying bare all that was within her.

And here was Michael, whose parents had quit hoping and believing in him. She saw the hurt in his eyes when he spoke of them. She admired him when she realized he had taken their behavior upon himself for not giving them a reason to believe in him until it was too late.

He told her about school—his chronic run-ins with the law and the court system for nonattendance. How he'd finally just dropped out of school altogether. He confided that, since he had never felt like he belonged anywhere, that he was a misfit no matter where he tried to fit in, he had followed the wrong crowd. He told of the regrets he had now, as he was paying a heavy price for his decisions.

Molly's heart reached out to him. She felt a kinship, a connection with him that was leading her to a place from which she could share more private details from her own life. From somewhere deep within, she felt a connection to this misfit who was so much like herself. It was an irresistible pull that she couldn't shake.

So Molly told him of her own trials, struggles, and eventually her battle with alcohol. He listened intently, patiently, his eyes gentle. Never once did she feel compelled to squirm under the spotlight of judgment.

She watched his eyes light up when he talked about Sara, sharing the quick-witted one-liners she was so good at. He told her about the fun he had with her at the zoo, about spending hours watching the zebras. How when he asked why she was so drawn to them, she'd replied, "They give me hope, Daddy."

"Hope of what?" he'd asked.

"That different colors of people can live together and be beautiful," she had answered dreamily.

Molly watched him, touched to the center of her soul when she saw the emotion he was feeling. Pure pride. And rightly so, she thought.

"Can you imagine? She's only ten, and she already has a concept of the real world. Her dreams and visions are so big. She has compassion way beyond her years."

Molly smiled, one leg tucked beneath her, sitting perfectly still, afraid to ruin the moment. He told Molly that they had begun going to church together on his weekends with her, and she had asked her mom if she could go to church with him every weekend, not only his scheduled weekends. Surprisingly, her mother had agreed, provided they had nothing else going on.

Sara's mom had married some rich doctor, he said, and yet Sara had never thought less of him. Instead she became protective of him. And in turn, he guarded his secret even more—yet that secret of his illiteracy chipped away daily at his self-confidence.

As they stood to leave after one of their coffee shop meetings, Michael asked Molly to have dinner with him that following Friday evening.

"I could introduce you to Sara. As a friend, of course," he added quickly. She agreed but then tossed an alternate idea his way.

"Maybe we could meet at your church on Sunday and go out for a burger afterward? Veggie, of course," she added and laughed. "Maybe that wouldn't be as threatening to Sara."

"That's a great idea," he agreed. "Would it be selfish of me to be just a little disappointed though?"

"I'm not following."

"Well, that means I have to wait two extra days to see you," he smiled.

Molly kept Madison up to date on her friendship with Michael, and Madison had told her she was dying to meet him.

"Why, so you can make him prove himself and scare him away? No way."

"Molly, I'd be lying if I told you I'm not just a little skeptical of his past."

"It's called trusting my instincts," she'd countered. "It's not fair to judge someone for who they were in the past. If that's what you believe, then I can only imagine what you think of me."

"It's just that—"

"Until I give you reason not to," Molly interrupted, "you need to trust me."

"Deal." But Molly heard the hesitation in her voice and wasn't convinced.

Michael called Molly Friday night while Sara was watching a movie. Molly was surprised at the flutter in the pit of her stomach when she recognized his number on the caller ID. Since their last meeting when he suggested she meet Sara, their friendship had risen to a new level. At least for her. She wasn't sure where exactly that was or what it meant, she just knew that it had changed.

"I was thinking…"

"Uh-oh," he groaned. "When a woman starts a conversation with 'I was thinking,' it's usually not a good sign."

"Is that so?" She laughed. "Now, as I was saying before I was so *rudely* interrupted…" She paused for effect. "What are you going to tell Sara about me so she doesn't get confused? Or get the wrong idea," she added, hoping it didn't sound like she was testing him.

"Confused or the wrong idea about what?"

"About sharing her dad with another girl."

"Is there a reason she would get the wrong idea?"

Molly tried to read his tone, to figure out if he was playing along or if he was serious. But she couldn't get an accurate read, and it unnerved her. Finally she answered, "None that I can think of. But then, I'm not a ten-year-old girl having to share my dad." After she said it a shadow crept into her heart. She missed her dad now. In fact, she would give anything to have the chance to share him.

"Molly, we're friends," he explained matter-of-factly. "Sara is a smart girl. She knows I don't live in a bubble. She understands I have friends."

"Opposite sex friends?"

"Yes. Unless there's something you want to tell me," he chuckled. "Now, is there anything else you're going to dream up to worry about or use to back out?"

"Nope," she beamed.

They talked for the next hour and a half until Sara's movie ended. Molly made an excuse to have to hang up when she heard the young girl's voice in the background. She didn't want to interfere with his time with his daughter when he didn't get to see her much to begin with. It occurred to her that she had seen him more that week than his own daughter had.

She hung up the phone and headed to her room. As she passed by the large oval mirror that stood beside her closet, she saw the silly grin plastered on her face. She knew what was happening and felt powerless to stop it. More than that, she didn't want to stop it.

She stared blindly into her closet, her mind running wild at the possibilities, like wild horses set free after being held captive, until she corralled them back in and focused on finding something to wear on Sunday. Should she go casual? Dress up? She rifled through her options, wondering why she was putting so much time and effort into what should be such a simple decision. After weighing both sides, she decided on a pair of cream-colored leggings with a tan, sleeveless blouse that hung below her bottom, and a pair of light brown knee boots. Madison and Max would flip. Not only was she not going barefoot or in flip flops, she was wearing boots. She laughed at the thought of it.

She heard Lily whine and turned to see the little dog's head cocked to one side, eyes wide, as if wanting to be in on the secret. Or was she telling her that what she was doing was wrong? She'd learned in her twelve-step program that making a life-changing decision in the first year of sobriety wasn't a good idea. But this didn't qualify as a life-changing decision. Or did it? Looking at it that way was somewhat presumptuous. Wasn't it?

She was driving herself crazy and scolded herself to stop it instantly. She looked down at Lily.

"Don't worry, little girl," she said, scooping up the little ball of fur. "No one will ever take your place. It's you and me. Forever." She kissed the tip of Lily's cold, wet nose and buried her face in Lily's white fur, then set her back down in the warm circle she had created on Molly's bed.

Molly spent Saturday getting lost in her writing and cleaning her house. She even met Jo for lunch. Jo was still being a mother hen, not quite as willing to trust Molly's decisions for her personal life as Madison was. But then, Molly forced herself to recognize that Jo was the one who found her in her worst possible condition. She needed to give Jo the time it took for her to regain her trust.

Before she knew it, Sunday morning had arrived. She hadn't heard from Michael since Friday night when they had spoken, so when the phone rang at eight o'clock, she took a moment to take a deep breath. Her stomach performed somersaults, and her hand trembled when the caller ID told her it was Michael.

She chastised herself for acting like such an immature child, muttering, "You'd think I was the one who's ten. We're friends. Just friends, Molly," she tried telling herself. And then the thought crossed her mind that Michael might be calling to cancel. A sinking disappointment filled her as she answered the call.

"Hello?"

"Did I get you up?" he asked.

"Of course not. Why do you ask?"

"You sound…different."

"No, I'm fine," she lied. "Do you need to cancel?"

He laughed. "Me? Cancel? Absolutely not. Why, are you looking for an excuse not to go? All you have to do is be honest and say so. No excuses necessary."

She laughed, feeling both relieved and somewhat foolish. "No, I'm not looking for an excuse. In fact I'm almost ready to leave the house."

"Well, then, the date is still on."

Molly's heart skipped a beat at the word "date." What in the world was wrong with her, and why was she acting like this?

"See you in a few, sunshine."

Yet again, her heart fluttered wildly at his nickname for her. It was then that she knew she was falling for this man whom she was supposed to be helping overcome an obstacle in life. And here he was helping her with one of her own. Life was strange.

She wondered if her parents were still orchestrating, somehow, the events of her life. Had it not been for their will and ingenious insight, she would never have met Michael. But, she reasoned with herself, there was certainly no guarantee that Michael thought the same way about her. He had said himself, Friday night on the phone, that she was simply a friend.

Right now, however, she didn't have time to think about it. She had somewhere to be. She grabbed her shoulder bag from the back of a chair and headed out into the fresh air and sunshine.

Chapter Seventeen

Max, along with Paul and Junior, had completed the project with Habitat for Humanity, then continued volunteering when he could. He was also in the throes of spearheading an AIDS awareness and support fundraiser. He had already raised ten thousand dollars, and the actual event hadn't even arrived. Mandi worked closely by his side, and he reminded himself daily how lucky he was. It was beyond him, how he had managed not to lose the one person who knew him for exactly who he was—the good, the bad, and the ugly—and loved and accepted him anyway. To think how closely he had come to letting his carelessness and playboy lifestyle play her right out of his life—it sent tremors of fear cascading throughout him.

He never tired of her company, whether they were talking, watching a movie together, or each doing their own thing. He looked forward to the bubbling enthusiasm that poured through everything she did, and he had to admit to himself that he even valued her opinion on professional issues. The sexy huskiness of her voice when she got frisky didn't hurt matters either. He smiled at the recent memory.

When he inadvertently fell back into the rut of being the selfish man he was before…before whatever it was he still couldn't explain that had changed him…Mandi would stand her ground, refusing to play along. She would go home or hang up the phone, whichever the case may be, but not without first telling him she loved him. She had gotten stronger, and Max had to admit that her strength was attractive. She accepted him as he was, like a defective piece of merchandise from a sale rack, knowing what she was getting and wanting it anyway. She didn't judge him, but she did them both a favor by not participating in the battle by compounding the issue with what would ultimately be her own hurt feelings.

He wanted—no, more than that—he needed her to know and truly believe he was in this with both feet, no lingering remnants of longing for the life he'd left behind. So when his phone rang, he would occasionally and casually ask Mandi to answer it for him. When the caller would happen to be a woman, something that happened frequently for the first few months, Mandi was gracious in her response to the voice on the other end, but he knew her well enough to be able to hear a hint of speculation and fear in her voice. And yet she refused to let it stop her from giving Max the phone.

As far as he was concerned, that was a significant sign of strength and trust. And he didn't want to destroy that trust. So when he would speak to the woman on the other end of the line, he would be sure Mandi stayed by his side, listening as he told the caller he wasn't available—at all. She told him once that he was like a little boy needing to be praised for doing the right thing. He'd laughed and said, "Yes, we never really do grow out of that."

Being single and playing the field had taken him nicely through his twenties, but now that he'd found "the one," he was done playing with the same intensity with which he had played. He was becoming more and more content and grateful for what he had right now at this exact moment. The concept was still so new that at times it was unnerving as he tried to figure out where it was all coming from. And he would remind himself of the old cliché that had taken on a whole new meaning to him: Never look a gift horse in the mouth.

Max and Mandi were planning their wedding for the following Christmas at his parents' house. It was his way of paying tribute to them and their well-thought-out will that he believed had miraculously brought him together with Mandi. The same will he had originally thought to be an outrage and an insult to both his person and his intelligence, had turned out to be a blessing. One he certainly had never seen coming.

Saying their vows at the farmhouse would somehow feel as if his parents were present to witness an event they likely thought they would never see in their lifetime. Which they hadn't. And for that, Max felt overwhelming disappointment. Yet, in an odd way, he was certain they knew now.

His practice was taking a large chunk of his time. He was wrapped tightly in the middle of a high-profile rape case. He worked through the details with ferocious intensity, giving it everything he could possibly give of himself, yet he felt somewhat unsettled. Uneasiness spread through his soul; at times he felt like it was wrapping its tentacles around his heart, squeezing tighter and tighter. A moment finally came in court when he had to ask for a short recess to go to the men's room to splash cold water on his face in order to regain his composure and continue. What in hell was happening to him? he wondered.

That evening when he got home, Mandi was there making him dinner. She had on a pair of jeans that fit her curves exactly the way Max liked, a light pink, sequined tank top, and her blond, bouncy curls were pulled up in a ponytail. She could see his preoccupation as soon as he walked heavily in the door. After a quick welcome, she watched him quietly, deciding not ask questions until they sat down. Max was grateful that she had come to learn his moods, when to question and when to be silent, giving him time to process, turning his thoughts over and over in his own head before he reached out to her. And she had always been okay with that.

Small talk accompanied dinner, and he was just about to enter into the territory of what was consuming him when she beat him to it. "Did something happen at work today?"

"This case I'm in the middle of." He groaned. "It's got me in the middle of something uncomfortable, and I can't put my finger on what it is." He put his fork down, clasped his hands, elbows on the table, and looked directly into her eyes. He stood up and walked over to the other side of the kitchen to lean against the counter. He braced his hands behind him, fingers curling around the edge of the countertop. He looked at her again, a cross of confusion and frustration. "I—this case—I can't tell you details…"

"I understand that," she assured him.

"I know you do." Max watched her, grateful she understood because it could cause huge and damaging rifts between them if that was something she couldn't accept. As long as he kept his secrets to professional issues, he knew he was playing according to the relationship rules. "It's not just about the win anymore," he said quietly. "And I don't know what to do with that."

He felt Mandi's eyes searching him, trying to hear what he wasn't saying. They suddenly opened into huge pools of emerald seas as she understood.

"Holy hell," she whispered. "I may be taking a giant leap here, but you don't believe he's innocent, do you?"

Max hesitated. Would she still think he was good if he admitted the truth he was afraid to even admit to himself? His eyes bore into hers. He was afraid to answer. Afraid of what it would mean for his record.

For him. Finally he spoke, barely a whisper. "No." He had told her the gist of the case—what he could tell her—and he knew she didn't pay much attention to the newspaper or TV news coverage. Especially about this case, because it tied her up in fits when she saw how he was being portrayed. Like the devil himself, in the flesh.

"I know how gentle you are and how good your heart really is," she said. "I know the good as well as the bad. What--"

"What bad?" he asked, feigning hurt feelings.

"Like I said," she replied, grinning, "I know the good as well as the bad, and--"

"I'm still stuck on the bad part," he insisted, trying to interject some humor. If even just a little bit. And perhaps, maybe just a little bit of him wanted to hear what she didn't like.

"Hard as it may be for you to believe, you aren't perfect," she said. "You're flawed just as much as the rest of us. Humanity is a fallen group. Right now you just happen to be out in the public eye during this case, your actions scrutinized and magnified by the media and advocacy groups that don't know the complete truth behind it all. They're unable to see the forest for the trees, and it's a truth no one, including me, will know until the case is over. The difference," she explained, "is that I know you."

She stood and walked over to him, took his hands in hers, and looked up into those blue eyes that seemed to see into her soul. "What are you going to do?"

"Knowing that takes things to a whole new level of difficult. A level I've not had to experience. Ever."

"You've never questioned whether a client was really innocent?" She asked, truly surprised.

"Oh, I've asked myself that before, sure. Even knew it a time or two."

"So what's different this time?" she asked quietly, wrapping her arms loosely around his waist, looking up at him.

"Because before I never cared whether they were or not." He looked into her eyes, expecting to see disgust. Horror. He was somewhat surprised that those were not what he found there, but he should have known better.

Mandi waited, watching, and he felt her acceptance. She tenderly cupped his face in her hands, looking deep into his eyes until Max was certain she could see the depths of his soul and the darkness that was there.

"Only you know what to do, babe." She paused. "And whatever that decision is, you will have to live with it. Is a win worth that?"

He leaned his head back against the cupboard directly in back of him, the one that jutted out from the rest, and the one he'd hit his head on more than once. He closed his eyes, keeping them closed for only a moment until the darkness became uncomfortable. He opened them and focused on the light in hers as he exhaled deeply.

"No," he finally whispered. "It's not. Not anymore."

"I'm proud of you, Maxwell Forrester," she smiled, and leaned in to embrace him. He rested his chin on the top of her head, and she inhaled the remnants of the Polo cologne he had put on that morning. "Hey, big guy," she said, voice husky. "What do you say we leave the dishes for later?" She pulled back and looked at him, a mischievous gleam in her eye.

"You wicked girl." He grinned, his own voice a low husky whisper. He slid one arm beneath her and carried her to his room.

He had something extremely unpleasant to do tomorrow. Something that went against his nature as he knew it. But for tonight, he was exactly where he wanted to be, with the woman he loved. Now, and for the rest of his life.

Chapter Eighteen

As the months marched forward, some of Madison's clients flourished and outgrew the need for her services on a regular basis. Rather than filling those time slots, as she had been quick to do in the past, she kept them open and free. Losing the income and momentum that propelled her forward in her career was no longer her main concern. Instead, she filled that time with activities that would create lasting memories for her kids, including Natalia in as many of them as possible.

Not only was Natalia an immense help with the kids, she was good company for Madison. With the arrival of summer, they took the kids to the zoo, various community pools, and took advantage of many of the neighborhood parks Madison had never really noticed before. Some of them she insisted must have been newly constructed, but Natalia was insistent that she had taken the kids there before. The kids, of course, backed up Natalia's claims. Madison had started out balking at the idea of her kids being in pool water with so many other children, imagining what lurked within the water, despite it being so highly chlorinated, which that in itself worried her. But Natalia talked her through to the point of allowing it, though she still wasn't completely comfortable. "Baby steps," Natalia had teased her.

They soaked in the sunshine on sunny days, went on picnics, and visited beautiful gardens, each picking out a favorite flower and learning the names of the flowers the others had picked. They walked along the river, feeding bread crumbs to the ducks and geese and swinging on the bench swings. The kids often ran ahead while Madison and Natalia brought up the rear, carrying their shoes loosely by their side. Madison finally understood the freedom that Molly loved so much.

When they arrived home, sun-kissed, exhausted, and happy, Madison read stories to the kids while Natalia made dinner. Phil spent more evenings at home now. He'd told his boss he wanted to spend more time in town and less on the road, and it was a request his boss was happy to honor as much as he could. There were still a number of accounts that he wouldn't allow anyone to handle except Phil. Not only did Madison understand that, but she was proud that her husband was such a trusted man at work. And she appreciated that time to spend alone with the kids. Or watching a movie with Natalia.

On quiet nights, Phil and Madison would light a fire in the fireplace, whether cool or warm weather, and sit side by side on the sofa. Madison would lean her voluptuous figure Phil so appreciated into Phil's strong frame, and he would drape his arm around her and lightly caress her shoulder as they quietly shared stories from the day. Sometimes there were no words needed. Simply sitting close, feeling the warm comforting presence of the other was more than enough. She felt blessed at the sense of newness that the past several months brought to their marriage. On warm summer evenings, they retired to the porch swing to admire the stars twinkling overhead, and they would find shapes in the stars as Madison had done as a child.

"I see the Little Dipper," she said, pointing her well-manicured finger.

"I see the face of a lion."

"No sir," she laughed. "That's a dog."

Now it was his turn to laugh. "I don't know what dogs you've been looking at, Mrs. Shaw, but none that I've ever seen."

She chuckled and playfully elbowed him in the ribs, staring into the vastness of the inky-black, star-glittered sky. The space seemed completely untouched by any human hand. Unmarked, innocent, but so far away. She remembered looking at the stars with her sister when Molly was all of four years old. Molly had sworn she'd seen Elmo from *Sesame Street* and was worried that he would fall and get hurt. Madison had to use her best big-sister reasoning to explain that it was just the shape of Elmo, and the next time she watched *Sesame Street,* he would be there, safe and sound. Molly hadn't been completely convinced, but it had been enough to stop her from obsessing about it. At least until she found something else to obsess about.

Madison smiled as she thought of Molly and how she was so different from that little girl light-years ago, yet so much the same. Phil looked over at his wife, then squeezed her shoulder in a hug.

"Quarter for your thoughts," he said gently.

Madison pulled herself back to the present and looked at her husband in amusement. "A whole quarter?"

"Yup," he grinned. "Inflation."

"I was actually thinking that's pretty cheap," she teased.

"It could go up. Depends on the economy."

She chuckled and lay her head back on his shoulder, crossing her arms in front of her loosely. "I was thinking that the more things change, the more they stay the same."

Phil was silent. The moon appeared to have a ring—at just the right angle, a myriad colors circled around it. A light breeze caressed them, and across the open field from their house, fireflies sparkled, making the darkness come to life.

Madison remembered catching fireflies when they were kids. Max would rub them on his ring finger, and the chemically produced light from the little beetle's abdomen would transfer to his finger, making it look like it was a glowing gemstone. Madison would get squeamish when he did that. She was content to catch them and keep them in a jar in her room at night, falling asleep as she watched them perform their light show.

Phil finally spoke. "What do you mean by that, my beautiful philosopher?"

"What we do to improve our purpose in life," she explained quietly, still watching the fireflies, "simply brings out who we already are and have been all along."

Phil remained quiet, encouraging her to continue. She'd grown to know his silence in these moments meant he was not quite understanding where she was coming from. And frankly, she wasn't even sure she understood herself this time. She wasn't sure if she was attempting to explain further for his benefit or trying to make sense of her own tumbling thoughts.

"Take us, for example. The more we've invested in our marriage these past several months, changing what could have become detrimental to our relationship if it had been allowed to remain status quo, has only shined the spotlight on what we already were and always have been. It was just unrecognizable from being tarnished from neglect.

"And Molly," she continued. "The more she has changed, the more I see her as she was before life began happening. She wasn't always an antisocial, antifamily little girl. That came later as life happened. And Max..." she trailed off. "Well, Max is just Max," she laughed, a deep, throaty sound. "He reminds me of Alex P. Keaton from the old sitcom *Family Ties*. Do you remember that one?"

Phil grinned at the comparison. "Yeah. And I'm not so sure I've ever heard a comparison quite so accurate. But the similarities in characters end there."

"What do you mean?"

"Because I can't imagine you and the *Family Ties* character Mallory being any more different. In fact, you're polar opposites." She chuckled.

They heard the screen door open and little footsteps on the porch behind them. "Mom?" Oliver's voice was a squeaky whimper, sounding younger than his six years. "I can't sleep. My tummy hurts."

Madison and Phil created a space between them, inviting Oliver to climb up between them, which he did. He curled up in a ball of blanket and hair, and buried his little body between them. Madison gently stroked his hair as he positioned his head on her lap, and Phil placed one protective hand on the little man's leg, which was now hanging over his own. He draped his other arm protectively around his wife. They looked at each other over the top of the little boy who created an indescribable, unbreakable bond between them—the golden thread weaving through their lives.

They sat that way, silent, smiling at each other occasionally, and swinging slowly until they were sure Oliver had fallen fast asleep. Then Phil gently scooped him up, whispering words of comfort when Oliver began to weakly protest, and carried him back to his bed. Madison watched them, thinking that she was the most blessed woman on the face of the earth. Peace blanketed her in warmth. Something that could only be the presence of God showering her with His grace.

They woke up the next morning to the alarm and Oliver's little form nestled in next to Madison. Phil was first to get up, tucking the sheet closely around Madison and Oliver as he planted a whisper of a kiss on her forehead. The smell of coffee wafted up the stairs, letting them know Natalia was already up and in the kitchen.

"What are your plans for today, Mrs. Shaw?" he asked quietly.

Madison lay the sheet back and stretched. Phil watched her appreciatively with eyebrows arched and a smile. "Appointments this morning. In fact, my first one is early today so Natalia is going to take the kids to school."

"Want to meet for lunch?"

"Can't."

"Ouch," he jerked back dramatically, then grinned. "My poor feelings."

"You're such a drama queen," Madison laughed, trying to be quiet but without luck. Oliver rolled over, perched on his hands and knees before sitting back, resting his bottom on his heels, and rubbed his eyes. She looked at him lovingly. "Natalia's got breakfast going, champ."

Oliver's eyes lit up at the mention of food. He rolled out of bed and scampered down the stairs.

"And why is my wife rejecting my invitation for lunch?" Phil pursued the conversation.

"I have other plans. And they include someone other than my husband," she teased.

"Wow! You sure know how to hurt a man."

Madison grinned and lay back down, one arm behind her head, the other reaching out for Phil. "I'm meeting with Samantha. We're going to the library today to work on a project she has due for summer school."

Samantha was the sixteen-year-old girl that Madison was mentoring through the community mentoring program for at-risk youth. She had had a rough life in her short years, and was just now barely allowing Madison to see what was inside of her. The things she kept hidden from everyone, the way she lashed out at those who got too close. The girl had so much fear of abandonment, rejection, and humiliation that it loomed over every other aspect of her life.

Madison had not yet introduced her to Oliver and Zoey, and at times she wondered what was really the driving factor behind that decision. Part of her was afraid to expose her own children to such raw pain and bitterness, and she also wasn't quite sure how Samantha would act toward them. The Momma bear part of her wanted to protect her kids from that part of life. They were enjoying their newfound friendships with their sponsored siblings through the child sponsorship program, but writing to those less fortunate and actually interacting with them seemed worlds apart. That, combined with the fact that Samantha was much older and would carry much more influence than the younger kids, kept the hesitation fresh and on the forefront.

Neither could Madison ignore the fact that this was Samantha's time, and she knew if Oliver and Zoey were in the picture, Samantha wouldn't get Madison's full and undivided attention. And that would be selling Samantha short.

Sam's relationship with her mother was hostile at best, and she had left Samantha alone much of the time since Sam was very young. That forced Sam to grow up faster than she should have had to. Her father had been out of the picture for several years, making an occasional quick appearance, staying just long enough to allow Sam to build up some hope that maybe, just maybe, this time he would stay around awhile.

Samantha also had an older brother who used to threaten her life when he lived at home. Once, he'd come very close to carrying out his threat—the knife was at her throat—when her father made one of his unexpected visits. But while her father's presence stopped the immediate behavior, he hadn't even so much as scolded her brother, and it left her empty, void of any feeling. Her brother had left that day and had not been back. As of this moment, Samantha didn't know where he had gone or if he was even alive. Samantha suspected he was in a gang, but she didn't care. Not anymore. Her heart was hard, and she wasn't about to let anyone crack it open. Not anymore.

When Madison first met Samantha, she had taken her on a walk to a neighborhood park. Samantha watched over her shoulder and jumped at any loud noises. None of it had escaped Madison's attention. Also evident was that, despite being a beautiful girl underneath what the world could see on the surface, Samantha lacked knowledge in basic hygiene skills. Her mother certainly hadn't given her the time it took to teach those basic things in life. She was a beautiful girl with long, wavy dark hair, and large brown eyes that were too large for her tiny, thin face. Madison began to work with her, and Sam's beautiful features began to emerge. No longer did she look like an unkempt, homeless girl, but a ray of sunlight peeking out beneath the clouds. Madison especially loved it when Samantha smiled. It was rare, but when it did happen, it gave Madison a glimmer of hope. It was the encouragement her heart needed to feel like she was making some kind of difference in this girl's life.

"So what have you guys got going on for fun? Besides just homework?" Phil's voice broke through Madison's thoughts.

"Hmm...I'm not sure yet," she said thoughtfully. "Maybe I'll see if there's anything special she wants to do."

"I know you have reservations about introducing Zoey and Oliver to her, but I don't think that would be such a bad thing."

"But what if..." Her voice trailed off. She felt like a snob for even thinking what she was about to say, but decided to go ahead and said it anyway. "What if...I don't want the kids to get hurt."

"And how is that going to happen?" Phil asked, brows furrowed.

"Samantha knows a lot of unsavory...characters. What if they see her with our children?"

"You can't protect the kids from life, Madison. Carefully placing them in a glass bubble is no way to teach them about life. You're not the one who keeps them safe even when you are together. The Big Guy upstairs does. Through you. But ultimately, it's not in your power and strength to keep them from the harm of the world."

"It's my job, Phil. As their mother. It's my job to protect them from whatever it is I possibly can."

"Not so far that it shelters them from living. From experiencing the life He intends them to have. To teach them life lessons that make them people who make a difference in this world. Robbing them of that is a terrible disservice and not fair to them."

"You think I'm a snob, don't you?" she asked, looking down and focusing on the wedding ring pattern of the quilt that lay folded back at the foot of their bed.

He sat down, breaking her concentration on the green ring in the middle of the blue. He lifted her chin with his forefinger so her eyes met his. "Not a snob, absolutely not. Just very protective. And I love you for that. Now, don't get me wrong, but 'let go and let God' is not just a cliché. It's wise advice. You can't control the world." She stayed silent as their eyes stayed locked. "Tell you what. Why don't you think about it, and the next time you meet, maybe I could pick up Zoey and Oliver, and we can meet someplace safe. We can all be there together."

"Deal," she said, one corner of her mouth turning up in a smile.

"Now how about I race you down the stairs for coffee?" he challenged her.

"Come here first," she said it so quietly that he had to bend down to hear her. And when he did, she quickly wrapped her arms around his neck, pulling him down on the bed. Then she hurried around him, grabbing her robe as she ran out the door and down the stairs, laughing. "I win!" she hollered at him as he made his way down the stairs behind her.

By this time Zoey and Oliver were at the bottom of the stairs, no doubt trying to see what kind of crazy game their mom and dad were playing this time. And when they saw their mother near the bottom, their father close behind, they clapped, jumped up and down, squealed, and cheered them on.

Chapter Nineteen

Michael and Molly continued to see each other, flourishing in each other's company. Their tutoring sessions, however, were now always held in a nearby coffee shop or the library. Molly needed that professional separation of boundaries in order to feel like she was doing what she was supposed to be doing. Michael had agreed with her that it was easier to maintain focus when they were in a public location.

He had told her one day how much he adored her, and her cheeks had flushed hot with embarrassment. She wasn't sure anyone had actually ever adored her before, and it made her feel somewhat exposed. After teasing her about learning how to accept a compliment, he had gone on to tell her that her free spirit, her dedication to her new life, and the way she interacted with his daughter made him admire her like he had never admired anyone ever before.

He admitted to her that he was so impressed with the fact that rather than be jealous of Sara's mother as past girlfriends had been, Molly showed respect for her, and she didn't try to take over the role of mother but was content with being confidante and friend, a role model for Sara.

"It's a beautiful thing to sit on the sidelines, watching the two of you together—the girl I love more than life itself and the woman who has officially stolen my heart," he'd told her. And she felt like she had to pinch herself a time or two to make sure she wasn't dreaming.

It was during one of their tutoring sessions at a little hole-in-the-wall coffee shop that Michael had introduced Molly to that their relationship experienced its first test.

They were sitting on a small leather futon in the corner of the room, facing each other, as Michael quietly read *The Catcher in the Rye* to Molly. It was one of her favorite classics, and one she was certain Michael would enjoy as well. As he'd realized how much he loved books, words, and all the different combinations of words laced together, his reading had progressed quickly. Molly sometimes worried it was too good to be true. She had fallen over the moon in love with someone—something she hadn't even known she was capable of—and so quickly that she hadn't even known it was happening until there was no turning back. The fact that this person shared her love of creativity and art—writing and books in particular— gave her a happiness she had never known.

As she sat, head bent, intently listening to Michael's soothing voice, the bell hanging above the coffee shop door jingled, signaling someone else entering what they had come to think of as *their* coffee shop. Molly startled and gently touched Michael's arm, signaling him to pause. Molly felt the color drain from her face and knew Michael saw it, too, as he watched her. A spot of color returned to her face as shame took hold.

The newcomer walked over and stopped where they were seated. Molly stood up, the slight tremor in her hands and voice betraying her as she spoke.

"Hi, John."

"Molly," John stated simply, quietly, with a gentleness that spoke too loudly his feelings for her.

There was an awkward silence until she seemed to remember Michael, who was now standing behind her. He reached around her to shake John's hand and she rushed to introduce them.

"Oh! John, this is Michael. Michael, John."

John's eyes looked deep into Molly's, imploring her to explain who Michael was to her, but Molly offered no explanation.

"How have you been?" John asked her.

"Excuse me," Michael interrupted, "but I really need to get going." He looked at John and said, "Nice to meet you, man." And before Molly knew what was happening, he was headed to the door.

Molly followed quickly after him. "Michael, wait! Where are you going?"

"Molly—this is clearly a two-party conversation, and I'm the third party who doesn't belong."

"Michael—"

"Molly"—he didn't turn to look at her—"we each have our own car. You don't need me here. It's awkward, to say the least." He turned now, and his eyes were so gentle that Molly wanted to fold herself into his arms. "Don't ask me to stay and watch."

"Watch what?" she asked as he walked out. "Michael!" she called, but the door had already closed. Molly watched him walk to his car, then realized she was holding his book in her hands. She held it to her chest and watched him as he backed out of the parking space.

"He's someone important to you?" Molly startled when she heard John's voice. She'd almost forgotten he was still standing a short distance away. She didn't know how to answer. And worse, she couldn't seem to find her voice at all. "I'm a big boy, Molly. Go ahead and tell me the truth."

"Yes, he is," she whispered. She saw pain slice through his eyes. "John—"

He held up a hand to stop her. "It's okay, Moll." He smiled sadly. "You can't force yourself to love someone."

"John, I did—I do—love you. Just not like that. I—I don't know how to explain it." "You don't need to explain anything. Except why you couldn't take just a minute to return even one of my phone calls. Just to let me know you were okay." Sadness consumed his eyes again. "I was worried sick about you."

"That's what Madison said." She looked down, guilt eating at her, and then back up at him. He deserved her full attention…and an apology was long overdue.

John continued, "I wasn't checking up on you, but—okay, yes, maybe I was. In fact, that's exactly what I was doing." She saw a glimmer of anger through the sadness and heard the defensiveness in his voice as he continued. "But if you would have returned my messages—even one—to let me know you were okay, I wouldn't have kept calling."

There was a definite flash of anger in his eyes now, and it cut clean through her heart.

"John, I'm not mad at you for calling Madison. If I were in your shoes, I probably would have done the same thing," she reasoned.

"You don't even wear your own shoes most of the time; you would never wear mine."

She felt relief wash through her at his attempted humor. She was grateful for the lightness, if even for the briefest of moments.

"It was wrong of me not to call you, and I know that full well. I was just going through so much. I felt like my feelings were eating me alive, and I didn't know which to confront and which to run from."

"So you chose to run from me? From us?"

"It had nothing to do with not wanting to talk to you or be with you. I felt like I had led you on. I felt awful. What do you do with that, John? With guilt that eats you up alive?" A tear threatened to escape, and she quickly turned her head to look out the window until the threat had passed. "So I ran and I hid. The thing I knew how to do best. I avoided having to face it and look at it. That was the only way I could get past it without drinking."

He remained silent, encouraging her to continue. They had taken a seat on the futon she and Michael had shared what seemed like years ago. She was careful to keep a respectable gap between herself and John, but faced him as she spoke. He deserved an explanation. And she was ready to give it to him. She was ready to face her demons. The guilt, the shame, the facade of bravado that she had hidden behind for so many years, trying to be "good enough." She was ready to put it to rest. Starting right now. Starting with someone she had wronged. Someone who didn't deserve her selfishness.

Molly tried calling Michael several times after she left the coffee shop and throughout the evening, finally leaving him a message to please call her back. By midnight she still hadn't received a call from him. Knowing he had to work early the next morning, she stopped calling, hoping his silence was because he was fast asleep. She wrote a few pages in her new book before calling it a night. Then she scooped up Lily and headed to bed. Instead of sleeping, though, she tossed and turned, waking from one dream after another, including one in which she and John were drinking together, then she passed out and woke to an empty house.

The next morning brought a fit of uncomfortable feelings stemming from somewhere deep within her. She found herself craving a drink so badly she could almost taste it. She made a pot of coffee, stronger than she had ever drank before, and her hands trembled so badly that she could scarcely hold the cup without spilling it. Finally she called her sponsor and headed out the door to meet with her five minutes later.

Molly had been shocked and relieved at the same time to find that Sharon, the woman whose family photos she had taken right after the funeral, was in her meetings. Sharon had welcomed her with great warmth and acceptance. She shared her experience and the strength and hope that she had gained over the past fifteen years. It had seemed natural to ask Sharon to be her sponsor.

Molly had nine months of sobriety under her belt this very day. She couldn't blow it now. Nor did she want to. She wanted to keep growing and journeying on the path she had discovered—a path of giving herself to God in ways she had never known before. The kind of giving of herself that brought peace she hadn't known existed.

After an hour with Sharon, she felt significantly better and threw herself into her work. She wrote, called Jo to tie up the loose ends on her next column, and did an impromptu photo shoot. And in the flurry of activities, she didn't even realize she hadn't checked her phone all day until she was on her way home that evening. There was one missed call and one voicemail waiting for her. She put the phone away, intending to check the message when she got home.

As she walked in the door, Lily came to greet her, all wiggles and kisses, begging to go outside. So Molly stood on the patio while Lily scoured the yard, investigating every new smell carefully. The sun was sinking low in the sky, and a beautiful hue glowed on the horizon. A gentle breeze brushed over her bare shoulders, and her simple black cotton dress brushed against her legs.

Her mind reviewed the events of her day, like a slide show presenting someone else's life. Nine months ago today, she had attempted to take her own life. Intentional or not, she couldn't even guess. And whether it was intentional didn't matter anymore, either. What did matter was how closely she had come to death that cold November night. How her mind seemed to have a will of its own—a dual thought process, one trying to suffocate the other. And that night, the enemy almost won.

Here it was now, the end of August, and she journeyed on, knowing she wasn't alone. She knew now what she needed to do when life got difficult and the bottle seemed to be the answer. She only hoped and prayed she would continue to be strong enough to do those things when the tide was strong against her, threatening to sweep the sand out from beneath her feet.

She'd managed to work in a meeting today, too, despite all she had going on. She'd realized a long time ago that that one hour in time could save her an entire life's worth of agony. No matter what she had to cut out of her day to make time for her twelve-step meetings, it was more than worth it. No matter what it was. If she wasn't sober, nothing else mattered anyway.

She sat in the porch swing on the patio in back of the house, one leg curled underneath her, the other foot swinging her slowly back and forth. It was a comforting motion. She laid her head back as she looked at the first sign of the moon in the sky. She thought of seeing John the day before and of Michael's quick exit. She couldn't shake the feeling that he was hurt, but she couldn't figure out why. She tried to figure out what would have caused his quick departure, but if her memory served her correctly, there was no conversation, just an awkward silence. John had just been there, and no one knew what to say.

As if on cue, her cell phone rang. The now-familiar number lit up the screen as she answered the call.

"Hi, Michael," she said a bit hesitantly. She was incredibly grateful to hear his voice.

"Hey there, sunshine." His voice was a warm caress in her ear.

Molly smiled, feeling relief wash through her. "I tried calling you last night."

"I know." There was a brief moment of silence before he continued. "Molly, I would really like to drop by for a bit. There's something I need to say."

The relief Molly had been feeling dissipated, and uneasiness took its place.

"Do I want to hear it? This isn't a "dear John" moment, is it?" she asked nervously, then wanted to kick herself for the innocent slip of the tongue and play on words. "Because I don't—"

"Molly?" Michael chuckled softly. "Don't let your imagination run away with you. Can I come over? I really need to say something. And it can't wait."

"Yes. I would like that." She responded quietly, looking at Lily who was looking up at her with betrayal in her puppy-dog eyes, as if she were wondering why Molly wasn't giving her undivided attention after being gone all day.

"I'll be there in ten minutes."

"See you in ten," she answered, a shiver of fear invading the excitement she felt to see him. She pushed the fear aside, picked up Lily, and sat swinging on the back porch until she heard the doorbell ring.

Molly opened the door to find Michael standing in front of her, looking more attractive than she could ever remember. Her heart about leapt right out of her chest as he moved in to give her a hug. She smelled the fresh scent of Irish Spring mixed with cologne that made her melt against him.

"Hello, sunshine," he whispered into her ear, brushing her hair with his lips. He pulled back and looked at her appreciatively. "Were you expecting someone else?"

Molly thought she noticed a shadow of something unrecognizable pass through his eyes as he looked at her. "You told me you would be here in ten. Who else would I be expecting?"

"I don't know." He looked over her shoulder into the house and back at her. "John?"

Molly tilted her head back and laughed. So that's what this had been about after all.

"And you're laughing…why are you laughing?" he asked, clearly not amused.

"Michael, can I get you something to drink? Lemonade? Iced tea? Soda? I think we need to talk. Or *I* need to talk. To explain."

Molly poured them both a glass of sweet tea while Michael stood close behind her. Close enough that Molly could feel the electricity that pulsed between them, making it hard for her to breathe. She led him back out onto the patio, settling onto the swing once again. The evening was so beautiful, and she wanted to share it with him. The quiet of nature that surrounded them, the moon, the stars lighting up the ink of the sky. It calmed her spirit as only a gift from God could do. The same God who worked good from all the parts of her life she had messed up.

Molly turned in the swing to face him, pulling her leg up, planting her foot on the seat of the swing with her knee nearly touching her chin. She stared into those gorgeous hazel eyes that held such wisdom and care for other people. The gorgeous hazel eyes that were unlike any she had ever seen before, and that held her heart.

"Do you have anywhere in particular you want me to start?"

"The beginning is always a good place."

She smiled at him. "Can I ask what it was that made you bail so quickly yesterday?"

"I didn't belong there, Molly. I told you that. It's clear how he feels about you."

"Felt," she corrected him.

"You're deceiving yourself. I saw it in his eyes."

"What you saw, Michael, was pain. But not pain from lost love—or even love not returned. It was pain from never getting an answer. Of feeling rejected without the courtesy of an explanation."

"Do you love him?"

"Yes." She saw the pain in his eyes, and she quickly added, "But not like that. Not in the way I love you."

Michael stared at her. "Did I just hear what I think I heard?"

"Yes, Michael. I love you. I love you like I've never loved anyone before. John and I—well, we are...were...friends. True, he wanted more and held on for me to change my mind. Looking back, I know I was leading him on, because I was afraid if I didn't, I would lose him and his friendship. In a sick way, I was very dependent on him. That's not love."

"Does he still love you?"

"He said he always will." She answered him honestly. She didn't want secrets to come between them, now or ever. "But he has also moved on; he's seeing someone else now. Yesterday...getting answers he never got from me before…I hope it's freed him to move forward in that relationship."

"Can you honestly tell me that you wouldn't be happier with him? It's obvious he has money—"

"Dude! Stop right there," she said sternly, her hand up instantly, palm facing him. "Love isn't something that can be reduced to money. And if you think that's what I want, you don't know me at all. I had my chance with John. Maybe you didn't hear me, but I don't love him that way. I love you. *You* are the one who makes me happy. *You* are the one I want to spend my time with. I want to share things with you that I've never shared with anyone. I want to get to know Sara better. If you will let me, that is," she added.

She realized she still didn't know why he had come over. What if he was here to break things off with her? Here she was laying her heart on the line, doing all the talking, and she didn't know where she stood with him right now. He seemed…uncomfortable. Maybe he was about to deliver news he knew would make her unhappy.

"Why are you just staring at me," she asked. She hadn't realized she was holding her breath until she breathed deeply, filling her lungs with the fresh night air.

"Molly," he began, his voice quiet, but deeper than she had ever heard, his hazel eyes bright in the now full moonlight. "I love you more than I could ever begin to tell you. I have never felt this way about another living soul. I want to spend the rest of my life with you, watching you with Sara, watching you fall asleep at night and waking up with you in the morning. You are the other half of my heart and soul—the part I've been searching for. I was so afraid I would never find you, but I knew I could never just settle for halfway."

Time seemed to stop. Words escaped her, and her heart beat so loudly that she was sure he could hear it. She watched almost in shock as he reached inside his shirt pocket and pulled out a ring. The diamond, sparkling and glittering in the moonlight, was one that the stars couldn't even compete with.

Everything seemed to be moving in slow motion as he got down on one knee before her.

"You have no idea how happy I am to hear it's not John or his money you want," he chuckled nervously, "because that means I don't have to try to convince you otherwise. Because I would have tried, you know."

Molly laughed, her brown eyes glimmering through unshed tears of happiness. "Is this what I think it is?" she whispered.

"That depends on what you think it is," he teased. "But it's me, asking you, if you will give me the honor of becoming my wife."

Tears ran unchecked down her cheeks as she threw herself toward him, wrapping her arms around his neck and sending them both tumbling onto the patio floor. "Yes!" she exclaimed. "Yes, yes, yes!"

Lily came over to join them, barking her existence into the moment, making sure they didn't leave her out.

Later that night, after digesting the realization of what had transpired between them, the love that had carried them to a whole new life, they talked about when and where they wanted to get married. They both agreed that they wanted something very small and intimate, sooner rather than later.

"So we can finally consummate this relationship," he teased her, brushing the hair off her neck.

"Michael, you do realize my sister and brother are going to think we're moving way too fast, right?"

"They probably will. But once they see how over the moon in love with you I am, hopefully that will make it okay with them. Besides," he added, "I've never been one to worry much about what other people think. Except you and Sara," he added as a caveat.

It was midnight when Michael stood to go home before they did something he knew Molly would regret. She had never hidden the fact that she was intent on doing things right. She didn't want to jinx what they had been blessed with, what had been brought to them by One much bigger and more powerful than either of them.

At the door, as he turned to leave, she asked with sudden concern, "How are you going to tell Sara? What if she's not okay with this?"

"Okay with it?" He laughed. "Who do you think helped me pick out the ring today?" With that, he planted a kiss on the tip of her nose before closing the door gently behind him.

Molly stood with her hand against the cool wood of the closed door, smiling like she would never be able to stop ever again. She locked up and made her way to her room, stripped off her dress, and lay in bed. The realization that she was going to become Mrs. Michael Stanza grew in her heart, bringing a smile larger than life. Her heart overflowed with love so intense, yet so peaceful, that she knew without question that it was right. In fact, nothing had ever felt so right in all her life.

When she finally slept, she dreamed of her parents. She saw them as if they were right before her, their love for each other making everything seem right. It was as if she were outside a window, watching them in the glow and warmth of the evening light as they danced in the kitchen, looking at each other with such pure love.

Scenes from her childhood followed, and she watched moments that had impacted her as she grew—moments that at one time had made her feel like the lone ranger in a family of people she never knew. But now she felt part of something wonderful. Part of something she felt blessed to have known.

She watched as she saw herself through the window as an awkward child not knowing how to interact with her mom. She wished that she could get in that window to help her little-girl self just reach out. To hug her mother. Then she saw the awkward teenager lash out at her father, and she desperately wanted to break through that window and shake some sense into that selfish girl. For a moment she forgot that she was watching herself until the girl turned and looked directly at her.

Molly knew it was a dream, and she tried to wake up, yet she also desperately tried to cling to a moment that seemed so close to her mom and dad. She wished she could go back and do things differently. She looked again and watched as her parents were now in what turned into her own house. They were standing in her bedroom, arms entwined, looking down at her as she lay sleeping. Molly wanted desperately to wake up, to reach out and touch them. They were so close. She seemed to go in and out of her dream, and she watched as her parents walked out of her bedroom, smiling at her, an aura of light encapsulating them.

It was then that she was able to wake herself up, to find her pillow wet from tears she hadn't even known she had cried. Her dream seemed so real and so alive. She could even smell the scent of her mother's favorite cherry blossom lotion wafting in the air she breathed. A scent that brought such comfort.

Molly sat up and swung her legs over the edge of her bed. She reached to turn on the nightstand lamp. There was no use in trying to go back to sleep now. Looking at the clock, she was surprised to see it was only one o'clock. She had been sleeping for little more than half an hour. She looked at her clock a second time to be sure she'd read it correctly and saw something purple and shiny that she was sure had not been there before. Or had it?

She reached out to touch the nine-month sobriety chip. A warm breeze swirled through the window, causing her curtains to flutter softly. She picked up the coin and felt the cool metal between her fingers as she lightly caressed it. She realized she hadn't picked up her chip at the meeting she'd gone to that day.

A chill traveled down her spine, though it was an oddly comfortable one. She tried to remember how the chip could have gotten there. Michael? But he hadn't been in her room. In fact, they had purposely avoided that temptation. Had he snuck in here when he had used the bathroom? But where would he have gotten it?

And then she remembered her dream, her parents standing next to her bed, lingering, reaching to place something on her nightstand. Her face paled, and her breathing quickened. A smile slowly curled her lips as she held the coin tightly in her hand. Could it be? Was it even possible?

Despite the time, she felt an urgent need to call Madison.

Chapter Twenty

Madison had just gotten Oliver back to sleep after a nightmare. His little body was curled up on Phil's side of the bed. Phil was out of town on a business trip with an account his boss wouldn't allow anyone else to touch.

She was finally drifting off to sleep herself when she realized her phone was ringing. The musical ringtone had stopped by the time Madison found her phone. In fact, for a moment she thought she'd been dreaming. She glanced at Oliver to make sure the phone hadn't awakened him, but he hadn't even stirred from the position he was in the last time Madison looked at him. He lay on his tummy, one leg pulled up, one arm flung off the side of the bed, the other tucked underneath him.

Madison picked up her phone to look at the missed call display, worried it might have been Phil. As she recognized Molly's number, the ringtone began to play again, and Madison quickly answered.

"Good morning, sis," she whispered. "Or is it even morning yet?" she asked, looking again at her clock.

"Madison, I'm sorry to wake you up, but the weirdest thing just happened. I don't know—"

Madison's heart became heavy as she listened to Molly's voice, packed with emotion. Surely Molly hadn't relapsed. What could possibly have happened to cause it? The man she'd been seeing? Madison knew Molly felt more for this man than anyone she had ever dated, but maybe she'd learned something awful about him. Madison's mind, now wide awake, was running circles.

"Madison? Did you fall asleep on me?"

She realized she had been so caught up with the "what if's" that she hadn't even heard the rest of what Molly had said. "I'm sorry. What, sweetie?"

"Where did you go just now?"

"At this hour, in bed?" She tried to sit up, still whispering as she slowly and quietly got up to leave the room so she wouldn't wake Oliver. "Just a minute…okay continue."

"Did I wake you up? Wait!" She interrupted herself. "Don't answer that. Dumb question."

"Yes, I would have to agree. Not one of your more brilliant questions," she answered, her voice tight with concern. "Oliver's been having nightmares, and I just fell back to sleep after getting him settled. I had to leave the room so my talking wouldn't wake him back up." As if she could sense Molly wondering why Oliver was in her room, she added, "Phil's gone on a business trip. He comes back tomorrow."

"Oh. Give him a hug and kiss from me. Oliver, that is," she added, laughing. "His auntie misses him."

"Enough to come do night duty when he has his nightmares?" she quipped.

"Say the word, big sister."

Madison could hear the warmth in her voice. "It's so nice to know my kids finally have a real relationship with their auntie and uncle."

"Even though we're crazy? What are his nightmares about?"

"Phil and I getting in an accident and leaving him," she answered, heartbroken. "That's pretty heavy stuff for a kid his age."

"Because of Mom and Dad? Aww, he loved his Grandpa and Grandma. But Maddie, does he even know the details?"

"Yeah...But how do you comfort a six-year-old about something like that and still keep it real? I mean, they're called accidents for a reason. They happen. Is it fair to tell him not to worry because nothing is going to happen, and then have him hate me and think I'm a liar if it does?"

"I have no idea. You're the one with the degree."

"Thanks a lot," Madison remarked dryly. "I can feel so confident dealing with other people's issues and drama, but I'm so completely clueless in making sure I'm doing what's right for my own family."

"So what have you been telling him?" Molly asked, curious.

"I've been using it as a vehicle to teach him about how God's children get to live with Jesus when they leave here. That Jesus is always with him, no matter what, so he will never be alone."

"Hmm," Molly answered thoughtfully. "That's heavy." Madison inhaled sharply. "I'm just saying I'm glad it's not me that has to try to figure out how to deal with a six-year-old on such a big issue," Molly added quickly.

Madison sighed. "So, what possessed you to call at this hour? Are you okay?"

"I haven't relapsed, if that's what you're worried about."

"I didn't—"

"—say that." Molly finished her sister's sentence. "You didn't have to. I know you, and I know that it's always in the back of your mind."

"I'm sorry, Moll. I know that's not fair."

"No need to be sorry. I don't know that I will never relapse," she answered truthfully. "I mean, I certainly don't intend to, but the bottom line is, I don't know. Not for sure. I take it one day at a time."

"So what's up?" Madison asked again, relieved Molly wasn't upset with her.

"A dream of my own."

"Do share. Unless it's x-rated," she chuckled. "Spare me if that's the case. Phil's gone, remember?"

"Eww! Madison…" she laughed. "It was about Mom and Dad, but not in the same way as Oliver's." She paused.

"Well? Are you going to tell me?"

"I'm trying to figure out how to tell you without you thinking I *have* relapsed and was lying about it. Or just plain crazy. But then again, maybe I am."

"Molly, for God's sake, just tell me," Madison blurted, stopping Molly's rambling.

"Do you believe in ghosts?" She didn't respond, so Molly assured her by adding, "I was telling you the truth when I said I haven't relapsed."

Madison chuckled, letting Molly know it was safe to continue. She told Madison about her dream, how real and vivid it was, all the way to being able to smell the cherry blossom body lotion.

When she was done describing every last detail of her dream, she was breathless from talking so fast and from the renewed excitement. Madison was silent, working hard to absorb what Molly had just told her.

"Yoo hoo! Maddie? Did you fall asleep?"

"No, sweetie, I'm here," she answered, her voice a hushed whisper.

Madison had felt her cheeks pale as she listened to Molly's story. Her dream. A dream that for some reason made her truly question if it was only a dream.

And then she realized where that question was stemming from.

"Molly, I have something to tell you, too." Madison went to stand by the bay window at the front of their house. She caught her breath at the sight of a gorgeous doe and her fawn, standing in the field across the street. They stood there so peacefully, grazing as if they didn't have a fear in the world.

Madison watched them as she continued, trying to hold onto reality as she spoke. "This morning I found two roundtrip tickets to the country Zoey's sponsored child lives in. They were on my dresser. I—I thought Phil must have put them there, but I couldn't remember seeing them before, and Phil has been gone for two days already."

"Did you ask him about it?" Molly asked, incredulous.

"No. I didn't want him to think I was crazy. Or maybe I was afraid of what it would mean if he didn't do it. That I truly was—or am—crazy," she laughed nervously. "But how else could they have gotten there?"

"The same way my nine-month chip got to me," Molly whispered.

They remained silent, neither knowing what else to say. Or if there even was anything else to say. It almost seemed that to say something would ruin the moment. The miracle. The warmth they both felt rush between the phone lines.

"Have you talked to Max?" Molly finally asked.

"No. You?"

"No. But knowing Max, he wouldn't say anything anyway. He would probably talk about it with Mandi. Which that in itself is a miracle. I mean, did you ever see the day Max would put someone before himself?" Molly asked with wonder.

"No. That, I can honestly say, I never thought I'd see. He's a changed man. Nothing like leaving it to the eleventh hour, but he's even started putting in some time at the homeless shelter. With Mandi, of course."

"Yeah, but is it thanks to Mandi, or thanks to Mom and Dad?"

"Thanks to God," Madison answered, the soberness of her voice speaking volumes more. "Thanks to God for working through Mom and Dad to reach all of us. So their death wasn't for nothing. You know what else? Max agreed to come to the farmhouse every Christmas, so we can keep the house."

"No sir!"

"Yes sir," Madison laughed lightly.

"Before we hang up, I have something else to tell you."

"I'm not sure I can take anything more," she laughed quietly, still in awe as her own life became her focus rather than the deer in the field under the stars.

"Hm. Okay. Good night then."

"Oh, don't even try that!" Madison laughed in unison with Molly.

"I'm getting married."

Madison sat down, grinning. Her world, her reality, had come full circle. For the first time since she was a little girl, everything seemed complete in her world.

"Hey, Maddie?" Molly interrupted her thoughts.

"Yes, sweetie?"

"It feels like things have finally been completed, doesn't it? I mean, no matter what happens, I know Mom and Dad will always be a part of it all. They are such a huge part of us. We're going to be okay, right?"

"Yes, Moll. We are. All of us."

30380696R00169

Made in the USA
Charleston, SC
13 June 2014